The Backside of Nowhere

by Alec Clayton

Cover art by Glennray Tutor
"Dream of Love" (detail), oil on canvas
www.glennraytutor.com
Cover design by Gabi and Alec Clayton

Cover fonts: ComixHeavy and Comix
Text font: Californian FB

First edition

ISBN: 978-0-9800322-6-0
Printed in the USA

DISCLAIMER
This is a work of fiction. All characters are the product of the
author's imagination. Resemblance to any person, living or dead, is
entirely coincidental.

Acknowledgements

Larry Johnson, a great poet and writer, read the complete manuscript at least three times and made detailed editorial corrections and suggestions. Thank you, Larry. And dear reader, run out right now and buy Larry's fabulous book of poems, *Veins*.

Thanks also to my good friends Linda Delayen, Margaret Ward and Jack Butler, and to my son, Noel, for reading the manuscript and offering suggestions and encouragement. And to my wife, Gabi, for suggesting the title and helping me design the cover.

Also by Alec Clayton

Fiction
Until the Dawn
Imprudent Zeal
The Wives of Marty Winters

Non-fiction
As If Art Matters

Books by Alec Clayton available online at

www.alecclayton.com
www.claytonworkspublishing.com
www.amazon.com

Water, Water

David Lawrence's many fans were surprised when he began performing his monologue, *Water, Water*, which ran six months Off Broadway before becoming a surprise hit on DVD. It showed that the popular actor had a subtle and sardonic genius and a depth of feeling that few fans and even fewer critics suspected. In his monologue, David Lawrence rants, "You know what I love about being a movie star? The money." And then, after a wink and a dramatic pause, "You know what I hate about it? Just about every damn thing else."

The audience laughs. On cue or spontaneously, it's hard to tell. Or is it canned laughter? The camera zooms in for a close-up. David runs his hand across his closely-cropped hair and says with a strong Southern accent (just a trace of Cajun), "Jesus, man. If y'all think you'd like to be a movie star, let me tell you, it ain't all it's cracked up to be." And he winks wickedly at the camera while projected behind him are films of David with his girlfriend, the actress Jasmine Jones. The obvious implication is that if making it with Jasmine Jones is a fringe benefit of being a movie star, then being a movie star is the greatest gig on earth, his protestations to the contrary not withstanding.

The montage quickly flashes a love scene from their film *The Witness*, followed by a photo of them speeding in his Jaguar and a blurred shot of them skinny-dipping in the surf. David and Jasmine met on his first picture, and the gossip rags have dogged their every move since. They're hot in the tabloids. They're together, they're not together, she's moving in with him, she wants to have his baby, they split up, he's seen with another hot young movie star, now they're back together.

David has three smash hit movies to his credit, *The Witness, Travlin' Light* and *Cold Justice.* In all three films he is the lovable but somewhat bumbling Southern lawyer Raymond Moon, who wins his cases by sheer good luck and gets the girl in the end. Teenage girls idolize David for his rugged looks and older women for his quiet manner. David says he doesn't like Hollywood parties, and he doesn't like going on talk shows, and he doesn't like reporters and photographers. But most of all he hates that the roles he plays are not the roles he envisioned when he studied acting in college. He wanted to do serious drama on Broadway. So far he hasn't been able to realize that dream, but he feels he has come close with his monologue.

In the monologue he talks a little bit about his life as a movie star, but mostly it's his story of growing up in the little town of Freedom in the bayou country near the Gulf of Mexico. As soon as the DVD hit the stores, David's mother bought a copy. (He had told her he would send her an advance copy, but he never did, and she wasn't willing to wait. "That boy would forget his own wedding if he ever had one," she liked to tell anyone who would listen, "and God knows I wish he would—have a wedding, that is, not forget it.") Shelly Lawrence didn't like the idea of her only son living in sin, although even she would be the first to admit that concept was old fashioned.

The whole Lawrence family plus David's old high school sweetheart, Sue Ellen Patterson, gather together to watch the DVD of *Water, Water.* There's David's father, Earl Ray, called Pop by almost everyone. Seventy years old and still strong, but nothing like in his youth when he lifted barrels of beer and loaded them on a flatbed truck, Pop is a magisterial figure with waves of silver hair and a neatly-trimmed goatee. He stretches his six-foot-six frame in an old recliner in front of the TV. Seated next to him is his wife, David's mother, Shelly, who at five-foot-four looks like a child next to Earl Ray. Seated on the couch and sharing a bowl of popcorn are David's beautiful sister Melissa and his not-quite-as-beautiful sister Mary, with Sue Ellen between them with the popcorn bowl perched on her lap. The three of them look enough alike that people often mistake them for sisters. All three are tall and statuesque with voluptuous figures and regal manners. Melissa is by far the most striking, but she works at it, always looking her best, even when relaxing with family. Her hair is thick and brushed to a lustrous sheen. Even now she's wearing lipstick and mascara, diamonds around her neck and on her fingers, gray cotton hip huggers that cling to her ass, and a little white tank top. When she gets up to go into the kitchen for a drink tantalizing bits of a colorful tattoo can be seen on the small of her back, and when she sits back down more hints of skin art peek out from her deep cleavage.

Sue Ellen's style is more conventional business casual, looking like she's just come from a board meeting but has shed her jacket. Her hair is shoulder length and she wears glasses. A loose blouse hides much of a figure that in the right clothes could rival Melissa's.

Of the three, Mary is the most casual. Dressed in ripped jeans and a simple plaid blouse, just as she was while cleaning house and cooking dinner that afternoon, she obviously feels no need to impress anyone.

Sprawled on an easy chair with his legs thrown across the arm is Mary's no-count husband, Buddy Boudreau. (It's Mary herself who insists on referring to him as no-count, usually following up with variations on the refrain: "but I love him nevertheless. He's like a bad puppy that's always piddling on the floor but he's so damn cute you can't stay mad at him. Ya know what I mean?")

Perched on the rug on their bellies with feet kicking in air and chins cupped in hands are Mary and Buddy's pre-teen daughters who are the envy of every kid at school because they are David Lawrence's nieces. Of course that envy is somewhat baseless because Patricia and Rhonda have never even met their famous uncle.

David opens the monologue with a quote from *Rime of the Ancient Mariner:*

> Water, water, every where,
> And all the boards did shrink;
> Water, water, every where,
> Nor any drop to drink.

The very deep did rot: O Christ!
That ever this should be!
Yea, slimy things did crawl with legs
Upon the slimy sea.

The girls go "Eeeych!"

David says, "Can you picture it? Dying of thirst with water all around, but you can't drink it because it's salt water. It's a metaphor I guess. That's what it was like growing up in Freedom. Both metaphorically and literally. There was water all around. Bayous, bays and creeks. And no one could tell the difference between the bayous and the bays or the creeks and the rivers or the gulf and the sound. It was just water, water, water— one body of water flowing ceaselessly into another. There was salt water, brackish water, fast-running water and stagnant water, mosquito- and snake-infested water, the chlorinated water of the swimming pool that seared my eyes like sausage in a pan. And there was so much rain. Flash floods, electrical storms, hurricanes. Thank God or Grandpa Lawrence, we lived on top of the only high spot in town. It was a manmade hill on the precipice of a manmade cliff on the banks of Little Bay. Granted, our hilltop fortress was not exactly the Matterhorn. We were like maybe fifteen feet above the water, but we were sort of kings of the mountain in our neck of the woods. The broad sunroom on the back of our house overlooked the water. If the house had been ten feet closer to the edge of the cliff, I could have done a swan dive off the back porch and into the bay.

"I lived through two hurricanes and I don't know how many flash floods. The last one they said was the wrath of God. People down there really believed that. Like God spends all day sitting around thinking what he can do to mess with a bunch of rednecks and Cajuns. I'm sure that at least seventy or eighty percent of the people down there believed that last big storm, the one when I was in high school, was God's punishment for our sinful ways."

Melissa says, "You tell 'em, David."

"He's right, you know," Sue Ellen pipes in. "He's got us pegged. And I remember that storm. Boy, do I ever! People thought it was the end of the world."

"Don't I know it." Mary puts her two cents in. "And I swear to God old Brother Fox down at Redemption Baptist, he still regrets that we survived that flood, and he just can't wait for whatever God's gonna throw our way next."

After enjoying a good laugh at the fundamentalists, they turn their attention back to the TV. David says, "If God was punishing us for our sins, it was the sin of hypocrisy, the sin of self-righteousness. Those are the real sins. But what the hypocrites down there thought of as sin was sex outside the bounds of holy matrimony (as if they weren't all doing it) and race mixing—mongrelization they call it—and homosexuality. There ain't nothing so devilish as a hairdresser. So sex, or shall we say unconventional sex, that's the big one, the numero uno sin. Murder? Nah, that's not really so bad, not if you have a good enough reason, anyway. Let someone screw with your wife or break into your home and you've got every reason to blast his lights out. But start screwing around with the wrong gender or the wrong race, and you bring on the big winds and high water. Sooner or later God's gonna get you for that crap."

He pauses. Takes a big sip of water from a glass.

"Floods and hurricanes, they kept life interesting. Hell, I lost my virginity in a hurricane. The big moment—you know, the big O—it came just when the wind lifted the roof right off the house where we were doing the deed."

"Oh my God," Sue Ellen moans, "I can't believe he's saying that."

"My oh my," Melissa chuckles, and Mary says, "Well it's true, isn't it?"

"Not really."

"Y'all did it in a hurricane just like he said."

"I mean it's not right that ... oh shit. Never mind."

"What?" the girls both ask.

"Nothing."

Shelly is glaring at them and Mary's daughters are waiting in anticipation of something deliciously dirty. Mary is silently praying that they don't ask her to explain what the big O is.

Melissa says, "She means it's not true that that's when he lost his virginity. That happened long before, didn't it?"

The three of them mock fight on the couch and spill a lot of popcorn. Sue Ellen blushes and won't say any more, and Shelly says, "That's quite enough. You girls are acting like you're ten years old." They're in their forties. Patricia and Rhonda are behaving more maturely, but are thrilled to see their mother and their aunts misbehave.

On the DVD, David has dropped the subject of losing his virginity in a hurricane but is still talking about stormy weather. He says, "Then there were the everyday summer squalls that were so regular you could set your watches by them. Every day in the summertime about three or four in the afternoon. First the humidity would start to come to a boiling point, temperatures and humidity both pushing a hundred. Then you'd see a cloud coming at you pouring rain over an area about the size of a football field. It'd be a ten-minute cloudburst followed by blinding sunlight. Everything washed clean.

"Almost half the year it was hot enough to go swimming. I'm talking right up till almost Halloween and starting again around Easter. We were practically amphibian. There was hardly a day I wasn't on the water or in the water, swimming or fishing or skiing. My father taught me to swim when I was one year old. You know how? By throwing me in the water. Sink or swim, that was his idea. And I swam. You better believe it. Yeah, I know, there's a million apocryphal stories about fathers throwing sons into the drink to teach them to swim. It's a popular myth down in Dixieland. But mine really did. You would have thought it would scar me for life. I don't know, maybe it did, maybe that was when I first started hating the old man."

"He oughta be thanking me, the little ingrate," Pop bellows. It's his first comment of the evening. He's been quietly sipping his highball and smoking his hand rolled Prince Albert tobacco. The room reeks of cigarette smoke, but nobody seems to notice.

David continues, "But I don't remember it; it was just something Pop boasted about later. It never kept me from my love of swimming. I was on the high school swim team, and I used to have almost daily races with Randy Moss. That's Randy Moss Jr., the sheriff's son. Now he's the sheriff. That's the way it goes down there, every boy becomes his father. Except for me. There was no way I was going to take after my old man."

"See! See what I tell you. The little ingrate." Earl Ray hacks into his handkerchief, grabs the remote and stops the video. He hands his empty glass to Shelly and says, "Refill us."

She gets up and shuffles into the kitchen to get them another drink, her fluffy pink slippers going swish-swish-swish across the hardwood floor.

A minute later, freshened drink in hand, Pop restarts the DVD. The camera pans to the wall behind David where there is a relief map of the bayou country, and then back down to David, who says, "We'd race across Little Bayou. It was about a mile to the other shore. Or at least we always judged it to be about a mile; I don't guess either of us ever knew for sure. There was a floating platform in the bay out behind Randy's house with a homemade springboard. It was made of planks and floated on empty barrels. My sister Mary would count down. She'd say, 'Get ready, get set, go!' And we'd dive together like twin rockets slicing the water, sucking air right before we went under, holding our breath until we thought our lungs would burst, pulling water with scooped hands. That son of a bitch could hold his breath for what seemed forever, but Ha!—I could hold mine forever plus a minute."

David is pacing on stage as he recites this tale, swinging his arms in mimicry of swimming. He sticks his face right into the camera lens and puffs out his cheeks froglike and strokes imaginary water. Rhonda and Patricia swing their little arms with him. Mary says, "He's lying now. Randy always won those races."

"But David could hold his breath longer," Sue Ellen says.

David says, "I stayed right with him, glancing to the side under the murky water to see when he would give up and break the surface. I knew he'd give up. He always gave up. That's the way Randy was, all show and no go. He was stronger, but I could hold my breath longer. (Sue Ellen says, 'See!') We'd always make it way out from shore underwater. Fifty yards maybe. Seemed like half a fucking mile, finally spouting like whales when we breached the surface."

The older of Mary's girls says, "He said fucking," and Mary says, "Remember? We talked about when it's appropriate to use adult language and when it's not." She had a pretty liberal policy about cursing. It's okay for grownups, and it's okay at home when there's just the family, but she taught her girls to respect the sensitivity of other people who may be offended by coarse language. It was a source of constant conflict between Mary and her husband who, she thought, was too uptight about it.

The monologue continues. "In the swimming pool I'd get them to time me. The longest I ever held my breath was seven minutes and thirteen seconds. I heard the world record is over fifteen minutes. Wow! I can't fucking believe it."

"He said it again," the girls say.

Buddy says, "Okay, that's enough. Somebody should have warned us this was a R-rated movie. I don't know if I want the girls watching this."

Shelly pauses the DVD. Mary says, "Oh, don't be such a prude."

"Well it's not right."

"Oh geeze, you're such a hypocrite."

The girls giggle. Shelly says, "Do you girls even know what that word means?"

"Yes ma'am," the older girl says. "It's a slang expression for sex."

"Does it embarrass you to hear your uncle talk like that?"

"No ma'am. Aunt Melissa uses that word all the time."

"And so does daddy," Rhonda puts in, "When he thinks we aren't listening. So I don't know what he's getting all in a huff about."

Buddy says, "All right. I guess I overreacted."

They revisit the discussion about when and where it may be appropriate to curse, and why. Mary tells the girls that *how* words are used is more important than what the words are. "I'm much more concerned with words that are hurtful. Like you should never call people stupid or fat or ugly."

The girls seem to fully understand and take their mother's intention very seriously. And they say their daddy is just being silly. He confesses that they're probably right. Then he says, "Hey, come on, girls, let's go get some ice cream while we got the movie paused."

After everyone has gotten snacks and made bathroom runs they restart the film. David takes a sip of his water and starts talking about another incident they all remember. "On the cliffside behind our house there were wooden steps that were dug right into the earth and ran down to the dock. Off to the side was a hard packed dirt trail that we could slide down after a rain or roll down in tractor inner tubes. I kind of ran and hopped and slid down to the dock barefooted. All I had on was a pair of cutoff jeans. One of those like, you know, with the pockets hanging out below where they're cut and your package showing if you don't watch out. You should have seen me. Tanned a deep bronze, long buttery blond hair bleached from the sun (with a little help from a bottle of Peroxide, something all the kids did back then). I walked out to the end of the dock. The boards under my feet were like hot coals, but hey, I could take it. I was one tough kid. I stood on the end of the dock and unsnapped and unzipped and stepped right out of my shorts. And my Jockeys. I stood there naked as the day I was born posing like some Greek athlete in the original Olympics, imagining who might or might not pass by in a boat and catch sight of me. Daring 'em, saying here I am, world! I thought I was pretty freakin' hot, if you must know. Plus, the possibility of being caught out there in my altogether was kind of thrilling. Randy's house was across the bay. It was far enough across that if Randy or his folks happened to be standing on their dock, which they weren't, they probably couldn't even tell I was naked, but somebody might come by in a boat. Maybe some girl from school. Maybe Mary Ann Wilson. She had the hots for me anyway.

We'd already made out pretty good in the swimming pool and would have gone all the way if we'd had some place to be alone. Okay, maybe not. I couldn't tell for sure if she wanted what she acted like she wanted that day in the pool, but even if she had we couldn't have done anything because it was broad daylight and there was a whole bunch of us together in the pool. I was still a virgin. We were just horsing around. She reached underwater and cupped my cock with her hand. Jesus. Shocked the everloving shit out of me. I'd never had a girl touch me like that."

Sue Ellen says, "Son of a bitch. He never told me about that."

"He could be making it up," Melissa notes.

David continues: "Maybe she wasn't really coming on to me after all. She had a whole troop of brothers, and maybe they played around like that. Maybe she was just playing gotcha. We were sitting together in the shallow end of the pool. She grabbed me first, so then I slipped a finger under the edge of her bikini. She let me rub her for about a minute, and she still had a hold of me. She wasn't just playing gotcha. I could see it in her eyes. Her face was all flushed, and the way she squirmed and rubbed on me... ooh whee. Damn. I was so flustered I didn't know whether to shit or go blind. But then she squirmed out of my grasp and kicked off with a laugh and started swimming to the deep end.

"For the rest of the afternoon we played around with the other kids. You know, the usual stuff. The girls would sit on the guys' shoulders and wrestle with each other, or the boys would make slings out of cupped-together hands and the girls would stand in our hands and we'd toss them in the air. All the boys and girls were flirting with each other, and the boys were copping feels whenever they could. One of the boys even tried to cop a feel from me, but I won't say who that was. And I never got another chance with Mary Ann. For the rest of the afternoon she darted away whenever I got close to her. We didn't even kiss or anything, and it never happened again. I never dated her. I should have asked her to go out with me that very night while she was still hot to trot, but I was so flustered I couldn't think what to do. I didn't exactly see myself as God's gift to women back then. Sure, I knew I was kind of good looking. After all, it wasn't like we didn't have mirrors in the house. And I had a muscular body. I worked out a lot. But I wasn't real sure of myself in those days.

"Bullshit," Melissa laughs. "He thought he was the cock of the walk. 'Sides, didn't he just brag about how good looking he was?"

"So while I was standing there buckass naked on the dock I had this brief little fantasy about Mary Ann coming by in a boat and seeing me, and I don't know how I imagined we'd get from her passing by in a boat to us wallowing naked in a bed of sea grass, but that's what I pictured. Of course her coming by in a boat wasn't likely to happen. And if she did, it would probably be in a boat with her parents, and I sure as hell wouldn't want them to see me naked. But then that possibility was kind of a thrill too, you know what I mean? In a weird sort of way.

"But the one girl that might actually see me was Sue Ellen Jamison, because she was my sister Mary's best friend, and she might well drop by the house. She did, quite often. And Sue Ellen was a lot sexier than Mary Ann to boot."

"Ah ha! Now it's getting interesting," Sue Ellen says.

The monologue continues. "She might not have been as pretty as Mary Ann Wilson. She had straw colored hair and kind of splotchy skin and a slight crook in her nose. But she had a better body. Bigger boobs, anyway. All the boys called her Knockers.

"I imagined Sue Ellen seeing me in all my bronzed naked glory. I imagined her coming down to the dock, rubbing her hands up my side. Next thing you know we're wallowing in the sea grass. My dick was overpowering my brain. I was on the verge of drifting off into a neverending fantasy fuck. So I told myself to cut it out and dive in the fucking bayou. I inhaled deeply and dove out into the bay. I sliced the water like a knife cutting into a watermelon. I propelled myself underwater like a submarine, picturing in my mind Johnny Weissmuller in an old Tarzan film. Finally breaking the surface a good twenty yards out like a missile fired from a submarine. Wait a second, let me see if I can think of ten more similes. (The audience laughs, so do Mary and Sue Ellen.) I took half a dozen hard strokes then turned on my back and floated lazily, looking back toward home. The sun was scorching hot, but there was a nice breeze and off to the southwest I saw black rain clouds spilling a cascade of silvery rain. It was the usual afternoon squall. It would sweep across the water and onto shore and pass over our house like a curtain in the wind, and then travel north to play itself out over the pine forests.

"I turned back over and started toward the opposite shore with a smooth crawl stroke, turning my head side to side with a gulp of air every other stroke. As I reached the lily pads and grasses over near Randy's dock I slowed down and dog paddled. Toes touched the ooze of the bottom. I slipped underwater and imagined myself as a fish gliding between the blades of grass. I felt along the silty bottom. I opened my eyes but could see only a few inches ahead. The water stung my eyes. I eased my butt into the bottom. It felt gritty on my skin. Grasses grazing my side felt like cold leather. Here the water was just deep enough for me to sit on the bottom with my shoulders and head sticking out. Minnows nibbled at my legs and toes. I tried to scoop them up in my hand but they darted away too quickly. I could see that the rain squall in the distance was getting closer, and it looked like it had grown larger. It was starting to look more ominous than the usual squall. It was now a solid wall of water, and the sky was darkening all around as if someone were gradually dimming the lights. I figured I'd barely have time to swim back before I got caught in the storm. Not that it mattered so much if I got rained on. After all, I was already wet. But if the wind and waves picked up it would be harder to swim. But the main thing was the challenge to beat the storm. Challenge was what life was all about—how far could I dive? Swim underwater? How long could I hold my breath? Could I go skinny dipping in broad daylight without getting caught? And could I swim faster than a storm that was hurling my way like a cliff of water?

"It looked like a much bigger storm than any we'd had for a while. Already the water around me was churning up in the wind. I pushed off with my toes digging in the slimy bottom and started swimming for home as hard as I could. My lungs felt tight. There was a cross current pushing me northward. If I couldn't beat it I'd hit shore a good ten or twenty yards past our pier where it would be hard to climb out on the slippery bank. Halfway across, my arms and legs began to grow heavy. I looked over my shoulder and saw the storm was closer. I wasn't going to make it. I had to make it. It was me or it. What the hell? It was just a summer rain storm, but it was fun to imagine it was life threatening. I pushed myself harder, harder, counting the strokes: one, two, three, four...

"The wind shifted. It felt cold against my face. The storm was about thirty yards behind me and catching up. Our dock was about thirty yards ahead. I had to make it. I had to, I had to. I stroked within twenty-five yards, twenty, ten, five. Three more strokes...

"I reached the dock and pulled myself up, flopping over the end of the dock like a reeled-in fish and scratching my belly in the process. Rain was peppering the water right behind me. I looked to the house, and guess what. Sue Ellen Jamison was there just like I'd imagined. She and Mary were standing in the back yard jumping up and down in excitement and shouting for me to hurry. Damn. She saw me naked after all. I didn't really want her to. Or did I? The idea was thrilling but the reality was sort of embarrassing. I grabbed up my shorts and pulled them up and started running, zipping and snapping as I ran, rain like machinegun fire at my heels, taking the steps two at a time, imagining I was a warrior attacking an enemy stronghold at the top of the hill, gunfire zipping overhead. I reached the back porch and leaped up to safety. Mary and Sue Ellen shouted 'Yeah, David!' and stepped out into the rain and spun around on the slick grass a couple of times before tumbling back onto the porch and falling into each other's arms in exhausted laughter.

"I grabbed the back of a chair and held on while trying to catch my breath. The porch boards wavered like heat waves. For a second I thought I was going to throw up. God, how embarrassing that would have been in front of Sue Ellen."

Rhonda and Patricia are mesmerized, as are the adults who cease interjecting comments and hang on to David's every word. He's telling a story they all lived through; they all know what's going to happen next, but they want to see how his retelling of the tale matches their memories. David talks slower now: "I was sweating and chilled at the same time. Mary and Sue Ellen ran inside and jumped onto the old couch by the back window where they could look out at the storm. Wearing shorts and T-shirts they perched on their knees on the couch and pressed their faces to the window to watch the storm. As soon as I was able to catch my breath a bit I went in and joined them. I pushed in between them on the couch. The hairs on my arm stood up in electric shock when my arm brushed against Sue Ellen's. She felt it too. We smiled at each other.

"We were in what we called the sun room. It was a long narrow room behind the kitchen with windows that ran the whole width of the house and a door in the middle that opened onto the back porch. The whole family used to love sitting on that porch after supper, watching the sun set over the bayou and then later after the water became placid watching the moon on the water as it undulated like a luminous milky disc floating on the surface of the bayou. Often in the summertime I slept out on that couch with the windows wide open and the perpetual breeze from the bay keeping me cool. I didn't like air conditioning. It got too damn cold.

"Mama came in with tall glasses of ice tea on a platter. We thanked her, took the glasses and continued to look out the window at the raging storm. Raindrops lashed the path up from the bayou. Splatters bounced mud drops froglike a good foot off the ground. The downpour was so heavy that we could no longer see the dock. The screen door on the porch kept banging open. Normally leaving that door open for even a few minutes would result in a swarm of mosquitoes. They said the mosquitoes on the bayou could pick up a full grown hound and carry him off, but they only came out for a short time around sunset, and we wouldn't have to worry about them as long as the wind was up. A tin sheet that had been propped against the back porch lifted like a giant square Frisbee and sailed out of sight.

"We heard the front door slam open, banging against the wall the way it did when someone opened it too quickly (how many times had Pop said he was going to put a doorstop there?). It was Pop coming in. We heard his heavy boots. He was running. I'd never in my life known him to run. He loped on long legs through the kitchen and out to the sun room and shouted, 'The store! We've got to save the store. It's flooding.'

"We all jumped off the couch not knowing what to do next. Pop said, 'David come with me. Sue Ellen, you too. Mary, stay here and help your mother. If the water gets any higher it'll be in the house. So ya'll just try to get as much stuff as you can up high.'

"He turned and started running back through the house shouting, 'Let's go! Let's go!'

"It was exciting. I loved it. Sue Ellen and I followed the old man. I was still barefoot and wearing my cutoff jeans and nothing else. Her shorts were brushed denim. Her T-shirt was emblazoned with *Hot Chick* across her namesake knockers. Plastic flip-flops flopped on her feet. She couldn't run in them very well so she kicked them off and left them where they flopped near the doorway, and we both ran barefoot into the storm. She slipped on the grass and fell flat on her face. I helped her up. 'You okay?' I asked, and she said 'Yeah, I'm fine,' and we ran on across the street, rain blowing into our faces like thousands of needles.

"The water was already ankle deep in the road. As common as flash floods were, I'd never seen it get so deep so quick. Our house was pretty damn high considering the whole town was pretty much at or below sea level. We'd never had any flood damage, but it looked like we were about to. I knew Sue Ellen was worried because her house sat in a bowl up past Little Don's on the far north end of the island where it flooded with just normal rainfall.

"The store was right across the street from our house. It was a wooden building made of whitewashed wood slats on a foundation one step up from street level with a broad front porch shaded by a red-and-white striped awning. When I say there was a porch, I don't mean it was up off the ground. It was just wooden slats laid across two-by-six boards on a flat concrete slab. The store was a lot closer to sea level than the house. Out front stood three gas pumps. Neon signs in the windows advertising Jax beer and Coca-Cola. Faded paper ads for Libby's Vienna Sausage, Moon Pies, Aunt Jemima corn meal mix. We knew Buddy would be there already. At least we knew he was supposed to be there. You never knew about Buddy. Sometimes he was where he was supposed to be and sometimes he wasn't. I'm talking about Buddy Boudreau, Mary's boyfriend. He was a Cajun from down below New Orleans. We all liked Buddy, but he wasn't the most responsible person in the world. Sometimes he simply wouldn't show up for work and we'd have to scramble to find someone to fill in for him. The funny thing was, Pop didn't seem to mind. He'd never let any of the rest of us get away with that kind of shit, but when it came to Buddy he'd say, 'Well, he's kind of funny that way. Where he comes from they don't keep regular hours.'

"I knew Freight Train would probably be there too. Freight Train didn't keep regular hours either, but he wasn't supposed to. He didn't work for us. He just dropped in to help out whenever he didn't have anything else to do, which in the summertime was most of the time. I'm talking about Murabbi 'Freight Train' Taylor. Y'all probably know him as the all-pro linebacker for the Raiders. He went to school with me. He was kind of a local sports hero and a gentle giant who, even in high school, could practically lift all the appliances in the store by himself if he had to.

"Water was already lapping the front stoop when we got there. The door was standing wide open and Pop was shouting for everybody to do what they were already doing, which was grabbing everything that could be water damaged off the lower shelves. Freight Train had half a dozen bags of dog food in his arms and was carrying them toward the back of the store where there was a storeroom with lots of high shelves. A couple of neighbors had shown up to help out. That wasn't unusual. The Lawrence store was the town store, even though there was an A&P and a Piggly Wiggly in town. People went to the chain stores for their major shopping but came to our store if all they needed was a quart of milk or a loaf of bread. If a customer wanted to buy something and Buddy or Shelly (that's my mom) or whoever was running the store happened to be busy, one of the regulars would just step behind the counter and ring them up. It was that kind of place. There were even a couple of easy chairs and a love seat by a pot belly stove where friends would gather and smoke and shoot the breeze. Cigarette butts gathered in an empty coffee can. Somebody had propped the door open with a gallon water jug so they wouldn't have to keep opening it. Buddy was down on his knees in the aisle lifting boxes and bags and piling them into waiting arms as they formed a kind of bucket brigade. Pop said, 'Let's start another line.'

"I took up position on the floor on the next aisle ready to pile stuff into Pop and Sue Ellen's waiting arms. The first things I grabbed, thoughtlessly, were plastic jugs. The old man shouted, 'Not the plastic, you fucking idiot!'

"I shouted right back, 'You want my goddamn help or not?' And he said, 'Don't you sass me, boy!'

"I shut up. I scooted down the aisle a ways and started loading cereal boxes. I wanted to kill him. If I'd been big enough and strong enough I'd a drowned him, held his freakin' big head under water right there where it was backing up on Liberty Street. But geeze, the old man was big. He intimidated the crap out of me. He had lorded it over me all my life, and I had this mental picture of him as bigger and stronger even than he really was, you know, as if six-foot-six wasn't big enough. I wanted so much to just bust him in the chops. He had no right to talk to me like that, especially not in front of everybody and not when I was trying to help him save his precious groceries. Like he really needed the damn store. Like he couldn't replace a few sacks of groceries. The store had never been a source of income for the family, but I guess it held sentimental value. It had been handed down from his father and grandfather. Pop liked to hang out in the store and shoot the breeze with his cronies. During the days leading up to elections the store became the unofficial precinct headquarters and Pop the unofficial party chairman. In the summertime he set up a target out back and archers practiced, and all year long hunters and fishermen swapped tales of big ones bagged or escaped to be caught another day."

By this point in his monologue David is berating his father pretty good. In front of the TV, Pop slouches further down in his beatup old recliner and crosses his arm in a pout. Everybody looks at him to see how he's taking this. It's no secret in the family that Pop and David have never gotten along. In the twenty some years since David left home the only thing he's ever said to Pop over the telephone has been "Let me talk to mama."

David continues his tale. "Within a few minutes the water was inside the store. I was sitting in it. It was an inch or two above the bottom shelves. Only a few boxes were soaked. Dry foods that we'd have to throw out. But we'd cleared most of the bottom shelves. Pop said, 'Let the stuff already wet go and start working on the next shelves up.'

"More neighbors came in and offered a hand. It was a regular party. The water reached almost to the second shelves and lapped our legs below knee level. It sat and swirled for a while. Dirty, murky brown water. A water moccasin swam in the front door and went shopping. Pop casually grabbed it behind its head and sloshed to the door and slung it out into the endless lake that was Freedom.

"Little by little the rain slacked off and then quit altogether. We kept moving stuff. We were wet up to our knees from the flood and our hair and faces were soaked with sweat. Dog tired. After a while Pop said, 'I think we're done here. Y'all go on over to the house and see if they need any help over there.' To the neighbors who had come by to help he said, 'Ya'll been a big help but you get on home and check on your own stuff now.'

"Sue Ellen said, 'I need to check on my mother if I can get there.' I could see in her eyes that she was scared.

"Pop said, 'Sure, honey. You go right on ahead. David, you best take her. Might best take the skiff. I don't think you can get there afoot.'"

There's a long pause. David walks to the edge of the stage and sits down with his legs hanging over. The camera pans to the audience and then back to David. He says, "Going out in the boat with Sue Ellen after the rain stopped was so weird. It was the peacefulness of it all that lent a dreamlike quality to the world we had thought we knew. The clouds were gone like there had never been any to start with, and the sun was blazing. Our whole town had been washed with dirty water. The banks of the bayou just never stopped. Boats floating in open water were held by lines that dipped underwater like fishing lines; what was not visible was that the ropes that vanished under the water were tied to submerged piers. Eddies and swirls of brown water carried debris in all directions. We took Pop's old homemade wooden skiff, a fourteen-footer with a square bow and flat bottom propelled by an Evenrude trolling motor. Sue Ellen sat up front. I sat on the back seat and operated the motor.

"I told her to keep a close watch for stuff that might be just under the surface of the water that could ram us and bust a hole in the boat.

"'Okay,' she said. She leaned forward to peer into the water, gripping the gunnels right and left, her shoulder blades angular and arms tense.

"We hit little whirlpools and cross currents that carried the little boat sideways. The engine was barely powerful enough to keep us heading in a northerly direction. There were other boats on the bayou and in the town, many of them piled high with stuff salvaged from flooded homes, and off to our left people were wading waist high, and in places even chest high, with boxes and bags held aloft. At the peak of Freedom Loop we headed into what passed for downtown. Here the water was maybe three or four feet deep judging by how high it came on waders. Everyone in town seemed to be outside, either in boats or on foot. I turned the motor off and tipped the shaft up, thinking it might catch bottom in some of the shallower areas. 'Grab a paddle,' I said.

"We drifted slowly, using the paddles to steer more than to propel the boat. We turned left onto Coffee Lane, stopping at the stop sign and looking both ways as if we were actually driving on the road. Simultaneously we realized what we were doing, and we both burst into laughter.

"The Jamison's house sat near the southern end of Coffee Lane close to where it met up with Liberty Street near Little Don's Diner. It was a ranch style, white shingle house. It sat in a deep dip in the road. The whole house right up to the edge of their roof was under water. Mrs. Jamison was straddling the peak of the roof. She was wearing a denim skirt and she looked like a cowgirl in a saddle. She waved when she saw us coming. Sue Ellen stood up in the boat to wave back, almost tipping us over. We paddled up close and turned the boat sideways. I was an expert paddler. I could maneuver a boat in close quarters even in the strongest of currents, but the current next to the house was as powerful as any I'd ever experienced. I could barely hold us steady. It took all the strength I had. 'Grab that line and toss it to your mother,' I told Sue Ellen.

"She picked up a length of nylon rope that was coiled in the bottom of the boat and threw the end. Mrs. Jamison reached to catch it, but missed. Sue Ellen pulled the rope in and tried again, and again. On the third try, Mrs. Jamison caught the rope. 'Okay, now tie it to the pipe,' I shouted.

"She looped it around a stove pipe at the peak of the roof and tied up her end, and Sue Ellen pulled it tight where her end wrapped around the bow cleat. Now at least the front end of the boat was secured. Then we had to do the same thing again with another length of rope in the back of the boat. Sue Ellen had to practically sit in my lap to throw the second rope, and when she did, all hell broke loose. The boat rocked violently, and Sue Ellen fell out, slamming against the side of the house and into the water. She grabbed the boat and hung on."

"I've still got a scar on my shoulder from that," Sue Ellen says.

David continues: "At the same time, Mrs. Jamison reached for the rope and slipped, and she came tumbling down with a huge splash. She scraped her leg up pretty good and got a big bruise on her hip, but we couldn't see that then. All we could see was that she was in the water and flailing her arms wildly. She screamed, and within a second or two she was swept away by the current, and Sue Ellen shouted at me, 'She can't swim!'

"Without thinking, I dove into the water and went after her. She was splashing like a fish on a line. It took no time at all to catch up with her, but then I had to get her back to the boat. I don't know how I managed to grab her and swim against the current with her added weight, but somehow I did it. I think she must have had the good sense to quit flailing about and maybe even help me swim by kicking her feet, even though she didn't know how to swim. I think it must be kind of instinctual. Anyway, we somehow got back to the boat. Sue Ellen was still hanging on to the side. I got in first, and then helped them both climb in, and we took the shorter route home—right down Liberty to Freedom Loop.

"While we were motoring back home, somebody stopped by our house and told Pop that there were looters robbing stores in town. We had not seen any evidence of looters, and knowing our neighbors and all, we couldn't really believe it. For the most part, we were proud of the folks in Freedom. All around town citizens were chipping in to help their neighbors, boating people to higher ground and helping to salvage personal belongings. But I guess not everybody was helpful. We heard that the looters hit the Piggly Wiggly first. The store was closed and sandbagged, water lapping three feet deep against the front windows. Looters broke the windows and grabbed armloads of groceries. One young man grabbed a cash register and loaded it into a boat. Looters also ransacked Ramsey's Electronics taking TVs and stereos. Word spread pretty quickly because just about everybody had CB radios and walkie talkies. The regular phone lines were out but that didn't stop the good ol' boys from calling each other. They were saying ten-four good buddy all over the place. This was back when that was all the rage, or maybe a few years after the fad died out. I'm talking about after the Carter years. Of course the first place people called was the sheriff's office, but that was useless. Sheriff Moss was vacationing in Hawaii.

"Pop called the sheriff's office and demanded they get someone down to his store to guard against prowlers. 'We'll git somebody down there soon's we can,' a deputy said; 'but right now we're awful short handed. I'm down here all by my lonesome and Sheriff Moss is out of the country.'

"'Well looka here, you redneck bumpkin,' Pop blasted back, 'You got a duty to protect the citizens of Freedom whether the sheriff's here or not. And just for your information, I happen to know that Randy Moss is lying on a beach in Hawaii right about now, and in case you didn't know it, that ain't out of the fucking country. It's part of the U.S. of A.'

"'Well I'm just as sorry as I can be, Earl Ray, but they weren't no way he coulda knowed it was gonna flood. Now I'm gonna git somebody down there just as soon as I can, and that's the best I can do.'

"So Pop and everybody at home went back across the street and waited in the store by the front door ready to fend off looters any way they could. Pop went into the back room and came back with a .22 rifle and a pistol. He handed the pistol to Freight Train.

"'Hey, I can't use this,' he said.

"'What? You ain't never shot a pistol before?'

"'Sure I shot a pistol, but not at people.'

"'Well I ain't asking you to shoot nobody. Just scare 'em off.'

"A little aluminum boat approached, coming right down the middle of Liberty Street. Two men stood up in the boat using large poles to propel the boat through the water. Between them was a large Sony TV box obviously stolen from Ramsey's. Pop and Shelly and Freight Train watched them approach. 'That'un up front's got a gun stuck in his belt,' Freight Train said.

"'Might be, but I betcha he ain't got the balls to use it. You can bet your bottom dollar on that.'

"'That's Malcolm Ashton,' Freight Train said. 'I know him. Shit, he ain't a bad guy. He's just a poor boy that's gone nuts on account of the flood and all. Seen himself a opportunity to cop some stuff he never could afford.'

"'Well he's gonna be dead if he comes much closer,' Pop said.

Mama said, 'Don't be too hasty, Earl Ray.'

"'You keep out of this, woman.'

"'I will not,' she said in no uncertain terms. Mama could be a feisty little broad. She might have been the only person within the confines of Freedom who had the nerve to stand up to Pop.

"Freight Train was trembling. Mama said, 'I know Malcolm Ashton's mama. She finds out what he's been up to she'll tan his hide, and whatever he steals, she'll just make him march right down and return it the next day, and she'll make him apologize too.'

"'Don't you think he knows that?' Pop said. 'He ain't likely to take anything home for his mama to see. He'll hide his loot and sell it next week or next month. That boy's clean beyond his mama's control.'

"The boat had come closer. The two boys were within shouting distance. Pop hollered at them, 'Don't y'all come any closer. I got a gun and I'll use it.'

"We came up behind them, putting along under the power of the little trolling engine. I killed the engine and let the boat drift up alongside the looters' boat. Pop shouted, 'Ram 'em, David. Hit 'em with your paddle!'

"I couldn't believe he'd say that. The boy in the front of the boat put down his pole and turned to his companion and said, 'Let's turn around.'

"'Are you kidding, man? We got a gun, and they ain't nothing but a old man and a woman.'

"'And Freight Train Taylor,' the other one said.

"I couldn't help but laugh at that. The whole thing was turning comical. I couldn't believe we were having an armed standoff with Sonny Staples and Malcolm Ashton. They were students at Booker T Washington. I could see that Malcolm was scared. Going up against Freight Train should have scared the bejesus out of both of them, but Sonny didn't have the sense God gave a billy goat. He was too boneheaded to be scared. He said, 'You yellow bellied chicken shit,' and he threw his pole down and lumbered up toward the front of the boat, rocking the boat like crazy, and he grabbed the gun out from his buddy's waistband and held it up with both hands trying to hold it steady against the wild rocking of the boat, and he pulled the trigger and the sound of the shot reverberated over the water and we saw the splash where the bullet hit the water a good ten feet off to the right of Pop's boat.

"'What the hell!' I shouted at Sonny. 'You're shooting at my daddy.'

"Pop lifted his rifle to his shoulder, and just as slow and calm as you please he took aim and shot a hole in their boat near the bow and right under the water line. Malcolm jumped in the water and started wading back in the direction from which they had come, holding his hands up and shouting, 'Don't shoot!' And Sonny fell to his knees in the bottom of the boat and threw his hands up too, and he starting begging for mercy.

"Their boat was slowly sinking. Pop shouted, 'Stand up, boy!' And Sonny stood up wobbly in the sinking rowboat, still holding his hands in the air. Pop pointed his gun right at him and said, 'Git naked.'

"'What?!' Sonny shouted back incredulously. I could see him take to shaking. Pop said it again, 'Git naked.' And Sonny took off all his clothes, and stood trembling. He put one hand over his little prick and kept the other one raised. His skin was sickly white with festering pimples all over his chest and back, and you could see where he'd blistered and peeled across his shoulders. Pop said, 'Now git out of the boat and follow your buddy there that's wading away.'

"Sonny climbed over the side and started after his companion. I tied onto their boat. I hollered at their backs, 'I'm going to tell your mothers,' and then I shoved off and cranked my motor again, and towed the sinking boat with its treasure of a brand new television to the store, where Freight Train lifted it out and carried it to the back of the store where the water had finally begun to recede. He said he'd return it to Ramsey's the next day.

"Pop still had some shouting left in him, and he turned it on me. He said, 'What kind of pussy are you? Why didn't you ram them like I told you to?'

"Mama came to my rescue. She said, 'Because I taught him to be a decent person, not some kind of caveman like his father.' She was seething with anger at Pop. She said, 'Not everything can be settled with brute force, you know, and this little show of macho bullying was sickening.

You're a better man than that, Earl Ray. Those are not bad boys. They just made a mistake, that's all. A little understanding will do them a lot more good than any amount of violence.'

"Pop shot back, 'It's just exactly because of wimpy attitudes like that that younguns turn to crime. This world is going straight to hell because people are not willing to stand up for what's right.'"

*

David's monologue goes on for almost two hours. He rambles on about life in the little town of Freedom, a town that was founded by former slaves with historic connections to old time rum runners, bootleggers, gamblers. "I don't know who all had their hands in who's pockets, and I never really wanted to know. But I know my family was pretty deep in the cesspool. That's why I got the hell out of Freedom a long time ago and never looked back. I know my grandfather on my mother's side was a crooked politician and my daddy had all kinds of connections with Mafia types."

The monologue seems directionless toward the end. He talks about having a blowup with his father when he was in college because he wanted to study acting and the old man wanted him to study something more practical like business. "I guess I showed them a thing or two," he bleats in a so-there tone that his family does not find particularly funny.

Pop says, "To hell with him. I don't care if it's another twenty-some years before he ever comes back home. If I'm lucky I won't live that long."

"You don't mean that, Earl Ray," Shelly says.

The Backside of Nowhere

When Pop and Melissa glide into the Golden Eagle Casino they cause a ruckus that could be matched only by their more famous relative, David Lawrence, with the sexy Jasmine Jones by his side. Dressed in a style she laughingly calls slutty-chic, Melissa looks like some kind of sexy film noir vamp. She wears a black fedora with a red silk band. The wide brim is tipped forward to cast a shadowed veil across her dark eyes. Her hair is not truly black but dark, dark brown tinted with Venetian highlights. It flows like oil across naked shoulders. Her black gown sparkles with red glitter that matches the rich red highlights in her hair. The gown is cleverly designed to look like it might expose far more flesh than it actually does. Men stare in anticipation as her breasts threaten to pop out and her long thighs scissor through an almost crotch-high slit in her skirt. What flesh is exposed—and there is certainly plenty of it—glistens like dark honey. A tattoo snake slithers from her cleavage. Dark stockings and high heels accentuate the curve of her calves. The eyes of every man in the casino follow her as she maneuvers through the crowd on the arm of the old man. He's bearded in white like the Spanish moss on the ancient oaks outside, and wears a white suit of a type long since out of style. He's tall and stately but walks with a slightly drunken stagger. While men stare lustfully at Melissa, casino employees and patrons alike greet them with smiling deference. They seem thrilled to welcome them into their establishment.

As if Melissa in all her gorgeousness and Pop with his height are not striking enough, they are accompanied by three hundred some odd pounds of muscle in the person of Freight Train Taylor, who splits off from their triad to grab a seat at the bar.

The funny thing about them evoking such awed responses as they sweep through the establishment is that they do it at least twice a month. While it may be true that the handful of local people and all of the employees in the casino know Pop and Melissa, more than half the casino patrons are there for the first time. They invariably think (hope) they are seeing a celebrity couple. They just can't quite place who they are. "Isn't she the actress that was in that movie with what's his name?"

"Yeah, yeah. And he's that guy that... you know, he looks like Burl Ives but he's tall and skinny?"

"He's one of those character actors that you see all the time but you never can remember his name."

"Right. Like... like what's his name."

Others assume she's a high-priced hooker and Pop is her sugar daddy, her pimp, or her John. And maybe she is a hooker. Even Pop doesn't know for sure.

Pop owns stock in the casino and his entertainment company (slot machines, juke boxes, pinball machines) supplies a lot of the casino's equipment. Furthermore, it is because of his political connections that the Golden Eagle has never had to worry about such inconveniences as fire and safety codes or payments to the state liquor control board. The locals have known the Lawrence family since way back when Pop was a kid. They know that Pop took Melissa into his home some twenty-odd years earlier when she lost her parents, and they know that Freight Train is Pop's personal assistant and bodyguard.

Melissa makes her way to an unoccupied slot machine, and the old man gives her a handful of coins. It's one of Pop's machines, custom designed for the Golden Eagle with magnolias, eagles and rebel flags on the tumblers. She puts a coin in and pulls the handle, saying "Come to mama." It whirs, comes up flag, flag, magnolia; she feeds it another coin, uttering incantations for a jackpot. This time it comes up magnolia, magnolia, eagle, then the same combination again. "Crap," she says. "Two out of three. Every time it's two out of three. So close but never a winner."

The old man says, "Nose out a sinner? What the hell does that mean?"

She laughs. She repeats more slowly, "Close but no winner."

"Oh," he says. "Well hells bells, whatdaya expect?"

Pop has a hard time distinguishing consonant sounds, and he refuses to wear hearing aids. Says they make ambient noises unbearable. He stands by and watches Melissa play the slots. Within minutes she's lost fifty dollars.

"That's enough," the old man says. "You gonna send me to the poor house sure as shootin'."

She shrugs. Fifty bucks is pocket change to Pop, and she knows it.

He walks away heading to the card tables. She follows, pouting. He goes to his favorite table, where they play what Pop calls "real poker" (five card draw, no wild cards). "This Texas whatever-the-hell they call it that's so popular nowadays is a girl's game," he snorts. He stacks five hundred dollars in chips on the felt. She sits by him. There's another empty chair to her left and only two other players at the table.

"If I lose this you got to promise to make me leave," he says, indicating his stake.

"Why bother? You never listen."

"What?"

"Never mind."

A bar girl brings a bourbon and water on the rocks and sets it in front of the old man. She places a Manhattan in front of Melissa. "Hey, Pop," she says. "Hey, Melissa. Y'all doing all right tonight?"

"Fair to middling," Pop says. He picks up his drink but sets it right back down when he's hit with a coughing fit.

"You okay?" Melissa asks.

"Yeah."

The dealer deals the cards. Pop fans his cards in his hands. Rearranges them. A pair of sixes, a jack, queen and a four. He discards all but the pair and draws an equally useless combination. There's a flicker of a grin on his face. He shows Melissa his hand and she shakes her head, no.

"I got nothing," he says, "but I'm willing to bet you birds got nothing either so I'll start this'un out with ten bucks."

The next player matches his ten, and the next one matches and raises ten. Pop sees him and lays his cards down. The fat man across from him wins the pot with a pair of jacks.

"See what I told you," Melissa says. "You never listen. I shook my head no and you took that to mean bet ten dollars."

He laughs and pats her hand. She says, "Don't you be all paternal with me. If you're just gonna throw your money away, I might as well go back to the slots."

"Now you just hold your horses, girl. You're my lucky charm. I need you here."

He downs his drink in one swallow.

From the lounge drifts in the sound of a Neil Diamond impersonator singing "Sweet Caroline." At the next table a group of young men wearing Hawaiian shirts along with women in shorts and halter tops, red from a day on the beach, are laughing loudly. Behind a mezzanine window, a casino worker overlooking the floor is wired to dealers and security and wait staff on the floor. To the bar girl who waited on them he says, "Pop Lawrence finished his drink, get him another," and before Pop has time to raise his hand to signal her, she's at his side with a fresh bourbon and water. At the bar some fifteen or twenty yards away from Pop's table, Freight Train sits quietly on his bar stool turned to face the gaming tables. He holds a tall glass of beer, which he sips slowly. People who don't know them or did not see them come in together would never suspect any connection between the three. Freight Train nods pleasantly when people speak to him, but doesn't say anything.

The old man wins the next hand with a pair of queens but then loses six in a row. He's down by a little more than a hundred dollars.

A young man approaches the table. He's wearing a fifty dollar haircut and a gray suit jacket over a dark red T-shirt. "Can I get in?" he asks.

"It's your money," Pop says.

The dealer nods, and the young man takes the seat next to Melissa. He smiles at her. "Hiya, sweet thing."

"Hey yourself."

His eyes go immediately to her cleavage. He picks up the cards that are dealt him and studies them awhile, and then he glances back to her chest. She says, "You having a bit of a problem keeping your eyes on your cards?"

"Can't help it, honey. You just look so fine."

"Beware," she says. "The snake bites."

The dealer deals out another hand. The new guy wins with a pair of jacks. He scoops his chips up and antes up for the next hand. Then he whispers to Melissa, "You with the old geezer?"

"No need to whisper," she says. "He's deaf as a doorknob."

"Anytime you're ready to ditch him, let me know."

"Thanks but no thanks. I kind of like the old guy."

"Whatever." He turns his attention to the card game. The cards seem charmed for him. The stack of chips in front of him starts to grow. Pop keeps losing but doesn't seem to care. He's in good spirits, joking, talking about football and politics, and tossing down the bourbon. Somebody brings up a recent installment of a popular radio talk show. The governor had been on. "The guv told it like it is," the fat man says.

Everybody agrees that Governor Blight is a good man. Sharp as a tack and tough enough to stand up to out-of-state big-money interests. Everybody but Pop. He says, "He's the biggest damn hypocrite since Billy Sunday."

The young man says, "Hey, I voted for him."

Pop says, "Figures."

Melissa says, "You're old enough to vote?"

"Funny."

Pop says, "The guv tells everybody he's in tight with the administration in D.C., like he's got some kind of special influence nobody else's got. Crap. He claims to be the friend of the little man while taking millions from big corporations, and he makes a big deal out of being all religious and stuff, but he'd sell his soul to get reelected. But I'll give him this much, at least he didn't give in to the damn homosexual agenda. Not that I got anything against homosexuals, mind you. Live and let live, that's what I say. They can practice their sodomy in the privacy of their own homes all they want and it ain't none of my say so, but when they expect law-abiding tax payers to foot the bill for their health insurance and when they want to mess with the sacred institution of marriage, well that's another kettle of fish altogether. That's how come I voted for him, even if he is a hypocrite and a buffoon."

"And he stood up to the wetbacks, too," the young man says. "Remember? The other guy wanted to put illegal immigrants on Medicare. Shit. Might's well pay for their abortions too. That's the problem with this country nowadays. Everybody thinks they're entitled. Even in the South. We're getting to be about as bad as the rest of the country."

Melissa jumps in. She says, "Y'all better go easy on the queers and the immigrants. I depend on them to make my hair and makeup so gorgeous."

"And it is gorgeous, too. I'll give you that much," the young man says.

"How would you know? You never looked at anything but my boobs."

Pop says, "Don't pay her no mind. She's got a soft spot in her heart for all the weirdoes and the sissies in the world."

"Why don't y'all shut up and play cards?" the fat man butts in. He's not just fat, he looks like freshly kneaded dough. He's an enormous man with puffy, bloodshot cheeks who has kept fairly quiet all night and who has lost even more money than Pop.

There's a moment of stunned silence. It's like in an old Wild West poker game and Pop is the gun slinger nobody dares mess with. Everyone looks at him as if expecting him to pull out a six shooter. He glares at the big man for a few seconds, then laughs and says, "You're the one that started this conversation. But what the heck, let's play cards."

They resume play, and the young man sitting next to Melissa continues winning. He picks up his cards and lays them down. He drinks his drink, some kind of fruity, rose colored concoction, and orders another. He lights a cigarette and lets it smolder in the ashtray. He keeps looking at Melissa's flesh, the deep cleavage and exposed thigh. He also keeps dropping sexual remarks. Pop can't hear much of what the guy is saying to Melissa, but he can decipher his tone and read her expression. He keeps a wary eye on her to see if she needs him to step in and rescue her. He kind of hopes she does. That's usually a lot of fun. It's not like they haven't run into enough men of his type before. They're usually little more than a mild nuisance.

After another ten minutes or so Pop asks Melissa, "Is this snotfaced youngster bothering you, honey?"

"Well, he is starting to make my stomach crawl just a little bit."

He addresses the young man. "Sir," he says. "The lady says you're bothering her. I'd appreciate it if you'd leave her alone."

"What's that, old man?"

"I think you heard me, son. I'm the one that's purt near deaf. I imagine you hear quite well." He points at the bar. He says, "You see that man at the bar? I'm talking about that big black man that looks like a gorilla. His name is Murabbi but everybody calls him Freight Train. You might of heard of him. He used to play football. He got hit in the head a few times too many and now he's kind of whacko. He's a funny kind of guy. He likes to hear things crack. Like bones and stuff. He likes to hear people scream. I don't know why. Just not quite right in the head, you know? He works for me. He's my bodyguard. He's kind of like a bulldog. You know how dogs can sense what their masters are feeling? Ol' Freight Train's kinda like that. If he senses that somebody's irritating the bejesus out of me, he kinda goes crazy. You know what I'm saying?"

"Yeah, I know what you're saying. But guess what, old man? You don't scare me one bit." For all his bluster, his voice is shaky.

Pop just smiles and shrugs his shoulders. All during this conversation the dealer has been sitting still with the deck face down on the table. Pop turns to him and says, "Deal 'em, Jimmy," and he deals another hand while at the bar, Murabbi, who has been watching, swivels back toward the barkeep and signals for another beer.

They play poker for another hour or so, then the young man, who has obviously not been threatened by Pop, lets the hand that's nearer to Melissa drop to the edge of her chair and graze her thigh. At first, just the side of his palm barely touching, but when she doesn't push him away he turns his hand and slips it up around to the inside of her thigh. She reaches down with her hand and places it on top of his, gently enough at first for him to think she's encouraging him. And then she squeezes with nails like cat claws. She digs in. She watches him grimace with pain, but he doesn't say anything. His pride forces him to at least try to save face. He refuses to shout out or curse or jerk his hand away. She grins at him and continues to quietly claw at his hand. Pop watches. He can clearly see what's going on, but he doesn't let on. Melissa and the young Lothario wrestle in silence underneath the table until he signals with his eyes that he's had enough, until he pleads with his eyes for her to let go, until she finally eases off and removes her claws. He removes his hand from her leg, lays down his cards and picks up his chips and pushes away from the table without a word and walks away. Once he has his back to the card table he looks at his hand. It is bleeding. Surreptitiously, still trying to act nonchalant, he reaches into a pocket for a handkerchief to stanch the bleeding. As he walks past the bar, Murabbi reaches out a hand to stop him. He speaks to him briefly and then lets him go. The young man walks quickly to the door and out.

The old man turns to Melissa and says, "You want I should have him knocked off?"

"Nah, just order his balls removed. That oughta be enough."

They both laugh, as do the dealer and the other players, although it's not clear that the other card players know why they're laughing.

Six Bourbons later Pop has lost half his stash. Melissa, who has been pacing herself with admirable restraint, is nursing her second Manhattan. The fat man across from Pop puffs on a fat cigar and then lays it in the ashtray. He's got it all wet and chewed to hell. "Anybody want to bet on the Ole Miss-LSU game?" he asks.

"I'll put a hunnerd on the Rebels," Pop says.

"What kinda point spread?"

"Two touchdowns."

"You got spaghetti for brains if you think the Rebels can beat LSU. They're nothing but a bunch a pussies."

"What'd you say?"

"I said the Ole Miss Rebels are a bunch of pussies."

Pop says, "I hear you talking but I don't see your money."

"Here's my money." He throws a wad of cash across the table. "Piss on the Ole Miss Rebels and piss on you too, old man."

"Piss on me? Is that what you say to me? Over a gentleman's wager you say piss on me?" He pushes back from the table and stands up. This time, sure enough, it's like a Wild West standoff. Any moment the gun's liable to come out. Pop circles around the circumference of the table in order to insinuate himself right in the fat man's face, drunkenly scattering cards and chips off the table as he goes. His face may show every bit of his seventy years and he may be too drunk to stand without holding on to the table, but with his superior height, Pop is an imposing sight in his anger.

His face turns red. He bellows, "Here's what I got to say to that!" Dealers and players brace for what's to come. Pop reaches down. Is he going for a gun? No. He unzips his pants and pulls his penis out, and he pisses on the fat man. It's a pathetic dribble that gets more on his own pants than on the fat man, but the message is clear. When he says piss on you, he means it.

Somebody screams; a bunch of people laugh, and the dealer scrambles out of the way. In seconds there are security guards on either side of Pop hustling him toward the door. They are laughing, and so is Pop. Melissa follows close behind. And Murabbi. Behind them the fat man heads toward the restrooms dabbing at his pants with a napkin.

When they get to the elevator the security guards stop. They let go of Pop. One of them starts brushing at Pop's jacket as if to smooth out any wrinkles they may have caused. He's giggling. When Pop staggers a bit the guard puts his hands on his shoulders to steady him. He says, "I'm sorry, Pop. I hope we didn't hurt you or anything, but you know you can't just go around pulling your prick out and pissing on the customers. It ain't right."

"You're right. I shouldn't oughta done it." He hardly sounds contrite.

"Well, I guess you can go back now. If you feel like it, maybe you oughta tell that fat fucker you're sorry."

"He insulted the Ole Miss Rebels."

"Well okay."

"Well okay. It ain't right. He insulted the Rebels."

"You're right."

"A course I am." He shrugs out of the guard's grip. He says, "I guess it's time for me to head out anyway. I'm too drunk to see the cards straight." It's a variation on the old I'll-drive-because-I'm-too-drunk-to-sing quip the guards have heard countless times, but they laugh along with him nevertheless.

Pop slings an arm around one of the guards, leans into him and starts staggering toward the elevator. The other guard helps steady them. Melissa slides in between them, slips an arm around Pop and says, "I got it from here, boys."

Murabbi sidles up alongside them. He looks like he's tickled by everything that's transpired. "Pissing on the fat man was a nice way to end the discussion," he says.

The elevator door slides open and they lurch in. Melissa sees that Pop's penis is still hanging out of his open fly. "Let me fix you here, Pop," she says.

She reaches down and takes hold of his limp dick and slips it back into his open fly and zips him up. She pushes G6 on the elevator. He leans against her with a silly grin on his face as if he's dreaming about some long ago peaceful moment. The elevator dings. The door slides open and they step out on the top floor of the parking garage. It's dark and almost deserted. Wind from off the ocean howls through the empty space. The night air is humid, but there's a chill of approaching autumn in the wind. There are only three cars parked on this level: a black Mercedes, a yellow Humvee and Pop's new red Corvette. Melissa has one just like it, but this night they came together. The Mercedes is Freight Train's. He says, "If y'all got it from here, I think I'm gonna head on home."

"Yeah, that's fine," Melissa says. She kisses him goodnight and he takes off. Pop and Melissa stagger to the Vette. He steadies himself with one hand on the top and bends to unlock the door. The keys slip out of his hand. "Shitamighty. I dropped the keys."

He bends farther, unsteadily, falls to his knees, feels along the floor, sits back on his haunches and drops his head to his chest and starts crying. "Shitamighty, they's under the car someaires."

Careless of her designer gown, Melissa sits down on the floor. She reaches under the Vette and feels around for the keys. "I got 'em."

"Oh, you're a darling," he sniffles, tears and snot dampening his beard.

"You want me to drive?"

"Nah, I got it."

"You sure."

"Sure I'm sure." Steadying himself with one hand on the door handle and the other pushing off the floor, he pulls himself up. She helps by reaching under his arms and lifting.

"I think I'd better drive."

"I can handle it. I drive better dunk then most people do sober."

"You can't even talk."

"Gimme the fucking keys." He snatches them out of her hand.

He fumbles around the lock again and finally manages to fit the key in, opens the door and gets in, and then leans across the seat to unlock the passenger side door for her. She goes around and gets in.

They sit there a while. She says, "Please, Pop. I really think you ought to let me drive."

He says, "How come you took up whoring? I didn't raise you to be no whore."

"You didn't have much to do with my raising and I ain't no whore."

"Seems like it to me."

She knows that to many people there might not be much difference between prostitution and the ways in which she allows men to take care of her. Melissa has never worked a regular job, but she always has money. She dates only wealthy men, and they like to buy her the nice clothes and jewelry she craves. She also inherited some money from her father, which was placed in a trust fund until she turned thirty. Until then, Pop doled out a monthly allowance. When she finally did come into her inheritance, she invested it. Her lifestyle indicates her investments were quite fruitful. Either that or her boyfriends give her cash as well as trinkets. Pop has never questioned her about it. He loves her unconditionally, more so even than the children he actually fathered. If she really is whoring, there are worse things a woman can do. She could be like Mary, living unhappily with a no-count husband the likes of Buddy Boudreau, or she could have abandoned her family the way David did.

She says, "I like men and they like me. That's all. It makes them feel good to spend their money on me, and I like making them feel good."

"And you like pretty trinkets."

"I certainly do."

He starts the car. She buckles her seat belt. He backs out of the parking slot, aims for the far end and jams the accelerator to the floor. The car rockets toward the far wall, which is not a full wall but a mere three-foot-high retaining wall of concrete blocks open to the night air six floors above street level. Melissa pushes back against her seat and slams on imaginary brakes. She screams, "Oh god!"

In six seconds he's up to fifty miles per hour. Rows of concrete pillars are a blur. He hits the brakes and gives the wheel a hard turn. Rubber screams on concrete and the Vette misses the wall by two feet. It's a tight-turning machine. "Whooeee!" he shouts.

Melissa shuts her eyes tight and squeezes the edge of her seat with all her might. He guns it again, heading for the other end. Just before he begins to turn again everything goes black. Something that feels like a steel band tightens around his left arm. There's a sudden pain in his chest and his eyes water. He's blinded by pain for a mere second, and then he's unconscious. They hit the wall at sixty. The collision shakes the whole building and the wall crumbles in a cloud of dust. The car bursts through and then stops. It teeters nose down and tumbles hood over trunk and is caught up as in a giant spider web by steel cables that hold in place a forty-foot wide neon sign that flashes GOLDEN EAGLE CASINO in colors that flow through the spectrum from red to violet to orange. The passenger side airbag deploys, Melissa's seatbelt holds, saving her from being thrown through the windshield. Pop's not buckled. His long frame is thrown over the opening bag and against the steering wheel. His neck whiplashes and his head slams into the windshield. The steering column crushes into his chest. He's unconscious already, his face a smear of blood. Melissa cries out, "Pop, Pop, are you okay? Are you alive? Pop? Pop? Oh my god, ohmygod. I can't feel my nose. My nose is gone."

She hears commotion above them. Feet pounding. People shouting. Someone shouts down at them, "Hold on. Help's coming."

She tries to answer, but her voice is a strangled squeak that doesn't carry much beyond the car.

She can't hear Pop breathing. "Are you okay, Pop? Can you hear me? Oh please, don't be dead."

She hears an irregular whirring sound like *fle-fle-fle-fle*. It's the wheels slowing to a stop. She thinks of hummingbird wings and then of the flapping paper sound from childhood when kids put pieces of cardboard in their bicycle spokes. These thoughts and these sounds seem to be far off and playing in slow motion. She begins to drift into unconsciousness. She sees herself as an eight-year-old. She's riding her bike. Sunlight slants through willows and oaks and stands of bamboo along the bayou. She's riding the dirtpacked trail on the side of Freedom Loop. The road is wet from a recent rain, and she aims at every puddle, thrilling at the rooster tail of water that fans out as she splashes through. She's dreaming. She knows she's dreaming because grown-up Melissa is watching a sweet little Melissa doing something she never did in a place she never was until she was much older.

She's not even herself, she's a little black girl with tightly braided hair festooned with colorful ribbons. She's at the Lawrence's store—or Pop's, as everyone called it, or just the store. The store is a low slung wooden building with a tin roof and a candy striped awning over a front porch that looks in her dream like something from a bygone era: an overturned wooden barrel, wicker chairs, a reach-in drink cooler with bottled soft drinks floating in icy water. Little fishes darting among the bottles. She climbs off her bike and carefully leans it against the sweet gum tree out front. Wet grass darkens her white sneakers. Calliope music. A merry-go-round. Melissa astride a magnificent horse, holding on with one hand and laughing, waving at all her friends. Her friends shout back. They call her Tashee. A bunch of old men are sitting on the porch. "Hey kid, how you doing? How's your maw? How's your paw?"

The Lawrence twins, David and Mary—all grown up even though in reality they're the same age as Melissa—say, "Hey there, Tashee."

"Hey yourself."

Mary says, "That a new bike?"

"Yeah. It was a birthday present."

"That's nice."

David asks her if she wants a drink. "Help yourself. You don't have to pay."

She reaches her hand into the icy water of the drink cooler and fishes out a Nehi orange.

She's just aware enough that she's dreaming to wonder why she had taken on a different name in her dream. She sees Murabbi in the store. He's a child (she never actually knew him as a child). He's growing into a man. He grows bigger and bigger and bigger like a balloon man expanding with helium. Or is she growing smaller? She's Alice in Wonderland. He leans over her. She watches herself cringe. He's cursing her. "You ain't nothing, girl. Little pipsqueak of a nappy hair bitch. You might think you're hot shit but you ain't nothin'."

*

She wakes up suddenly. She glances around to see where she is. White walls, a television mounted on brackets up high, flowers, Mylar balloons wishing her a speedy recovery. She's in a hospital bed. She's wearing a hospital gown, and she has a hospital bracelet on her wrist. It looks to be early morning judging by the sunlight slanting in through the blinds. The overhead light is turned off, but there's a bedside lamp and green and blue and red glowing numbers on machines hooked to her arms. Murabbi is there. He looks gentle and sweet as he always does, nothing like the frightening monster of her dreams. "Hi, honey," he says. How are you feeling?"

"Like a goddamn freight train ran over me."

"Hey, I didn't touch you," he laughs sympathetically. "You just ran off the top of a building, that's all. You have a broken nose and a few cuts that are pretty minor, but you're going to be fine."

"What about Pop?"

"He had a heart attack, and he's banged up pretty bad, but he's alive."

"I'm surprised you're not with him."

"Well, he's sleeping now." Murabbi is fanatical about his responsibilities as Pop's personal assistant. He seldom leaves his side. Even when he does, he seems to have an infallible sense for when he's needed and often gets there before he's called.

Melissa looks at the clock on the wall. It's 6:45. "Is that a.m. or p.m.?"

"It's morning, honey."

"Really? I don't think I've ever been awake this early."

"Maybe you'd better try and go back to sleep. I probably oughta check on Pop anyways." He pushes up out of his chair and steps to her bedside and leans over to kiss her cheek.

"Watch the nose," she says. "It hurts like the dickens." And then she closes her eyes to accept Murabbi's kiss, and he walks out.

*

In L.A. it's a quarter till four. David wakes to the insistent ringing of his phone. It's playing "Dixie"— programmed by his girlfriend, who likes occasional reminders of her Southern roots even though she has never shown any more interest in going home than has David. He has told her more than once that programming that song in the ring tone was cruel and unusual punishment— for what, exactly, he has never said.

"You can always reprogram it," she tells him, but he hates to admit he doesn't know how. Technology befuddles him.

He squints at the green glow of his bedside clock before groping in the dark for the phone. It must be an emergency, anybody calling this early. Unless it's his goddamn agent calling to try and convince him to do commercials for Purina or, God forbid, some male enhancement pill. That son of a bitch knows no boundaries. David gropes for the phone and flips it open. "Hello."

"Did I wake you?" It's his sister Mary.

"Of course you woke me. It's two hours earlier out here and we're civilized. We don't get up with the roosters."

"It's Pop. He's in the hospital. We don't think he's gonna make it."

He kicks off the sheets and swings his legs off the side of the bed, sits up and rubs his eyes. He says, "Exactly why is it you think I should give a rat's ass?"

There's a pause on the line. Mary is momentarily shocked at his venom, but then it all comes flooding back to her, the constant fights, the outrageous accusations. She remembers that David hasn't spoken to the old man in years. She's long since resigned to accept that he'll never forgive and forget. She sighs and says, "Well maybe for Mama's sake. If you don't care about him, pretend you do. For Mama. Despite it all, she still loves the old man."

"Yeah. Well, I guess there's that."

Next to him, Jasmine stirs awake. She pulls herself up and turns on the lamp on her side of the bed. Her face is splotched red. Under the lamp's glow he sees the spray of freckles that is hidden by makeup in all her movies. He thinks they're cute, and he feels privileged to be one of the few people privileged to see her without tons of goop on her face. Her tousled hair is thick, silky and golden. She grabs a Camel filter from the pack on her nightstand and lights it, and reaches across the bed and slips the lighted cigarette between his lips. Then she turns and stretches back across the bed to fish out another one for her. She's naked on top of the sheet. As she twists away from him he admires the shape of her hip and the contour of her arm, which remind him of *La Grande Odalisque* by Ingres. He could envision doing her in oil if knew how to paint. He's happy to be living with her. He's happy to be rich and famous and still amazed after three successful pictures to think that he's actually a movie star who gets to sleep with a starlet whom half the men in America dream about.

He takes a deep drag on the cigarette and coughs.

"Still smoking, huh?" comes the voice over the phone.

"Yeah," he snorts derisively at his own stupidity. He's been trying to kick the habit for ages but just can't seem to do it. If Jasmine would quit too, he could probably do it. They could do it together. But then, she is going to be leaving soon to shoot a picture in England. Maybe when she gets back, if they're still together. He coughs again and crushes the smoke out in his ashtray. "How's Mama handling it?"

"She's a mess."

"Yeah. Figures."

Jasmine gets out of bed and pads barefoot to the bathroom and washes her face in the sink. David watches her through the open door and ponders, as he has a million times, how unreal it is that millions of men and women have gazed upon that same naked body in fully nude sex scenes in two movies—breast implants, tummy tuck and all. It's magical the way she has remained twenty-eight for fifteen years. He tries to imagine what her fans would think if they could see her like this, but he can't quite envision it. With hair mussed and no makeup she presents a picture of vulnerability that he thinks is more lovable than her public image.

"Are you still there?" Mary asks.

"Yeah, I'm sorry. I was distracted a moment. What happened to Pop?"

"He drove his car off the top of the damn parking garage at the Golden Eagle. It woulda killed him but there were some steel cables that caught the car and kept it from falling to the ground. Melissa was with him. All she got was a busted nose."

"Thank God she's all right."

"Yes, thank God. But David, we need you. Mama needs you. Can you come?"

"What good would it be for me to be there?"

"For Pop, probably nothing. No, that's not true. I think he'd love for you to come, even if he'd never admit it. So would I. But the main thing is it would mean the world to Mama."

There's a long and uncomfortable silence while David watches Jasmine brush her teeth, and finally he says, "All right. Yeah. I guess I can come. I'll catch the earliest flight I can."

He says goodbye to Mary and snaps the phone shut. Jasmine comes back into the bedroom. They both slip into underwear and lightweight robes and head to the kitchen where Jasmine makes coffee and David heats sweet rolls in the microwave and butters them, and they breakfast on the deck while the Southern California sun begins to burn off the early morning mist. Unlike the world he grew up in, the only water here comes from automated lawn sprinklers and the crashing of surf on sand.

Jasmine wants to know all about his father and his sister. "Just why is it you hate your father so much, and if he's so terrible why doesn't she hate him too?"

"To answer the first part, he's just a first class bastard and a bully."

"Did he beat you?"

"No, but he threatened to, and he was... I don't know, I guess what you call psychologically abusive. He's just an old fashioned macho man, and pretty powerful, too, in our part of the world. He was used to having his way. He expected to be obeyed. I'm pretty sure he slapped Mama around some, and I even suspected for awhile that he molested Mary, but she denies it."

"Denial is pretty common."

"Uh huh."

"What about the woman that was with him? Who is she?"

"My other sister. Sort of. She was never legally adopted into the family, but she was our sister nevertheless. Is, I mean, still is. I can't help thinking of them in the past tense."

"Tell me about her."

"Well, it's been about twenty years, and I don't know what she's like now. But she was one hot lady back in high school. Beautiful. Really beautiful. She could be a star if she wanted to. Sort of exotic looking for the bayou country. None of us ever knew anything about where she came from. She just showed up around about our junior year in high school. She looked like she might have come from the South Sea Islands, Hawaiian maybe or Tahitian. Maybe even a little African blood mixed in there somewhere. Actually, she said her parents were Hawaiian, but there was something weird about what little she said about them. I always felt like she had fantasized her whole past history so much that she didn't even know who she was. She was pretty wild, too. Pop brought her home one day and announced that we were going to take her into our home. She had lost her parents in a tragic accident. They were killed in a plane crash in the Rockies."

"Damn."

"Yeah."

She wipes crumbs off the glass tabletop into her cupped palm, gets up and goes to shake the crumbs out over the deck rail. "What's home like? Just another sleepy little Southern town?"

"Not hardly. Well yeah, in some ways Freedom is just another soggy little village. It's in the bayou country near the Gulf Coast. We always called it the backside of nowhere. Small, yeah, but not like other little towns. My daddy kind of ran the town. Him and the fucking sheriff who lived across the bayou from us and was one corrupt son of a bitch. He and Pop never liked each other, but they were both political animals and they knew when to fight and when to play along with each other, or the system or whatever. I guess they were both pretty cagy. Pop owned the general store, which his daddy owned before him and his daddy before him. It wasn't much of a store. Mostly what they sold was Nehis and Moon Pies and Vienna sausages and shit like that. In the early days it was a front for bootleg whiskey, which was the real family business before liquor sales were legalized. The old man had his hand in all kinds of questionable activities all over the coast. Legitimately, he supplied and maintained slot machines and juke boxes. Behind the scenes he had a hand in gambling before it was legal, and I don't know what all. Prostitution? Drugs? Organized crime? Yeah, probably all of that. Doesn't all that stuff usually go together? And my mother, well, I always thought she was as innocent as a baby kitten, but her father was another corrupt politician who had the cops and government officials by the collective balls, so she probably wasn't as naïve as I imagined.

"Colorful family."

"Yeah, well, all of Freedom was pretty damn colorful. The whole coastal strip was like a little Las Vegas. For the longest time, even long after prohibition was repealed in the rest of the country, booze and gambling were wide open, although officially illegal. They used to say it was the sheriff and the Baptist preachers that kept the coast dry and wet, if you know what I mean. Folks down there have been paying off the cops forever.

"The town of Freedom was founded by former slaves shortly after the Civil War. They called it forty acres and a mule, the rule under which freed slaves were granted land. But I found out much later that that was kind of a crock. People liked to romanticize it. Actually, the forty acres law only applied to certain areas on the East Coast, and it was repealed right after the war. But anyway, somebody down on the coast gave some emancipated Negroes some land, or they homesteaded some land or something. It was marshland, swamps, bayous, nothing anybody could farm. But I guess they were industrious people. They turned to what they could do: fishing, shrimping and rum-running. It was a town built on shellfish and booze, run by what was affectionately called the Negro Mafia—smalltime hoods for the most part, and not all black despite the name. The real power was with a handful of crooked politicians. I don't know exactly what role my old man played in all of that, but if it was dirty and lucrative he had his hands in it someway. And his daddy before him. That's my proud legacy."

She starts laughing.

"I guess it is funny," he says.

"No, not that. I was just thinking it's no wonder you took up acting. You grew up in a movie. By-the-way, you're starting to talk real Southern again. Do you know that when you talk to folks from home you slip back into a Southern accent?"

"You too. I've heard you."

It was true. Jasmine, from a little town in Georgia, and David had each noticed that trait in the other. They had both worked hard with a dialect coach to get rid of their accents because it was hard to get a role in a movie when you sounded like Gomer Pyle. Unless you were playing a Gomer Pyle type. Ironically, the first role David was cast in was as a good ol' boy in a courtroom drama set in Mississippi, and after that he had been typecast and never got to use his hard earned accent-free voice. His character, Raymond Moon, was a big hit. He was supposed to be a supporting character, the lovable sidekick, but he turned out to be more popular than the lead, so there were a couple of spinoffs with David's character as the lead.

Back inside they turn on the TV to catch the morning news and are surprised to see that Pop's accident is the lead story. It's not often that a car wreck all the way across the country makes the news on the West Coast, but his father's wreck had the kind of dramatic visuals broadcasters love to run on a slow news day, plus the added bonus that the victim was related to a famous movie star. There is a clip of the car trapped in a network of cables with a camera shot from a helicopter that makes the six-story height look twice as high. Black clad rescue workers rappelling down the side of the building look like something out of a heist movie. "Damn," David says, "would you look at that?"

It's a long, long news segment, almost as interminable as one of those chase scenes they're always shooting live from a TV helicopter. He watches them hoist first Melissa and then his father out of the car and up to the roof of the building.

"Can you book me a flight?" David asks. He no more knows how to book a flight online than he knows how to reprogram his cell phone ring tone, so Jasmine goes online and buys a first class ticket to Atlanta for the following morning. From Atlanta there are daily flights to Carver Field in Freedom on what the locals call a puddle jumper, a six passenger Cessna.

"How long are you going to be gone?" Jasmine asks.

"Till we know whether he's going to live or die, I guess."

"Well, we start location shots in England next week, so I don't know when I'll see you. I'll call you."

*

David steps off the jet in Atlanta and blurts out to no one in particular, "Jesus, Joseph and Mary, how do you people stand this heat?"

A breezy voice behind him responds, "Been a while since you've been back down South, huh?"

"Not near long enough." He looks over his shoulder to see who's talking, expecting some college girl from the sound of the voice. It's Sue Ellen Jamison (or whatever last name she may be going by now, assuming she must be married). He can hardly believe his eyes. She's wearing a pink skirt and a white blouse, shoulder length blonde hair and just a hint of makeup. Her luggage consists of a single suitcase and a laptop strapped to a rolling carrier. She's wearing glasses. That's something new. She looks her age, forty-two, which he has decided is the age at which women look their best. He's not sure when he thinks men look their best. At his age, 42? But probably not, he thinks. Most men are beginning to turn gray or bald at 42, and he thinks they look better when they get all the way silver or all the way bald. He was pleased with his own appearance at thirty, but now he's beginning to think he might look better if he could speed up the aging process just a tiny bit (and then maybe stop it altogether). Of course if he really wanted to he could dye his hair silver. But Sue Ellen, wow! She looks great. And that's exactly what he tells her as he grabs her with a big hug. He blurts, "Jesus, it's good to see you. You look great. I almost didn't recognize you. It's good to see you. Did I say that already?"

She laughs, "I certainly didn't have any trouble recognizing you. But you do look a little different in person."

"That's what my fans always say. I think they're always a bit disappointed when they see me in person."

She says, "Catching the puddle jumper to Freedom?"

"Yeah." They walk toward the Cessna as they talk. He shades his eyes from the glare. She says, "Maybe your fans have outlandish expectations. If you ask me, you look just like you always did."

"You too, but better. Something's different."

"I had my nose fixed?"

"Fixed how? Why?"

"Don't you remember? It was crooked."

"Oh yeah. I thought it was kinda cute that way."

"And I colored my hair."

"Ah, that's it. It suits you. You're a real beauty."

"As good looking as Jasmine Jones?"

"Better. Shitfire, I musta been an idiot letting you get away."

"Bull hockey." She slips her glasses off and puts them in her purse. She pulls her shoulders back. He notices that she's making an effort to put her best features forward, with only a modicum of subtlety, despite passing his compliment off as bull hockey.

They're both sweating by the time they board the little plane and take off. They reach for handkerchiefs almost simultaneously, wipe their brows and laugh at the thought of what kind of picture they must make. "You think we could choreograph that any better?" he asks.

They're the only passengers on the Cessna. Between Atlanta and Pensacola they catch up on the past twenty-odd years. She tells him she has been married and is now divorced with two teenage sons, twins, and a daughter.

"Twins, huh? Wow! Just like me and Mary."

"Yep. I even thought about naming them after you two."

"Why didn't you?"

"Well, for starters, they're both boys, so I don't think either of them would have wanted to be called Mary. And then I didn't think my husband would be too crazy about me naming them after you. Actually, we did name one of the boys David, but after his grandfather. The other one's named James. The girl is Jeri."

"Who's their father?"

"Jimmy Dale Patterson."

"Jimmy Dale! My god, I can't believe it."

"Yeah, I know. Me either. But it's the lord's own truth."

"He's not still wearing plaid pants and shirts held together with safety pins, is he?"

"Nope. Now he dresses like Tiger Woods."

"So did you name James after his daddy?"

"Uh huh. It was a compromise. He wanted to name one of them Jimmy and the other one Dale."

They're quiet for a minute. They listen to the drone of the engine, and then David starts to laugh at a private thought, and quickly stifles it.

"What?" she asks.

"Nothing."

"Aw come on."

"I was just remembering." He pauses, doesn't finish the thought.

"What?"

"Knockers."

Sue Ellen says, "Oh my god, do you have to remind me?"

"Well you did fit the description. Still do." He makes a show of assessing the knockers in question with an evil leer and nods as if expressing satisfaction that, yep, they're still rather outstanding.

The plane lands briefly in Pensacola and picks up a man who looks like a traveling salesman circa 1920, complete with suspenders, sweat soaked white shirt and a white straw hat. He takes off his hat and practically bows at Sue Ellen. "Hot day, ain't it, ma'am?" he says.

"Ain't they all?" she answers.

They take off again and are soon flying along the coast. David looks out the window at the dark water, which turns much lighter near shore where small whitecaps break. He remembers wading in that tepid water and scouring the beach with a metal detector, finding a few old coins and a smattering of junk items such as forks with broken tines. Seldom anything worth keeping. There's a little archipelago near the coast, and the shallow water between the islands and the mainland beach is generally calm. There were never enough waves for surfing. He remembers seeing people sunbathing with their reclining beach chairs set far out in the shallow surf with the cooling water lapping their backsides.

He says, "I still can't get over running into you like this. It's like a one in a million chance."

"Oh, I don't know. You're going home to Freedom. This is the only flight, and I catch it a lot. Besides, we would bump into each other at the hospital or at your folk's place. I still visit them, you know."

"No, I didn't know that. I was going to look you up. I already thought about it."

"Well there you go. Now you don't have to."

She had actually expected to see him on the flight and had been looking forward to it. She worked for a drug company with headquarters in L.A. and Atlanta. A lot of her work could be done by telephone and e-mail, and she still lived, most of the year, back home in Freedom, but also spent a lot of time in L.A. and Atlanta. She had been in the L.A. office when she heard about Pop's accident. The reason she expected to see David was she heard on the news that he was going home, and unless he was going to rent a car, the puddle jumper to Carver Field was the only way he could get home.

Sue Ellen was his first, if not his only, love. He can recall every moment they spent together, especially the two times they made love. The first time had been after a football game when they were juniors in high school. Like most kids, they did it in the front seat of his daddy's car. He's pretty sure it ranked as one of the most disastrous first times ever (he should have told the tale in his monologue). For a long time before they actually made love they discussed the pros and cons of whether or not to do it and if so when and where. Once they made up their minds to go through with it, they planned it out with care. Here's a condensed version of their discussions, pared down from talks that went on over the course of several dates:

"When are we going to do it?"

"After the homecoming game."

"On the beach?"

"Yeah."

"In your daddy's car?"

"I guess so."

"Don't forget the condom."

"Hell, I'm gonna fill the glove compartment with 'em just in case."

Along the beachfront there were pullout parking areas every quarter mile or so. During the day they were mostly filled with the cars of tourists and beachcombers, but at night there were plenty of parking places. David pulled his daddy's Pontiac off the highway and yanked up the parking break. He cranked the driver side window down an inch or two to let in some of the cool fall air, and they faced each other and said, "Okay, here we are. Let's do it."

He scooted out from under the steering wheel and over to the middle of the front seat. It was a big car. There was plenty of room. They put their arms around each other, and they kissed, and he reached his hand under her blouse. "Are you sure you want to do this?" she asked.

"I'm sure. Are you?"

"I think so."

"You think so?"

"I know so."

"You sure?"

"Yes."

"Then let's get on with it."

They started frantically trying to undress one another. He was hurrying to get the deed done before she changed her mind. She was anxious for the same reason. Four shaking hands groping in the dark could not manage to unfasten her bra, so she tried to jerk the bra over her head. A snap or a strap or something got caught in her hair. "Shit! Shit!" she grumbled. "It's caught. Help me here."

He reached in the dark and pulled her hair trying to untangle the offending undergarment. She slapped his hand away and said, "Never mind. I'll do it. You get out of them pants," which he tried to do in a rush but couldn't manage because he hadn't bothered to take his shoes off. His shoes got caught up in his jeans, so he gave up and left his jeans and his underwear wrapped around his ankles, which made it very hard to maneuver in the cockpit of the car—the roomy, roomy front seat that seemed to be growing ever more constricted with every passing second. Elbows and knees and bunched-up clothing seemed to be everywhere but where they belonged. It was as if they were caught up in a tumbling clothes drier. And when they finally managed to get the necessary body parts uncovered and he situated himself between her legs and entered her, he finished in no time flat.

"That's it?" she said.

"I guess so." He gasped, as shocked as she was by the suddenness but winded and sweat-soaked nevertheless. He pulled out and reached down to roll the rubber off. He said, "Oh shit! Christamighty!"

"What?"

"It ain't there."

"What?"

"The rubber. It musta come off."

"Come off! Jesus Christ, how could that happen?"

"Well I don't know." He started groping around underneath them on the seat. "Maybe I didn't put it on right."

He realized that he must not have rolled it down all the way and confessed that he'd never put one on before and didn't really know how to do it, which she said was actually "kind of sweet... but Jesus, where'd it go?"

"It must be still in you."

"How do we get it out?" she asked.

"I suppose you just have to reach in there and fish it out."

"Me?"

"Well yeah. I mean, it's your..."

"But it's got your stuff in there."

After the act, they were rather disgusted by the messiness of body fluids—something they'd given only cursory thought to before.

"Don't watch me," she said. She reached between her legs and felt around and extracted the limp, inside-out condom, pinching it between thumb and forefinger and flipping it disgustedly at the car window. But the window on her side was rolled up, so it splat against the glass and fell in her lap. "Eee-euw! Get it off!" He picked it up gingerly and rolled down the window and started to throw the used condom out, but suddenly stopped his arm mid-swing, because standing outside the car with a flashlight angled upward enough to make visible the self-satisfied leer on his face was a uniformed policeman. David was caught wet handed holding the rubber, his pants down around his ankles. The cop flashed the light into the car. He aimed it at Sue Ellen's breasts, and then down to her lap where her hands were frantically and simultaneously pulling up her panties and pushing down her hiked-up skirt. He got a good look at her before she managed to cover up, and then he blinded them both by aiming his flashlight at their faces again.

"You're Pop Lawrence's boy, aincha?" the cop asked.

"Yes sir."

"Well looka here, son. This ain't no good place to be making out. They's muggers that patrol this beach at night looking for just the likes of you kids." His voice was deep and authoritative, and yet casual. Just as he had been lackadaisical and unashamed about copping a good look at Sue Ellen's nakedness before she managed to cover up, his manner of speech seemed to imply that while serious about the threat of muggers along the beachfront, he was casually friendly with David who, after all, was the son of an important man in the area. David felt sure that there was no threat to them.

The cop said, "There's been two reports just this week. There's a group of 'em, at least two men and maybe three, depending on which report you believe. They hit on younguns that's making out, and they don't just rob them. They beat up the boys and then have their way with the girls. No kidding. That's how come we patrol down here now. We ain't trying to keep y'all from fucking—excuse my French, Miss. We're here to protect you. Onliest thing I'm trying to say is y'all need to find some other place to do your stuff. Now y'all go on and get out of here, ya hear?"

"Yes sir," they both said. Sue Ellen had looked down at her prayer-grasped hands in her lap the whole time the policeman was talking. She could not bear to look him in the eye. The cop turned off his flashlight and walked away heading toward another car that was parked in the next parking spot farther down the beach. David searched the area for the cop's car, finally spotting it across the road in the parking lot of an apartment complex. It looked like he had parked on the far side of the highway in order to be able to approach parked cars without his headlights giving warning of his approach, meaning that while he might be sincere about warning parked couples of the danger they were in he was also hoping to be able to catch the men who were accosting lovers, assuming he had not made that part up. Or maybe it was evidence that he was out to get a little thrill by watching them make out.

David was still holding the limp condom. He shook his finger out the window and it fell to the sand.

"Let's get out of here," Sue Ellen said.

He cranked the engine and pulled onto the highway. She asked him to find the nearest place with a bathroom so she could wash herself out.

"I got to get it all cleaned out. How long does it take for sperm to swim upstream?"

"I don't know."

"If I wash out immediately, do you think it will keep me from getting pregnant?"

"Yeah, sure. I guess. Geeze, I don't know about that kind of stuff."

"Oh God, oh God, it better."

Tourist traps of all the usual types were wall-to-wall along the beach drive. He pulled into the nearest open diner and they went in, and she rushed right through to the women's restroom, leaving him to explain to the waitress that they weren't going to order anything but she just had to go to the bathroom.

"The bathrooms are for customers only."

He glanced around. There were no customers. "This is an emergency," he said. "Besides, she's already in there. If you want to go in there and pull her out, then you just be my guest. But she's been known to scratch and bite and pull hair."

The waitress was adamant. She said, "Then you got to order something to make it right."

"All right. I'll have a Coke."

"Will that be takeout?"

"Yes."

"And will there be anything else?"

"No, dammit."

She served him a fountain Coke in a paper cup, and as it turned out, he was glad to have it. He hadn't realized he was thirsty, but he was suddenly bone dry. He swigged it down in desperate gulps.

Sue Ellen came out of the restroom and said, "Take me home, please."

They lived in dread for the next three weeks. They spent as much of that time together as they could, but didn't have sex again. They were relieved when she finally got her period. After that, they decided not to take any more chances. "Not ever?" he asked.

"No, certainly not forever, but not until... well, until it feels right, I guess."

They still loved each other. There was never any question about that. But they were young. They had plenty of time. They were afraid of another slip-up, or "slip-off" as he put it. Sue Ellen, who was not very religious but did believe in a god who sometimes pokes his business in human affairs, was afraid that the condom slipping off had been a warning from God not to take chances. Even if she could be assured there would be no more such accidents, there was always the chance that a condom could leak. Unlike many of her classmates, she had actually believed the health teacher, Miss Montoni, when she said condoms were only fifty percent effective. Not having sex, however, was not difficult for them, because what they called not having sex meant no missionary style or any other style humping with genital insertion. Hand jobs and head jobs didn't count.

They finished school, and in the fall they went off to separate colleges. They called each other and wrote, and got together during holidays, but the time when it felt right to finally make love again seemed never to come, not until a full two years later when they found themselves together at a hurricane party. It was traditional for people who owned beach houses to throw hurricane parties to ride out the big storms. Of course a lot of people had been killed trying to ride out Hurricane Camille back in sixty-nine, but that had been a once-in-a-lifetime storm, and everyone knew nothing like that would come again. At least that's what they thought in sixty-nine, and still thought in the early eighties.

It was the Labor Day weekend. For a whole week Weatherman Donny, the hot-shot new weatherman on Channel 7, had been reporting a hurricane making its way across Haiti and the Bahamas and up the east coast of Florida, People from Tampa to Pensacola were waiting pending evacuation orders. And then Weatherman Donny announced that the storm had changed directions and was heading toward the Gulf Coast with top winds of seventy to eighty miles per hour and forward motion at twelve miles per hour. The eye of the storm was aimed right at the Moss's beach house. Randy's parents were in Europe (his father working on his reputation as the sheriff who was always on vacation when he was most needed at home). Randy had assured them that he'd leave the coast if the storm reached category two. But he knew that riding out a category two would be the greatest thrill of all, especially if he could do it with a house packed with drunken fraternity boys and lusty sorority sisters.

The on-and-off friendship between David and Randy was at its lowest point at the time, and David would not have gone to Randy's hurricane party if another friend had not dragged him along, telling him simply that they were going to a party but not who's party it was. Sue Ellen was there under similar circumstances, having been invited by other friends, not Randy.

There was loud music and a keg of beer and people were snorting coke and smoking marijuana, and the wind and rain outside was fierce. David and Sue Ellen found each other and clung together. "This is no fun at all," Sue Ellen shouted over the music and the loud chatter and the howling wind. Lightning flashed outside. A deafening clap of thunder shook the house, and they heard the crack of tree limbs splintering. Lightning struck a transformer a block away and fire flashed high in the sky and the sound of it was like the crash of speeding automobiles. Everybody ooohed like spectators at a fireworks display.

David and Sue Ellen went upstairs and found an empty bedroom and went in and shut the door behind them and pushed a heavy dresser up against the door for safety from the storm and from the storm of drunken partygoers who might try at any moment to crash in on their sanctuary. They held each other tightly and they kissed. Mouths open wide, tongues probing. He gripped her soft butt cheeks and pulled her groin into him. They tore at each other's clothing. They stripped naked and fell onto the bed and made love to the sound of roaring wind outside. The wind grew louder. Windows rattled. Rain hitting the glass sounded like buckshot. Screaming guitars from downstairs and the throb of bass and drums shook the floor. And suddenly, with a horrifying whooshing and ripping sound, the roof blew off above their bed. In one big section, it simply lifted off and sailed away, and torrential rain poured down on their naked bodies, and they scampered off the bed and crawled underneath it where the darkness was like the bowels of a cave, and they held on to each other and laughed until they cried. And then the wind slowly subsided and the rain became a gentle patter, and they crawled out from under the bed as if entering an alien world. "Oh fuck," she gasped. "That was intense."

Feeling their way in the dark, they scooped up clothing from the floor— "What a icky, icky, feeling," she said, "slipping into wet clothes"— and got dressed and went downstairs. On the ground floor there was not a single window with glass intact. Furniture was overturned and water stood ankle deep on the buckled hardwood floor. The whole ground floor was awash with glass shards and cigarette butts and ashes and books off the shelf, and someone's shirt had somehow ended up hanging off the blade of a ceiling fan. All of this they saw as if through dark glasses, helped by the flickering light of candles as someone rounded up a few and set them ablaze with their trusty Zippos. The deck outside the glass doors was simply gone. It was eerily quiet after the howling wind. The clouds overhead drifted apart and a full moon cast its silvery light on the water. As far as they could see out over the now gentle water, bits and pieces of jagged wood bobbled on the waves, all seen in silhouette and shadow. Inside, a couple slept on the couch, his leg hiked over hers and one arm trailing in the standing water on the floor. A woman huddled in a corner crying and shaking while her boyfriend tried to comfort her. There was a makeshift bandage on her arm leaking blood. Two men were trying to clean up the debris-strewn floor with a broom and a mop. Randy Moss sat on a bar stool by the Halloween glow of a lantern surveying the damage and looking a lot like the cop who had approached them on the beach two years earlier. He was singing a song they couldn't recognize. He lifted his glass to David and Sue Ellen as if proposing a toast as they came downstairs and passed through the room. They ignored him and sloshed through the water and out the door. Outside was utter destruction as far as they could see. They stepped over the trunk of a fallen tree and made their way to her car, which was miraculously unharmed by the storm other than a few scratches. "I think it's okay," she said, "Where's yours?"

"I didn't drive. I came with Johnny and Chuck. Look over there." He pointed to an upside-down Ford jammed against the broken hull of a thirty-foot shrimp boat a good hundred yards away from the broken pier where the boat had been moored. "That's Chuck's car."

"I guess I'll have to take you home, if we can get there."

They had to drive across lawns to avoid gaping places where pavement was mangled, and they were forced to take a long detour because of an unusable bridge, but they eventually managed to work their way away from the coast and into the vicinity of Freedom, where the storm damage was much less severe. Her headlights picked up paper, cans, bottles and small limbs in the road, but only a few of the street signs had been blown down, and it looked like none of the houses had been destroyed. Driving along Liberty Street, they saw the blazing lights of Little Don's Diner. It looked like half the town was there. It was four o'clock in the morning, well past Don's usual closing time. Little Don's was almost solid glass across the front with a row of six booths inside the window. One pane had been shattered and already a plywood panel covered it. Otherwise, there appeared to be little damage. Inside, every booth was filled with customers. Everyone was talking excitedly about the storm. David's sister was there with Buddy Boudreau and Melissa with her latest boyfriend, Scooter Davis, and another couple that David and Sue Ellen didn't know. Mary told everybody to make room so David and Sue Ellen could squeeze in.

They ate bacon and eggs with grits and toast, and drank many cups of coffee. Everyone had tales to tell about what they had seen and heard. "Where were y'all?" Melissa asked David and Sue Ellen, and they broke into laughter, and Sue Ellen's face turned red.

Melissa said, "Ah ha!"

David said, "We were at a party at Randy Moss's beach house. There ain't much of his house left."

"Good," Melissa said. "I hope he got his ass blown out to sea."

"Afraid not," David said, "When we left he was singing some stupid beer-drinking song and toasting the survivors."

"And just what were you two up to when the shit hit the fan?" Mary teased.

"That's for us to know and you to find out," Sue Ellen said.

And Melissa said, "Oooh! You did the deed in the middle of a hurricane. That must have been something."

*

They circle low over the field. The plane banks, and David peers down at the sparkling water of the bay. Spread out from the water's edge are flat expanses of seagrasses like Kansas wheat fields only shiny green. Wooden piers and boat houses jut out over the water. He spots his old home and the family store, the town and the schools, and then farther to the north open fields with clumps of oaks and maples and huge magnolias and small forests of shortleaf pines. A suburban development has sprouted up to the northwest where once upon a time the view from an airplane was solid pine forest as far as the eye could see. Circling in over Carver Field they see the gray strip of runway and the red tin roofs of the hangars and the office with the windsock on the corner, a scattering of cars in the parking lot. The sky is milky blue, almost white. They sit down with a little bump and taxi to a stop in front of the office. David glances out the window before unbuckling and standing up. "I see they've still got that stupid sign on the roof," he says. The sign says, *If you love Freedom, You're home now.*

The heat slaps him in the face once again when he steps out of the plane, although at ninety degrees Fahrenheit and with a breeze off the water it is somewhat cooler than it had been in Atlanta. A television reporter and cameraman meet him on the tarmac. "Mister Lawrence, excuse me, sir. But would you mind if I ask you a few questions?"

He notices that the cameraman is waiting for his answer before filming. "Jesus. Y'all actually ask permission?"

"Yes sir. Welcome home."

"Thank you."

The cameraman hoists his camera to his shoulder and takes aim. The reporter gives him a roll-camera signal. He says, "Well sir, I guess the first thing I ought to ask is, is this lady here your companion?"

David breaks into a broad smile. He even licks his lips. He says, "Believe it or not, this beautiful woman was my high school sweetheart and to this day the only woman I ever loved. And you can quote me on that."

Sue Ellen takes his arm and beams at the camera. The reporter says, "Does that mean you're breaking up with Jasmine Jones to take up with your childhood sweetheart?"

Panic. A sudden slap of reality. For all his experience with reporters, David has yet to learn that he can't simply blurt out with the first thing that comes to mind. He can't get it through his mind that reporters don't recognize when he's joking. "Hold on a second. You probably shouldn't use the part about the only woman I ever loved. Just cut that. Okay, keep rolling and use this..." he clears his throat, his voice drops an octave.

"Believe it or not, this beautiful woman was my high school sweetheart, and I was overjoyed to run into her on the flight from Atlanta." He throws an arm around Sue Ellen and kisses her chastely, then says, "Jasmine Jones will have my fucking balls if you broadcast that first part, and I *know* you can't use what I just said on the air." (Surely, he reassures himself, these polite Southern reporters won't simply bleep the f-word and go ahead and broadcast that.) "Off the record," he says, "was it Jasmine that told you I was coming here?"

"Well I wouldn't know about who told what. We got a call from our network affiliate in L.A., but didn't nobody say who tipped them off."

David tells the reporter that he has come home to be with his father who was in an automobile accident. The reporter says they're well aware of the accident. It's been all over the news. He asks a few routine questions about upcoming film projects (there's nothing definite in the works for him, but his monologue is going to run on HBO again, and he plugs Jasmine's new film, a revision of *Tom Jones*).

"So you and Jasmine Jones are still together?" the reporter then asks.

"Well she's off to London and I'm here, but we parted with the intention of coming back to one another."

"Do you intend to marry her?"

"We don't have any definite plans one way or the other. We just take it one day at a time."

After the reporter politely thanks him and ends the interview, Sue Ellen says, "That was interesting. I wonder how he'll spin it."

"It'll be a brief item on the local news, and they'll replay clips from the accident. And then the tabloids will pick up on it, and they'll be claiming that I'm having an affair with my old high school sweetheart, and you, my dear, will be the next worldwide sensation."

"I don't believe it."

"Oh, believe it, honey. That's the way it works. You just better hope there are no nude pictures of you floating around anywhere, because if there are they'll be all over the Internet by this time tomorrow."

"Oh God, no. Maybe. My ex-husband took some, but I think he destroyed them."

"He's not the kind of sleazebag who'd actually sell them to *Hustler*, is he?"

"No. Never. What about Jasmine? Is she gonna be pissed at you?"

"Nah. She's going to think I was having a jolly old time with a reporter who shouldn'a been asking about my love life in the first place."

"But he didn't. You brought it up."

"Oh yeah. I did, didn't I?"

They've made their way around to the front of the building where her car awaits. It's a sensible family car, a three-year-old Honda mini-van, forest green, a Booker T High Pirates sticker on the back window. "What now?" she asks. "Is somebody picking you up?"

"Mary."

"Oh, I'd like to see her. I could wait with you. Maybe we could grab a bite to eat."

"Good idea. Is Little Don's still here?"

"Little Don will be here after the Apocalypse."

"Great. I'll call Mary's cell and tell her to meet us there."

They climb into Sue Ellen's car and she cranks up, and immediately some terribly obnoxious music blasts from her CD player. Whatever godawful stuff her kids had been playing. "Oops, sorry," she reaches to turn the volume down.

It's a short drive to Little Don's. Freedom looks a lot like he remembers it: muddy ditches alongside the road, brambles, cattails, the giant oak right at the sharp turn onto Liberty Street, small clapboard houses with children's toys scattered in the yard, the same old profusion of potted plants on Widow Simpson's front porch. But there are a few more houses than he remembers, and a new strip mall, a cell phone tower where they used to play ball—and what really amazes David, new condos lining the banks of Bujold Bayou.

On the way to the diner Sue Ellen talks about her marriage to Jimmy Dale Patterson. "He actually turned out to be a much more conventional adult than we ever would have imagined. Kind of boring, to tell the truth, but he was a good father. Still is."

"All I remember is he tried to start a punk rock band with the Simpson boy and Malcolm Ashton. They were god awful. I can't believe you married him."

"I can't either, but what was a girl to do stuck down here on the backside of nowhere with no prospects?"

"How long did it last?"

"Way too long."

"So how come you broke up?"

"Who knows? Just one of those things." She tells him that she and Jimmy Dale were comfortable with each other but there was never any real spark. The divorce was amicable and sharing time with the kids works very well for both of them. She says she enjoys her job as a sales representative for a pharmaceutical company. She's been with them since before her marriage, makes pretty good money and gets to travel a lot. Plus she gets a lot of drug samples. Her children are in high school. When her business takes her out of town overnight they stay with their father. He's a plumbing contractor. Fortunately they both have a lot of job flexibility. "He's really good with the boys, but I think he's kind of scared of Jeri."

"Jerry?"

"Jeri with an I. That's my girl. Jimmy Dale doesn't know what to do with girls. He's overly protective, scared to death some boy's going to get in her pants. So she never dates when she's staying with her father. She doesn't want her dates to have to undergo his scrutiny."

Sue Ellen pulls up close behind a city bus. David notices a printed ad on the back of the bus: *Big wheels keep on turning, our slots keep on burning. Golden Eagle Casino.*

"Golden Eagle," he says. "Isn't that the one Pop drove off of?"

"That's the one."

"Way I hear it, the fucking casinos have ruined the coast."

"How would you know? You haven't been here since before they came."

He thinks he detects a little bitterness in her tone. He says, "Yeah, I know. But still."

"When we were kids the coast was all cheap amusement parks and souvenir shops and night clubs. Now it's cheap amusement parks and souvenir shops and night clubs and casinos. Not much difference except the casinos have brought in lots of money. Big, big bucks. And your old man is getting a lot of it."

"Yeah. Like he needs it."

*

Little Don's looks just like he remembers it, a metal box in red and white with huge windows and a sign shaped like a shark's fin jutting out from the front and lapping half the roof—fifties modernism. Inside, the shiny chrome has been dulled by decades of smoke and grease. The vinyl on booths and barstools is torn and taped. The one big difference, which takes David totally by surprise, is that his picture is plastered all over the one section of wall where a chalkboard menu once hung. Posters from all three of his movies and an old photograph of him with Don taken when he was fifteen years old.

They step inside. The air conditioning feels good. Immediately Little Don rounds the counter and grabs David in a bear hug and exclaims, "Welcome home, boy." A good foot shorter than David, his head presses against David's sternum and David's chin rubs his bald head.

"Thanks, man," David says, "it's good to see you. You're looking good." He thinks that Don must be in his eighties by now, but he doesn't look much older. Or, as he revises his assessment, Little Don looked ancient twenty years ago but he doesn't look any more ancient now.

"Hey, I was really sorry to hear about your old man. Have you seen him yet?"

"No, not yet. I just got off the plane."

"Okay. Well you must be hungry after your flight. Howzabout I fix you one of my burgers? On the house."

"Sure. That'd be great. But Mary's coming. I think we'll wait till she gets here. Maybe I'll get a beer while I'm waiting. Do you have anything besides Jax and Budweiser?"

"You name it, we got it. Porter, stout, pilsner."

David laughs, "Damn Don, you've really come up in the world since I've been gone. Next thing I know you'll be serving bagels for breakfast, with lattes."

"We do. New York style bagels and ever kind a coffee you can think up. Ain't no moss growing on this ol' coot."

"Well ain't you sumpin'? Awrighty, I think I'll have me a stout."

They scoot into a window booth while they're talking. David smiles in pure delight at Little Don's enthusiasm. He's forgotten how exuberant he can be, how downright loveable. He's one of the few survivors of the old Freedom, the Freedom of local legend. Close Little Don's and the whole place would be just like any other Southern town. Bury him and the history of the town would evaporate like the morning dew.

*

The freed slaves who founded the village of Freedom were accustomed to hard work but unaccustomed to making their way in a world of white men. Before migrating to Freedom, the former slaves thought their former owners would respect their newly granted freedom, but they quickly found out the white devils knew how to get around the law in any number of ways and virtually reinstate slavery. Any number of ways? Yes, but only one was needed, the simplest of all—vagrancy laws. Anybody could be arrested for vagrancy and forced to toil on work gangs. So even though the big cotton plantations were gone, there was a lot of other work to be done throughout much of the Southland that was once done by slaves and was now done by prisoners who had been arrested for the crime of being poor and black.

But Freedom was not much like the rest of the South. The place was a low lying island unsuitable for growing any of the crops the new settlers knew how to grow, so they turned to fishing. Shrimp and crab became their new cash crop. Not that they knew how to catch them or process them or market them, but they soon figured it out.

Also among the founders of Freedom were rum runners from the Caribbean, pirates, thieves, murderers, drunks, and a handful of poor white sharecroppers who were even more lost and afraid than the former slaves. These few whites who cast their lot with the black settlers were survivors from the Confederate Army, a good many of them deserters. They were hard-working and decent sorts, and they quickly discovered that the poor blacks were more welcoming of them than more affluent white people had ever been. But these more affluent white people did not settle in Freedom, and the way of life that governed the rest of the post-war South did not apply. Until midway through the twentieth century the area, which to anyone outside of a thirty-mile radius might as well have been a foreign country, was a haven of racial harmony in a divided South. But with newfound wealth and leisure following World War II—not to mention the availability of air conditioning, which made the South livable at last—a few wealthy whites from the North discovered that the quiet bays and bayous around Freedom were great spots for vacation cottages. These were factory owners who lived part-time in Freedom to escape the harsh winters in the north, commuting back and forth to peek in on their factories from time to time. One family, the Ostermans (locals took to calling them oystermans) had owned and operated a small wagon manufacturing plant in Ohio. Seeing that the fisherman families in Freedom needed boats, they turned their wagon-building knowledge to boat building, and a whole new industry bloomed in Freedom. Part-time Freedom residents and the burgeoning boatbuilding industry created a class divide between the white leisure and management classes and laborers both black and white. A new all-white school named Freedom School was opened and the original, all-grades Freedom School was renamed Booker T Washington and became a predominantly black school. The majority of the white families, with the notable exception of the Lawrences and Boudreaus and Jamisons and a few more descendants of the original white sharecroppers, transferred their children to Freedom School. In 1966 the town shut down the public swimming pool as the only way of preventing blacks and whites from bathing in the same water—for fear the black would rub off, the more liberal citizens joked—and Strickland's Cafe, one of Freedom's two eating establishments at the time, remodeled to provide separate dining areas for blacks and whites with a pass-through kitchen in the middle. The only other place to eat, Little Don's, remained adamantly integrated. Little Don put up a sign that read: *All races, creeds and nationalities welcome. No Bigots.* Don became a symbol for the racial harmony that had once been the pride of Freedom but which in the late sixties to early seventies was all but dead.

*

Little Don stands five-foot-three and weighs close to two hundred pounds, with a barrel chest, massive biceps and a gut like a medicine ball. In the seventies he sported an Afro, but now he's bald on top with gray fringe around his ears and bright round eyes that make him look something like a bream. He had been a boxer in his youth, and he bounces on his feet like a boxer while taking orders in the diner. He walks back and forth to work every day for the exercise. Now he bobs and weaves by the booth with a white cloth draped over his arm and order pad in hand. He says again how happy he is to see David and tells him how good he looks and says he's seen every one of his picture shows.

Sue Ellen says she'll have coffee. In a moment Mary drives up in her flashy red Mazda convertible and parks right outside their window. "Fancy car," David notes.

"It's the new family trademark. Pop and Melissa and Mary all three drive red sports cars," Sue Ellen says, adding as an afterthought, "Of course Pop's is totaled now."

Mary waves from her car, unties the scarf that's holding her straw hat to her head and lets her hair fall down around her shoulders. She steps out of her car in her worn coveralls and a sleeveless T-shirt. David watches her stride to the door. Sunlight glints off the glasses that dangle from a chain around her neck. She comes in and greets David with a big hug. They look more like identical twins than the fraternal twins they are. Identical eyes and noses and chins, but her cheeks are puffy with weight put on over the years that he's avoided with exercise and diet. If he ever doubted that a tendency to put on weight is in his genes, his twin sister provides all the evidence he needs.

"Welcome home," she says. "It's really good to see you. God I've missed you."

"Looks like you've been working your garden."

"Yep."

She greets Sue Ellen and then says, "I got to run to the little girls' room before I order."

The word twittery comes to mind, which is not a way David would have ever described her in the past. Watching her walk away, he notices that she has sort of a high-hipped, flat butt. Has that always been the case? He can't remember, but he makes a mental note: I'm sure glad I was the boy half.

When she returns she scoots into the booth next to Sue Ellen so she's facing her brother. But she quickly—twittery again—changes her mind and scoots around to his side saying, "I just gotta hug you one more time."

David says, "I didn't realize how much I missed you till I saw you."

"Yeah, well, you only got yourself to blame. You're the one that can afford to travel all over the world but can't seem to find his way home."

"I know. But I just had to stay away. You know why."

"From Pop, you mean."

"Yeah, from Pop. Not to mention Randy Moss and all the right wing nut jobs."

"Right. Meanwhile, the rest of us are pretty nice people and we missed you."

Little Don returns to their booth to take their orders, burgers and fries for the women and catfish and hushpuppies for David, crisp with big chunks of onion in the hushpuppies. More cholesterol than he's had in the past month.

A couple of teenage girls approach and shyly ask, "Are you David Lawrence the movie star?"

He acknowledges that he is. They ask for his autograph and he obliges.

After the girls go back to their booth Mary updates David on the accident. "It's a miracle they weren't both killed. Melissa busted up her nose. Oh my goodness, she was the prettiest girl ever around these parts. Now I guess if she wants to look as pretty as she did before, she'll need plastic surgery. Otherwise she's okay. Nothing else hurt. But the old man's a mess. His head rammed against the windshield, and his chest and knees crashed into the steering column and dashboard. He got a big gash across his forehead that took about six stitches, and his nose was busted. Not so bad as Melissa's, but pretty bad."

Mary fiddles with her silverware while she's talking. She says, "His lip was cut and two teeth broken. You know how proud he was of still having all his teeth. Maybe you didn't. Anyway, yeah, he's gonna need false teeth, and his right knee and hip were mangled up something fierce. He's got a big freakin' cast on and can't move for shit. Speaking of shitting, he ain't done that since the accident neither. That's what mama told me. He's laid up on his back. Can't even turn over on his side. But the biggest worry for the rescuers was his heart. He definitely had a pretty good heart attack, they said. Pretty good was what Doc Duvall said. That's the way he talks. If it's really bad he says it's a good one."

For a few seconds David's mind wanders. He notes the familiarity with which Mary mentions Doc Duvall. Apparently he has been the family doctor for many years. David remembers their old doctor, Doc Riley, and wonders what's happened with him. "He passed away six years ago," Mary tells him.

Mary continues filling David in on Pop's accident. "He was kind of slipping in and out of consciousness when they got to him. They put nitro glycerin under his tongue and gave him oxygen even before they got him out of the car. They strapped him to a stretcher and lifted him by wench to the roof, where they loaded him into a helicopter."

Sue Ellen butts in to say, "Getting him out of the car and onto the stretcher was an amazing thing to watch, and they got it all on film. Men all strapped up to cables like something out of an adventure movie."
"Yeah, I saw that part on the news," David says.

"In California? It was on TV way out there?" Little Don asks. He's hovering over their booth.

"Yeah," David says.

Mary says, "The helicopter freaked him out. He told mama. Of course he wouldn't admit it to anybody else. He told her the helicopter gave him flashbacks to Vietnam."

David and Mary think back to the countless times they have heard the thum-thum-thum of helicopter blades while watching television reports or movies about Vietnam. None of them are old enough to actually remember the war, but the sounds and images have been broadcast throughout their lives.

Sue Ellen says, "I didn't even know he was in Vietnam."

"Yeah, he was, but he never talked about it." The only thing David knew about his father's service in Nam was that he had been medivacked out of the jungle with a bullet in his stomach.

There's a sudden stillness in the diner. The whole time they've been there a wall-mounted television above the bar has been broadcasting a local newscast. Something on the news has caught the attention of one or two diners and suddenly, as if responding to a silent cue, everyone stops talking and turns their attention to the television. The anchorman says, "A hundred thousand people dead in Myanmar, and many more may still be found as workers sift through the rubble left by the storm. The United States launched its first relief airlift today after prolonged negotiations with the isolated country's military rulers, who have been accused of restricting international efforts to help cyclone survivors at risk of disease and starvation. An estimated 1.5 million people are on the brink of a massive public-health catastrophe, the British charity Oxfam warned." Pictures of the disaster flash across the screen: homes turned to rubble, bodies floating in ponds and streams.

The picture changes to another kind of rubble, in this case an urban scene, the same kind of destruction but in another place. The anchorman says, "A string of tornados across America's heartland leaves death and destruction in its wake in Kansas, Missouri and Oklahoma."

"Jesus, it's everywhere. The weather's gone crazy," Sue Ellen says.

"It's global warming," Mary says. "A month ago it was snow storms in Southern California and floods in places that have never flooded before."

The anchorman says, with absurd cheerfulness, "Speaking of weather, let's go to Weatherman Donny and the Channel 7 Storm Tracker report to see what's happening closer to home."

A slightly pudgy and still youthful looking Weatherman Donny comes on, standing in front of a weather map of the region. It's the same weather guy David watched back in the eighties. His brushed hair flows back from a center part. "He looks like Lassie," David says.

Weatherman Donny says it's hot in Freedom.

"Well yeah, we kinda had that figured," Mary scoffs. They chat on about the weather for a while, agreeing that global warming is causing weather anomalies all over the world, but not agreeing about what's causing global warming or what should be done about it.

Little Don says, "It's all the junk we send up into space."

David changes the subject. He asks, "How's mama handling everything?"

Mary says, "She seems to be all right, considering what all's happened. Not that she hasn't been a nervous wreck, she has. What do you expect? And she's pretty much plum wore out now, but I think she's okay."

"You mother's an angel," Little Don says.

"Yes she is," Mary says, "and so are you. You've been a great help."

No sooner had word got out about the accident than Little Don showed up at the hospital with food for Shelly and any other friends or family members who might be there. "Nobody should have to eat hospital slop," he told them. Plus, he gave his daughter Beulah more food to take to the Lawrence place. Both food packages were loaded with fried chicken, cold slaw, potato salad and fresh made biscuits. "Ain't no sense in anybody having to cook at a time like this," he said.

Mary teases, "The way you've been doting over Mama, if I didn't know better I'd swear you were in love with her."

Don says, "I am. I been in love with yo mama since befo y'all was a twinkle in your daddy's eye. I told your daddy as much. Told him right out he didn't deserve the likes of Shelly Barbour. She was the songbird of the South, she was a angel walking."

David and Mary have heard the stories about their mother the singer but never heard her sing in public. That Shelly, her life back then, had always been legendary and a little bit unbelievable to David and Mary. They vaguely remember her singing at home, snatches of songs now and then, usually more humming then singing. And they know there had always been a grand piano in their living room, but she hardly ever played it. The one song David can remember her playing on it is an old tune called "Wang Wang Blues." But when they were growing up the piano just took up space.

But Little Don remembers listening to Shelly Barbour sing at the Jump 'N' Jive, a blues joint long since closed down. "We weren't no more than sixteen or se'mteen. Shouldn'a even been lowed in no honky tonk. It was around nineteen and fifty-eight. Ol' Luther Smith brung her in that first time. He walked her right up to the bandstand and he said sumpin' to the piano man. That was Randolph Bright. And then old Randolph he announced her like she was a celebrity or sumpin'. She stepped up there in the light, and she was the prettiest vision I ever seen. Skinny little thing with a upturned nose, and when she sang, it was like Miss Bessie Smith herself was there, like Bessie's achy black voice coming out of that little white gal. It sounded like a world of hurt in that young heart. I don't know where that come from in such a sweet young thing."

*

Shelly Barbour was what people liked to call a poor little rich girl. Her father was in the state legislature and like so many of the people who wielded power on the coast, he had his fingers in multiple business interests, some legit and some not so. Colonel Barbour, he was called, although his military rank was of questionable legitimacy at best. He was a retired colonel—or perhaps an honorary colonel, nobody seemed to know for sure—in the Gulf States Militia, a ragtag military unit rumored to have connections with the Klan, which was not recognized by any governmental body but was allowed to march as a unit in Veterans Day and Confederate Memorial Day parades. He doted on his only child and was the first to say, with pride, that she was spoiled rotten. "I just cain't help it. That girl tugs at my heartstrings, and I give her everything she wants."—everything but love and personal attention. The colonel seldom had time for either his wife or his daughter.

The Barbour home was an antebellum mansion set deep on a manicured lawn facing the beach but a good two hundred yards back from the busy coast highway. Majestic live oaks and magnolias, a bearded weeping willow and a single chinaberry tree stood sentry in a widely spaced array on the lawn. Shelly loved to climb the trees and search the horizon for ships, imagining sometimes there were pirate ships and other times fantasizing a mariner husband sailing home at long last after a voyage across the sea. She practically lived in the enveloping arms of a favorite live oak beginning when she was first able to reach the lower limbs and pull herself up and continuing until she was almost grown. When she outgrew pirate fantasies, the tree became her favorite place to hide away while reading and re-reading the novels of Jane Austin and Willa Cather, and the poems of Emily Dickinson.

The house was fronted by a broad columned porch with a trellis on one end woven with honeysuckle vines. There was an orchard in the side yard that in the heat of summer was aswarm with bees. On summer evenings the family could sit on wicker chairs on the porch and listen to a symphony of katydids and crickets and frogs while swimming in the cloying perfume of honeysuckle and rotting fruit. A driveway skirted the house and led to a three-car garage in back that had been converted from an old carriage house. There had also once been servant quarters in back, but they had long ago been torn down to make room for a tennis court and a swimming pool. Growing up, Shelly was given lavish parties for her birthday every August, hosted by her mother with the help of domestic servants. The kids played tennis and danced to phonograph records and swam in the only private swimming pool any of them had ever seen. The only year there wasn't a party was her twelfth, when she had the mumps. Colonel Barbour never attended any of the parties.

She was not allowed to leave the property alone. "It's too dangerous for a young girl," her father said. "Besides, what could you do in town that you can't do right here at home?" A driver took her to school in the morning and picked her up in the afternoon. The driver also dropped her off and picked her up at the movie shows, but only if she was accompanied by her mother or another trusted adult. She graduated high school having never dated and having been kissed only once, by Leroy Johnson underwater in the swimming pool at her fifteenth birthday party.

Most of the kids who came to her parties hardly even knew her. She invited everyone in her class, first at Church Street Elementary and later at Ross Academy, the exclusive girls school she attended beginning in the seventh grade. They came out of curiosity about the Barbour family and their estate, and because of the swimming pool and the lavish spreads the Barbour servants were known to put on. Even the famous Leroy Johnson—famous for having kissed every freshman girl at Ross Academy—came to that one party and kissed her that time only to keep his record intact. Her only real friend was Lucy Kirby.

Shelly and Lucy had been best of friends since their first day of class at Ross. At lunchtime that first day Shelly sat alone while the other girls laughed and talked in small groups at other tables. She noticed Lucy because she was the loudest, and all the other girls seemed to hang on to her every word, as if she were older and more experienced and they could learn from her the ways of the world. She wore the same green plaid skirt and black vest as the other girls, but somehow she made her school uniform look daring. She was short like Shelly but looked more grown up.

Twice during lunch Shelly noticed Lucy looking her way. None of the other girls paid her the least attention. After lunch there was a half-hour recess. The girls gathered together on the side of the school. Shelly wandered around the school yard sliding her feet in the dirt and kicking at rocks. She found a swing set and sat down in one of the swings and kicked the dirt some more. Again she saw Lucy look her way. She saw her leave the chatty group and come toward her. "Hi," Lucy said. "You mind if I swing too?"

"Not at all."

"I'm Lucy Kirby. What's your name?"

"Shelly Barbour."

"Ohmygod, you're Colonel Barbour's girl?"

"Uh huh."

Lucy pumped hard to make her swing go high, huffing and talking in bursts and shouts. The first thing she said after the introductions was, "I bet you're a virgin, aincha?"

"Well of course I am. My gosh. What a crazy thing to say."

"Well you never know," Lucy said. "I just thought we oughta get that straight right off the bat if we're gonna be best friends."

Shelly couldn't figure out which was more shocking, the virgin question or the best friends part. But Lucy had answers for both questions before they were even asked. She said, "In case you're wondering, I'm a virgin too, but I don't plan to stay that way long. And I know we're going to be best friends because you're quiet and you keep to yourself. I like that in a friend. It shows you think for yourself and you don't run with the herd."

Just as Shelly suspected, Lucy was far more experienced than any of the other seventh graders. She had already gotten drunk once, on seven and seven (Seagram's 7 and 7-Up) — "I should have waited till school started, then it would have been seven and seven in the seventh"— and she had kissed six different boys and went steady with one, and even let Leroy Johnson touch her titty once.

Lucy taught Shelly how to kiss. She taught her how to angle her head just so and how to use her tongue and avoid banging teeth together. She mixed Shelly her first highball (she managed to down only two small sips) and taught her how to smoke and how to dance. In the seventh grade, if girls dated at all, they were chaperoned dates, but Lucy bragged that she dated a boy in the eleventh grade who had his own car, and they parked on the beach and made out, but didn't go all the way.

In the summer after tenth grade Lucy and some friends, not including Shelly, went water skiing. There were four kids: Lucy and Mary

Hardy, another girl from Ross, and two boys, the infamous Leroy Johnson and his brother, Kip. Leroy's dad drove them out to the lake and also drove the boat, a brand new seventeen-foot Chris-Craft. The lake was crowded with boats that day, circling the lake and crossing one another's wakes like a swarm of giant water bugs. Mister Johnson had bought the boat just a few days earlier and had never before driven a boat. He had a hard time launching it and getting the motor started, and it took him a few minutes to get the hang of steering, not understanding that you turn an outboard motor in the opposite direction from the way you want to go. A couple of times he steered dangerously close to other boaters. The other drivers cursed them, and their wakes rocked the Johnson's boat.

After a while he seemed to get the hang of it. They were all having a good time taking turns skiing. The boys went first, and then Mary Hardy. Lucy was riding the bow of the boat, hanging onto a cleat and bucking like a cowgirl on a bronco when Mister Johnson steered into the big wake of another boat at a dangerous angle. If he was going to cross the wake, he should have headed directly into it, but he hit it sideways and their boat almost capsized. He panicked, turned quickly to the left and then back to the right. The sudden turns threw Lucy off and into the water. She hit the water head first and dove as deep as she could, instantly knowing that the boat might run over her. Trying desperately to turn away from her, Mister Johnson turned the stern, and thereby the motor, right at her. If he had turned the other way, Lucy would not have been hurt. If she had not had the good sense to dive, the propeller might have hit her head. As it was, it sliced her leg from thigh to ankle like a deli slicer through sausage. She surfaced in such a billow of blood that she looked like the victim of a shark attack.

Shaken and desperate, but finally knowing what he had to do, the driver of the boat steered to where Lucy was treading bloody water and idled the engine and pulled her into the boat and took her to the boat launch where, being in a state park, there was a ranger on duty who called an ambulance. They rushed her to the hospital, stanching the blood flow as best they could on the way. There was no possibility of saving her leg.

They couldn't even salvage the pieces from the bottom of the lake. Lucy lost her leg, but was fitted with a prosthetic limb with which she could at least walk.

"I never liked dancing anyway," she said to Shelly from her hospital bed.

But Shelly knew better.

Lucy refused to let anyone pity her or make fun of her. If anything, the other girls in school looked up to her even more because of the prosthetic leg and her courage in not letting it be a tragedy. She learned to walk with barely a limp, and yes, she even taught herself to dance again—to dance well enough that if her classmates had not known she had a gimpy leg they never would have suspected.

In her senior year she was forced to transfer to a public high school because her father lost his job and could no longer pay for the private school, and she and Shelly did not see each other as often after that. Despite her boast in the seventh grade that she wouldn't be a virgin for long, she still was when she graduated high school. That summer she got a job carhopping at a drive-in restaurant where the carhop girls zipped around on roller skates. Teaching herself to skate on her false leg was not easy, but she did it. In fact, it was typical of Lucy to go for a job that offered such a physical challenge.

While carhopping that summer she fell in love with one of the boys who flipped burgers. They dated for a few months and she thought for sure he was going to propose to her. And then, just when she was almost certain he was going to pop the question, she found out that he had been sleeping with another girl, and the other girl was pregnant and he was going to marry her.

During their junior and senior high years when Shelly and Lucy were best friends Shelly's parents continued to think of Shelly as a little girl. They never thought of her as a girl who wanted to date or go to a dance or do any of the things other girls her age routinely did. It never dawned on Colonel Barbour or his wife that their little girl might be practicing the art of kissing with her friend, Lucy, or that the two of them might be spending their after-school hours yapping about boys and about who may or may not have gone all the way.

Twice and twice only Shelly spent the night at Lucy's house. She went to only one high school dance, without a date and chaperoned by her mother, who was shocked to see that her daughter's friends looked a lot like grown up men and women and that the way they danced looked a lot like preludes to sex. A lot of Shelly's classmates got married soon after graduating high school, and yet her parents still had a hard time thinking of her as anywhere near grown.

At home, Shelly seemed content to read her books and talk to Luther, the Negro gardener, about her dream of some day becoming a professional singer. Luther played phonographs for her of great blues singers like Bessie Smith and Billie Holliday and Alberta Hunter, and Shelly would sing along with a voice that was surprisingly husky. Even knowing how much she loved to sing the blues, Luther was shocked when she asked him to take her to the Jump 'N' Jive and let her sing. Luther's nighttime job was tending bar at The Jump 'N' Jive.

"Law, chile, you sure you wants to go to a place like that?"

"Why not? What's wrong with it? You'd be there."

"Yessum. But I can't be watching you all the time. They be dirty dancing and drinking, and they's boys there that it ain't no telling what they might try with a pretty little gal like you."

"Do you mean colored boys?"

But Luther said, "I mean boys of any color. They's white boys and colored both that comes to the Jive, and they all be after the same thing when they see a gal like you."

"I think I can take care of myself. I'm not a kid, you know."

"That's just the problem," Luther mumbled.

If Little Don remembered her being "sixteen or se'mteen" at the time, he was off by a few years. She was twenty. But her parents still treated her like a child, as did Luther, taking his cue from her parents and from her child-like looks.

It took a lot of cajoling to talk Luther into taking her to The Jump 'N' Jive. Once she convinced him, then they had to wait until a weekend when the colonel was going to be gone, and they had to come up with a way to keep her mother from being suspicious. An accomplice was needed—in addition to Luther himself, whom she swore to secrecy. The perfect accomplice was naturally her friend Lucy, who not only loved a good conspiracy but who had already been to The Jump 'N' Jive at least once as far back as her junior year at the academy—proof positive to the head mistress at Ross that they had miserably failed in their attempts to mold Miss Lucy Kirby into a proper young lady.

Lucy's parents were going to be gone over the Labor Day weekend, so Lucy would have the house to herself and could stay out as late as she wanted. Since Colonel Barbour was out of town, his driver was not available to take Shelly to Lucy's house, so Luther volunteered. That was a serendipitous happenstance which made it easier for Luther to escort the girls to the club, but he could have picked them up at Lucy's house anyway. Lucy asked her mother if she could spend the night at Lucy's, and Luther offered to drive her. Naturally they didn't tell her that Lucy's parents were going to be out of town.

"No'm, I don't mind taken her," Luther told Mrs. Barbour. "I's going to Freedom, and Miss Lucy's house is right on the way."

They picked Lucy up right after supper. From her house to Freedom was a twenty-minute drive, and from there they had to cross the bridge over Bujold Bayou and wind along a long and dark two-lane road through the pine forest to the little jive joint north of town. There were no street lights and very little traffic. Before heading into the dark forest, the road snaked through marshlands where, in the dark, Shelly could not tell land from water. Moss draped trees flashed ghostlike past the car. "How far is it?" she asked.

"Just about six more miles," Lucy said.

"It seems like we've already gone a hundred miles.

Luther laughed. "It be six miles going but jest three miles coming back."

"How can that be?"

"It's magic."

Soon he said, "It be just around the next curve now." And sure enough, they rounded a curve and saw the low-slung building with dimly lit windows and a neon blue Jump 'N' Jive sign on top. It looked like a chicken house. Dark humps of cars were bunched on the side of the building like boulders washed up in a storm and left at the bottom of a cliff. Inside it wasn't much lighter than the night. Red bulbs in mock Tiffany shades hung from the ceiling. Spotlights in red and white illuminated a corner stage where an old black man played boogie woogie on an upright piano. Dancers were jumping and swinging, women's hips gyrating. A blue-gray haze of smoke filled the room. It took Shelly's eyes awhile to adjust to the dark. To her eyes the dancers were a stroboscopic shadow show. The dance floor was crowded with black couples, the few white couples in the joint were seated at tables near the bandstand, seemingly content to watch and listen. There was one young white man seated alone at a table by the piano. Since he was partially in the penumbra of the spotlight focused on the piano, Shelly got a good look at him. He was wearing a light blue sports coat over a black turtleneck sweater and a black beret cocked at a jaunty angle. His nose was straight and thin, and his jaw angular. His hand practically engulfed the glass he held and his legs stretched far out from under his table. He smiled at Shelly and gave a slight nod of his head when Luther sat them at the table next to his. Luther got them settled in their seats, asked them what they wanted to drink, a soft drink for Shelly and whiskey for Lucy, and then took his place behind the bar.

Smoke irritated Shelly's eyes. Randolph the piano man went into a bluesy rendition of (appropriately) "Smoke Gets in Your Eyes" and then was halfway through a blues she didn't know before Shelly's eyes adjusted to the dark. She watched the piano man, fascinated by the large rings that sparkled on his fingers as he pounded the keyboard. Luther set their drinks on the table, and when Randolph finished his song, stepped up to the piano and said something to him that she could not hear. And then before heading back to the bar Luther leaned down and whispered in Shelly's ear, "He's gonna call you up. This is your chance to shine, sweetheart."

The piano player lit a cigarette and took a big drag, then sat the burning cigarette on the edge of the keyboard, which was already scarred from countless cigarette burns. Into the microphone he said, "Ladies and g'nmen, we got a special treat for you tonight, a real songbird in her first appearance. Y'all give a big welcome now to Miss Shelly Barbour. Come on up here Miss Shelly."

There was a smattering of applause, and Lucy urged Shelly to her feet. Shyly she took the microphone in hand and said, "Thank you."

She asked the piano man if he knew "Can't Help Lovin' Dat Man."

Lucy, now alone at her table immediately in front of the piano, listened with rapt attention. So did the tall man at the next table, but beyond those front tables there was a constant murmur of talk. The crowd was ignoring her. Until after the first few bars when her voice penetrated the crowd and one person after another began to take notice. Not everyone, but a lot of the people began to grow quiet. A few of the dancers quit dancing and stood in front of the stage. There was something mesmerizing about such a guttural yet sweet voice coming from such a little white woman—Colonel Barbour's sheltered little sweetheart of a daughter singing about heartache and longing as if she had lived a lifetime of hard work and two-timing men. In her voice was the sweetness of gurgling spring water combined with the crying of a wounded animal. She sang the blues not from the usual places of hurt poorer people might know all too well, but from the privacy of a gilded prison. The crowd applauded and shouted and whistled, and when she thanked them and went to sit back down they shouted for more. She let them coax her into singing another song.

Again they applauded long and loud. After the applause died down and she returned to her table, the young man with the beret stood up and stepped over to their table and said, "That was wonderful. I'd like to do something to show my appreciation. Can I buy you a drink?"

Shelly looked up. It was a long way to his smiling face. She said, "Thank you, but I don't drink."

"Well what's that there in your glass?" he asked.

"A Coke."

"All right then. How about another Coke?"

"Okay. That would be nice."

He turned to Lucy. "How 'bout you, ma'am. Can I buy you a Coke?"

"You could buy me a whiskey."

He laughed. "Sure 'nuff, sweetcakes. One Coke and one whiskey coming up."

He went to the bar and ordered the drinks from Luther. Luther filled a heavy glass with Coke from the fountain and poured whisky and water, lots of water, in a shot glass. He said, "Dem young girls is under my protection."

"Yes sir, I understand. I promise you my intentions are honorable."

He returned to the table. "I'm Earl Ray Lawrence. You probably never heard of me, but you mighta heard of my daddy. His name's Earl Ray too. He's the man that keeps the juke boxes and the pinball machines working and keeps the liquor flowing to all the clubs on the coast."

"Don't forget the slot machines and the whores," Shelly replied, surprising herself with her daring. "I know all about it. My daddy's the one that makes sure the law looks the other way. You might of heard of him, too. Colonel Raymond Barbour."

"Well I guess you've one-upped me now. If my daddy's the prince of the underworld, yours is the king."

"I wonder what that makes us," she said. She was just a little bit intoxicated with the whole illicit atmosphere and the sexy music and the handsome young underworld figure who bought her a Coke and leaned over her table so solicitously from his great height. She almost wished she had ordered a whiskey. "What a wild night this is," she said.

Mary has heard this tale a time or two. She says. "That was Pop. I remember mama telling us about that night. He quoted Emily Dickinson."

Clayton – The Backside of Nowhere

"That's right. 'Wild Nights! Wild Nights! Were I with thee, Wild Nights should be Our luxury!'"

"She said she'd never in her wildest dream imagined a bootlegger in a honky tonk quoting Emily Dickinson."

The Dickinson quote and the banter that followed were lost on Lucy, so she turned her attention to the piano man and drank her whiskey. It dulled the phantom pain in her leg.

Afterwhile Earl Ray looked toward the bar and muttered, "Uh oh, trouble."

"What is it?" Shelly followed his glance and saw that Luther behind the bar was talking to a uniformed officer of the law.

"That's Randy Moss, the county sheriff. He's a blowhard, but he ain't gonna bother us."

Inside Little Don's, Mary comments," He's still a blowhard. Or his son, anyway."

"Always has been," David says.

Little Don is getting peeved with the constant interruption. He says, "Would you let me finish the story?"

David and Sue Ellen laugh. They tell him to get on with it.

*

Shelly slouched down in her seat to hide from the sheriff. It looked for a moment as if she would slide completely under the table. She said, "He's been out to the house before. He knows me. God, I hope he doesn't see me."

"Well it's a little too late to try and hide now. He's spotted you already, and he's coming this way," Earl Ray said.

The sheriff came over and plopped both of his heavy hands on the table and leaned forward between Earl Ray and Shelly. The butt of his holstered pistol was almost touching her cheek. With an oily and muffled voice he sneered, "Looka here, looka here. Little Earl Ray Lawrence in a nigger nightclub with none other than Colonel Barbour's little girl."

Earl Ray said. "Bug off, Sheriff."

Shelly was astounded that he would speak so smart-alecky to the sheriff. Was he that sure of himself or was he putting on a show to impress her? Shelly was beside herself with fear. She practically got down on her knees to address the sheriff. Her voice shook. "Please sir, don't tell my daddy," she begged. "I'm not doing anything wrong. This is just Coke I'm drinking. I swear. You can taste it and see for yourself. And you know Luther." She pointed at the bar. "He works for my parents. He brought me here. He didn't want to, I made him. And he's watching over me just like he was my own daddy."

"Well now, I'm just looking out for you, too, honey. You just be careful who you talk to in here. Now young Mister Lawrence here, he's okay. And Luther, he's all right too. He's a good nigra. But some of these young bucks? You know what they do to a young white gal if you give 'em half a chance? They'll slip a knockout drop in your Coke and next thing you know, fore you can whistle Dixie they'll have you out in a car with your panties pulled down." The way he said it, it sounded to Shelly like he was dreaming of slipping her that micky himself.

He turned his attention to Lucy, who crossed her arms over her chest when he looked at her. He said, "What's your name, gal?"

"It's Lucy," she said.

"Lucy what?"

"Lucy uh…" Her first impulse was to make up a last name, but she decided not to bother; if the sheriff knew Shelly's father he could easily enough find out who she was. She said, "Lucy Kirby."

"Well I've got my eye on you, Miss. If anything was to happen to Miss Shelly, some of the blame would have to fall right smack on you. You git my drift?"

"Yessir, I think so."

Earl Ray said, "All right, Sheriff, you can go on about your business now. We all get it. You're here to protect us. Ain't nothing gonna happen to these girls."

*

The club didn't close down until two o'clock in the morning. "You had enough?" Luther asked Shelly as they were walking to his car.

"Not by a long shot," she replied, weary sounding but still with a note of excitement. "I want to come back and sing some more. I want to sing a whole show."

"I don't know 'bout none a that," Luther said. He unlocked his car and held the back door open for the girls to get in. They both crawled into the back seat.

Luther cranked up the engine and pulled out onto the road, his low beams searching through the fog ahead. Half a mile down the road they passed a car parked on the side of the road. Luther slowed down and signaled to pull off. "Dem folks might need some help," he said. But before he could come to a complete stop the parked car pulled out on the road and passed them. "Strange," Luther murmured.

A few minutes later they drove past a little store and Luther said "That there's the Lawrence's store. The young man y'all was talking with? His daddy owns that store."

The car that had passed them was now parked in front of the store and two other cars were waiting at the stop sign to merge in behind them.

"Lots of traffic for two o'clock in the morning," Shelly said.

Luther said, "Sumpin's going on and I don't like it none neither."

Then the blue and white flashing lights of a cop car came on. "Uh oh," Luther said.

"You weren't speeding, were you?" Shelly asked. Both girls turned to look out the back window.

Luther said, "I reckon I better pull over."

It was Sheriff Moss. He eased to a stop behind Luther and the car that had been following close on his bumper passed them and pulled off to a stop ahead, thus boxing them in. The sheriff got out and approached Luther's car with his flashlight wavering. Luther watched him in his rearview mirror. He also saw in the mirror, from far behind, that the car that had pulled off in front of the Lawrence store was now coming up behind them and pulling to a halt behind the sheriff. "I got a bad feeling," Luther said.

Sheriff Moss poked his face through the driver's side window and aimed his light at Shelly. "Miss Barbour, I need to ask you to get out of the car, please ma'am."

"Did I do something wrong, Sheriff?"

"Just get out, please."

Nervously Shelly climbed out of the car, and the sheriff escorted her back to his vehicle and instructed her to get in on the passenger seat. "I've been instructed to take you home, Miss. It's for your own protection."

"Wha... what about Lucy and Luther?"

"They'll be just fine, Miss. Don't you worry 'bout them."

"What do you mean by instructed? By whom?"

"By your daddy, Miss."

He must have called her father.

Feeling as if she were a prisoner being carted off to jail, Shelly looked out the side window as they drove off. She saw that two of the men from the other cars were holding Luther by his elbows, one man on each side of him, escorting him to one of their cars, and that the two other men were escorting Lucy in the same manner but to the other car.

"That was the end of it," Little Don says. "If there was any other end to it nobody ever knowed, although there sure was a lot of rumors about what might have happened after that. Lucy and your mama both said that was the end of it, but Luther went missing, and I mean for good."

"I'm going to ask mama about that," David says. "She told us about that night, but she never told us what happened with Luther after they carted him off and I never thought to ask. Surely she must know more than she told."

*

It's three o'clock in the afternoon before David and Mary get to the hospital. Sue Ellen had gone home from Little Don's but said she would visit soon. The door to Pop's room is open just a crack, and David can smell smoke before he pushes it open.

"Hey, sweetie," his mother says, a huge grin lighting up her face. She stands up from the chair beside the bed. She looks smaller even than he remembers. Her hair is now solid silver, her arms thin with knobby elbows, large blue veins in her hands. She shakes her finger at him schoolmarmishly but smiling hugely all the time to assure him her scolding is all in fun. She says, "You certainly took your own sweet time getting here. Now come over here and give your mama a kiss."

David hugs her and bends forward to kiss her cheek. She tastes of powder. He remembers when he was eight years old standing by her dresser and watching her powder her face and paint her lips. The powder was a dusty rose color and smelled sweet. He remembers asking her if he could put some on. She lifted him to her lap and let him powder his face. It got in his nose and made him sneeze.

"Not so much," she said as he raised a cloud of powder. And then they heard the front door open, and she lifted him back off her lap and quickly wiped the powder off his face saying, "Better not let your daddy see you like this."

His old man would have whipped him for doing such a sissified thing. They knew that because it had happened before. The old man blundered into the bedroom once to find his wife turning his eight-year-old son into a girl with lipstick and rouge. It was a game of make believe they sometimes played. Earl Ray snatched her lipstick tube out of her hands and threw it against the mirror, and he snatched David up and swatted him with his bare hands. David tried to scurry away. The old man shouted, "Don't you run from me, boy. You come back here and stand still and take it like a man."

Sniffling, David tried his hardest not to cry out loud, because he knew his daddy would whip him even harder for crying. He stood still while his father whipped him with his doubled-up leather belt.

After he had administered about six hard swats to David's rear end Shelly said, "That's enough," and Pop stopped whipping him.

David ran out of the room. As he was leaving he heard his father shout at his mother, "I'll not have you making a sissy out of him."

Putting on makeup with his mother's help had been a harmless and playful way for David and his mother to bond. It had never been, as his father feared, the harbinger of some kind of gender confusion, or of homosexual urges (two entirely different things, and which of them, he wonders, would have horrified the old man more?). He finds it curious now that the smell of his mother's powder brought back this long forgotten memory. But he thinks it's ironic considering that makeup is a part of his profession. He idly wonders what his father might think if he knew that before every scene he filmed he had to sit for a makeup artist to paint his face. Worse yet, he muses, what would the old man think if he knew that even John Wayne wore makeup? Would that shake up the old man's view of the world?

The old man grumbles, "Are you even going to say hello to me? I'm the one that's hurt, you know."

He looks at his father. His head is propped up on a pile of pillows. One leg extends out from the sheets in its cast. His lip is swollen and there is a nasty scar on his forehead and a bandage on his nose. He's all hooked up to plastic tubes buried right in his chest, and another tube going to his nose, and a saline drip and a blood pressure cup attached to his arm and some kind of little clamp with a red light on his finger, and there are lighted-up graphs and numbers that David assumes tell the doctors and nurses how close to death the old man is. He can't make any sense of the numbers but he's seen enough television to know what it means if the up-and-down lines go flat.

"So how are you?" David asks.

"About three quarters the way into my grave. Thanks for asking."

Pop coughs hard and winces with pain. Tears come to his eyes and he reaches with a bare arm to wipe them off. "Jesus, that hurts."

He grabs at his chest. "They went and cracked open my fucking chest. Can you believe it? They didn't need to do that crap. Broke me open like a goddamn walnut shell."

Shelly says, "Do you have to curse so much?"

"You let 'em crack your fucking chest open and see if you don't cuss." He crushes the cigarette out in the ashtray.

David says, "If you don't quit smoking you're never going to leave this hospital."

Shelly says, "I tried to tell him. He won't listen to me."

"I can't believe they let you get away with it. For Christ's sake, they provide an ashtray."

"Naw, they didn't provide the ashtray. Murabbi grabbed one from the waiting room and brought it in."

Murabbi grins sheepishly. He's standing quietly by the window silhouetted against the light. Almost as tall as the old man and a lot heavier, he practically blocks the whole window. In the distance as seen around his bulk is the silvery blue water of the Mississippi Sound, shrimp boats on the horizon. It's downright bucolic out there, but a storm's brewing inside Pop's hospital room as everyone tries to speak at once.

David says, "Hey Freight Train."

Murabbi makes a move to greet David, but he stops to let Shelly finish what she's trying to say. "They've told him about a jillion times not to smoke, but he won't listen. He tries to hide it, but of course they can smell it when they come in."

Pop says, "Aw, git off your high horse." To David he says, "Your grandpa lived to be eighty-nine and smoked like a stovepipe, and I known guys that never smoked a day in their life and keeled over from a heart attack at forty-three. So don't tell me 'bout no smokin's gonna kill me."

Murabbi finally gets his opening to greet David. "Hey there, Bub. It's good to see you. Welcome home." He reaches out one massive hand and David's hand vanishes in his grip.

After six seasons with the Oakland Raiders and more concussions than he can remember, Freight Train had decided to call it quits while he still had part of a brain. For a short time after ending his football career and coming back home he was treated like royalty. He was offered jobs in sales and public relations on the basis of his popularity as a sports figure, sales managers assuming that men would fall all over themselves to buy from an all-pro football hero. He took a job as a car salesman but quickly learned that he was not cut out for that. All the bickering over price made his head hurt. Customers would come onto the lot with an almost worshipful attitude toward their football hero and go away saying things like, "It don't matter how many tackles you made, you're just another sleazy used car salesman now."

He tried selling insurance for a while, but that didn't work out either. Then he got a job as a security guard in one of the casinos, and finally Pop Lawrence asked him to be his personal assistant and bodyguard. He had been working for Pop for about five years. Long before that, he and David had been teammates at Booker T Washington High, and in more recent years they had spent some time together carousing nightclubs in L.A. during the brief time when the Raiders were located there.

For a short time he was married to an exotic dancer, stage name Lilith Fair. She managed to hide her drug addiction from Murabbi until after they were married and after they discovered she was expecting a child. Murabbi couldn't stop her from taking drugs, but he was able to keep it somewhat under control until after the child, Abdul, was born. Post-partum, however, Lilith's drug abuse became uncontrollable. Murabbi divorced her and won custody of the child and brought him back home to Freedom when he retired from football.

Almost grown now, Abdul is playing on the same high school football team David and his father played for, and he's working as Buddy Boudreau's assistant in the Lawrence store—meaning he pretty much runs the store because Buddy is seldom there. In Pop's hospital room Murabbi asks David, "Are you keeping in shape, buddy boy?"

"Oh yeah. In my business you have to. I mean, unless you always want to play the heavy. No pun intended."

"Maybe we can do some running together while you're here."

"Maybe."

After the initial greetings, there's an uncomfortable silence in the hospital room. Nobody seems to know what to say, and David won't even look at his father. Afterwhile Shelly asks David if he's working on a new picture.

"Not yet, but there are some things in negotiation."

"Well I hope you get something good. And don't let 'em talk you into any more of them dirty pictures. I Sewanee, the things they won't do in pictures nowadays. And the language! In my day people simply didn't talk the way they do now, not even in the raunchiest honky tonks, and believe you me, I played one of the raunchiest there was."

"Don't worry, mama. I'm not going to do any porno films." He's tickled at her unique mixture of innocence and worldliness. Singing jazz in a juke joint but getting all prudish about sex scenes he wouldn't even call soft core. He wishes he could go back in time and see what she was like back when she was singing. Come to think of it, he'd love to do a movie based on those days. He could play his own father, the sleazebag.

Shelly says, "Well I don't know what you call porno, but if that last picture wasn't pornography, then I don't want to see what is. I seen that last picture. You and that Jasmine Jones making out like bunny rabbits for the whole world to see. I declare, I never thought I'd live to see the day my only son showed all his business in a movie for the whole world to see."

"That wasn't really me, mama. It was a stand-in. I don't think anybody wants to see my naked body anyway."

"Nobody but half the girls in America," Freight Train says.

David says, "If you watched it again, mama..."

"Again! I couldn't hardly stand it the first time."

"But if you did you'd notice that you never see our faces and our bodies at the same time. And do you know why? Because it wasn't us. They used stand-ins for me and Jasmine both. That's the magic of Hollywood. It was our faces but somebody else's bodies."

"I don't get it. Do you mean they cut and pasted your heads onto other bodies like with a computer?"

"No, not like that. If we watched it together I could show you."

"Oh no, I'm not going to watch that again. 'Sides, even if it wasn't really your naked body, everybody in the world *thinks* it was. So it might as well have been. Somebody with your face was exposing his penis."

Mary sees his last comment as an opportunity to tease him. "I guess they had to use a stand-in so they'd have somebody that's actually got something to show. I've seen all your business, as mama puts it, and what I seen looks like something you'd put on a fish hook."

Pop laughs at that until he starts coughing again and grabs his chest in pain. He chokes out, "Get a nurse!"

Shelly pushes the nurse call button and David runs out to the nurse station. It's only a few steps down the hall. A nurse rushes in. She looks at Pop and then at the meters, and then back at Pop. "We're all tangled up here," she says, affecting an attitude of calm efficiency as she lifts the oxygen tubes from around his neck and untangles it and reasserts it in his nostrils, and lifts his arm and fiddles with his blood pressure cuff, and looks back up to see what his pressure is reading now. David comes back in the room. He sees that Pop is breathing heavily. There's a look of panic in his eyes such as David has never seen. Numbers on the machines go crazy. The old man's blood pressure shoots up and then plummets. He starts sweating in rivulets. His skin is white and clammy to the touch. Shelly wipes his brow with a towel. The nurse says it's his blood sugar. She rushes out of the room and quickly back in carrying an orange colored drink in a plastic container with a bendable straw. They hold the straw up to Pop's mouth. His head is drooping. He can barely suck the drink up through the straw, but he does manage to down a few sips, and almost immediately the color comes back to his face and be begins to look more alert. He smiles weakly. "I'm okay," he says.

"Thank god," David says. "That was scary."

"What'd she want?" Pop asks.

"What did who want?"

"Mary."

"Nobody said anything about Mary."

"You said Mary called," Pop grumbles.

"But I'm right here," Mary says, and then she realizes what's going on and explains, "He said scary, not Mary."

To David she explains that Pop has lost a lot of his hearing. "He hears the sounds but he can't distinguish all of the words. He mixes consonants up and guesses when he doesn't hear clearly."

*

Pretty soon Pop drifts off to sleep again and all but Shelly leave the room. They settle in a lounge area where they have a little more room to stretch out and make themselves comfortable. The TV in the lounge is turned to the Channel 7. Weatherman Donny's reporting on forest fires in Florida and California, and floods in the heartland. "Every time I see a TV that guy's on," David says.

"Seems like everybody around here is addicted to ol' Weatherman Donny," Freight Train says. "I pretty much tune him out."

"We all do," Mary says. "He's like a drone in our collective subconscious. We all trust that if he has anything important to say our internal alarms will go off and we'll tune him back in."

David is seated in a lounge chair facing a large window overlooking a parking lot and stands of longleaf pines. He hears a familiar voice from behind. It's a woman's voice as throaty as a bass clarinet. She says, "My god, look what the cat dragged in."

He turns to greet Melissa, flashing her a big smile. "How are you, honey? God, it's good to see you."

He stands up and greets her with a hug and a chaste kiss on the lips. She says, "I'm not doing too bad except for this broken schnoz. But the pain relievers they've got me on, they ain't half bad."

"Enjoy them while you can," he says. He tells her that even with the swollen and bandaged nose she is the most beautiful creature between Dallas and Mobile.

"That's what you said the last time I saw you, and that was twenty-something years ago. You were a big liar then and you still are." They easily fall into the flirtatious banter they had habitually engaged in when they were kids.

Mary interrupts them to ask who's watching the store.

"Abdul," Freight Train says.

Mary says, "Buddy's supposed to be running the store, but God knows where he got off to. Working on one of his endless and fruitless get-rich-quick schemes, probably."

Nobody in the family seems to quite know what Buddy's role in the family business is. Ostensibly he runs the store, but he's seldom actually there. He depends on Abdul, or Mary when Abdul is in school, to keep the store running. Buddy seems to always have better things to do, mostly running errands for Pop and chasing after his own dreams and schemes; making deals, negotiating. Pop says Buddy is a natural born salesman. He's homey and likeable, with a bit of Cajun in his speech, and he has a way of putting everyone at ease. Pop once said of him, "He can spend an hour talking to a customer and the customer will come away feeling like he's been patted on the back when all along ol' Buddy be sticking it up his ass."

Mary suspects that sticking it up somebody's ass might very well be what Buddy is doing half the time he's off who knows where. She caught him once with some girl in his office in the back of the store. He swore that was the first and only time, but she's pretty sure there have been others and probably always will be; but she's willing to shut her eyes to whatever he might be doing behind her back. She knew he was a skirt chaser even back in junior high school when he first moved to Freedom from the little watersoaked town in Louisiana that the Boudreau family came from. Like David and Randy, Buddy had been a fiercely competitive athlete, but his chosen sports had been wrestling and karate. He wasn't the biggest or strongest boy in school, not by a long shot, but he was the quickest on his feet and slippery as an eel. He was fast with the girls as well. More than one girl at Booker T had been known to say, "I don't know what it is about that boy, but it's just about impossible to say no to him."

Mary certainly knew that was true for her.

*

Abdul, not Buddy, is the person who keeps the store in operation. Without him, the store would never be stocked with the things people want and it would never be open dependable hours. As is, it's little more than a tax write-off. It costs more to keep it open than it makes. But the store had always been operated in a slipshod manner, even long before it was the Lawrence store. Selling groceries had never been the store's primary function. Its primary function had always been to serve as a front for wheeling and dealing of another sort, from bootleg whiskey to the making and breaking of politicians. In their county, the metaphorical smoky room where political deals are sealed is for real. It resides in the back of the Lawrence store. The original owner was Big Ben Rogers, Sugar Rogers' ancestor. The first Lawrence to run the store had been David's great-grandfather, Jedadiah. Jedadiah's father, Joshua Lawrence, was an itinerate preacher who roamed the Southland preaching hellfire and brimstone on riverbanks and in little community churches. The biggest church he ever preached in had a congregation of twelve, and the longest he ever stayed with any church was six months. On three separate occasions Joshua was either caught in the act or suspected of sleeping with the young daughters of congregants. In each case he escaped town barely ahead of the law or a lynch mob. He was called by the Lord (or escaped the law) to preach in villages from Georgia to Texas, always dragging along with him his only son, Jedadiah (who never knew who his mother was).

Jedadiah was a likeable kid who made friends easily. But since they moved so frequently, his friendships were always fleeting, and he never knew any kinfolks. All the boys he met while growing up seemed to have a whole bunch of brothers and sisters and cousins, and talked about them a lot. So in order to fit in a little better and appear more normal, he made up a couple of cousins—Jethro and Randle. He told people these cousins had moved away up north.

Jedadiah was fifteen years old when war broke out between the states. He volunteered for a Confederate Army brigade out of Mississippi and ended up in the Battle of Antietam Creek under the command of Brigadier General Shanks Evans.

In the war he made friends with a boy named Jimmy Smith, a small town boy from Georgia. Jimmy was the only son, but not the only child, of the village blacksmith. He had six older sisters, each about a year older and ten pounds heavier than the next, from Annabell (eighteen years old and 180 pounds) to Amy Lynn (twenty-six and 240). Between the six of them—only half of them married—they had a dozen children. "My daddy, he fathered most of them kids hisself," Jimmy said.

Jimmy Smith's fat sisters were just about the wildest and surely the most hell bound women Jedadiah had ever heard tell of. Often at night when the fighting and marching was over for the day Jimmy would tell Jedadiah stories about his fat sisters and all their drinking and whoring and running wild. After a while, when Jimmy started getting their names mixed up, Jedadiah figured out that he was making the stories up. But he never let on. If he did, Jimmy might stop telling those stories.

At one point during the battle at Antietam Creek the armies called a truce to gather up the dead and wounded. Jimmy and Jedadiah, wearing rags for uniforms and toting weapons for which they had no ammunition, surveyed the bodies left strewn on the ground. As the elder Earl Ray Lawrence described the scene to his son, it looked like a field of giant uprooted root vegetables, the tattered, torn, mud- and blood-encrusted bodies looked more like gnarly roots coming out of the ground than anything laid upon the ground. The wounded howled in pain, and unseen dogs in nearby woods howled as if in sympathy. Wandering the field with his buddy as if in a daze, turning over lumps of bodies to check for any sign of life, stumbling over detached arms and legs and entrails, Jedadiah murmured, "What's it all about? What's all this killing for? It don't make no sense."

Corporal Smith said, "They say we's fighting to protect the Southern way of life."

"What's that mean?"

"Plantation living, I reckon. Fancy balls. Slaves working the fields, lifting the load, serving your meals."

"But I don't own no slaves. I ain't got no plantation, I ain't e'm got no wife to go home to. I don't know 'bout no Southern way of life. I don't know 'bout but one way of life and that's jes to follow my ol' man while he preaches the gospel."

A Union soldier passed by within a few feet. Like Jimmy and Jedadiah, he was looking for survivors among his comrades in arm. He tipped his hat. Jimmy and Jedadiah said "Hidy."

Jedadiah said to Jimmy, "Them Union boys is just like us. Hell, I had cousins that moved up north. They's Yankees now. Does that make them the enemy? We used to go fishing together in the crick. Now, for all I know, they could be lying dead in that there crick, kilt by one of us."

"I know," Jimmy said. "We all got cousins or uncles on the other side."

"It don't make no sense."

Later that day Corporal Smith was killed. He would never again tell tales about his fat sisters. A Union soldier rammed him through the gut with a bayonet. He might well have been the same Union soldier who tipped his hat to him earlier. He would have bayoneted Jedadiah too if Jedadiah hadn't fallen down. He stayed on the ground and pretended to be dead until the fighting stopped. That night Corporal Jedadiah Lawrence simply walked away from the battle field never to return. If anybody saw him escape, nobody bothered to raise a call. More than likely, if anybody did see him sneak away they just didn't give a darn. He wandered from village to village over the next weeks and months, hiding from soldiers on both sides. He was wary of all white men, in uniform or not. He trusted only women and Negroes. Hiding whenever possible during daylight hours, he would approach houses at night and beg scraps of food or sometimes a place to stay for a day or two. A barn or a shed. Eventually somebody told him that the war was over and he didn't have to hide any longer. But he continued his wandering ways, picking up what work he could here and there, and finally ended up in the newly-formed town of

Freedom, where he got a job picking up whiskey off a boat that docked in the bay and delivering it by wagon to a distribution point forty miles away. His boss was a Caribbean islander named Big Ben Rogers. Big Ben smuggled tax free liquor into the country loaded off ships in the bay and distributed to bootleggers throughout the coastal area. He also owned the general store. Big Ben's children and grandchildren would become leaders of what became known as the Negro Mafia. Big Ben took a liking to Jedadiah Lawrence. He liked his quiet and diffident manner. He put him in charge of the store in Freedom where he sold staples such as sugar and flour and coffee, and sometimes candy, and some tools and clothes. Locals called it the Come Back Tomorrow store, because Jedadiah never seemed to have in stock what people needed when they needed it. Mostly his business took place not in the store but out the back door.

Pop Lawrence never knew how it came to be, but Jedadiah's son T.J. (Pop's father) became sole owner of the store sometime during the 1920s or 1930s. By the time Pop was a boy working for his father in the store, it had been renamed Lawrence Grocery and Mercantile, and, as the only store within twenty miles, served as a community center, polling place and post office for Freedom. Booze was still their main business, however. They still sold bootleg liquor out the back door; because even though prohibition had come and gone, local liquor laws were up to the states, and Mississippi remained dry until 1966. Selling liquor illegally was much more profitable than selling it legally. The legalization of liquor sales did not exactly provide a huge boost to the tourist industry, but casinos did. And the distribution and maintenance of pinball machines and juke boxes, a somewhat profitable sideline for Pop, blossomed into the hugely profitably business of slot machines.

*

It's suppertime. The setting sun is painting the bayou behind the Lawrence house fiery orange. Mary drives David and their mother home, finally forcing Shelly to take a break from sitting watch by Pop's bed. She had wanted to stay in the hospital. She had complained, "It takes so long to get home. I'll just have to go right back again in the morning. And what if he takes a turn for the worse?"

But Mary insisted that she go home. "You need a good night's sleep, mama. You won't be any good to him or anybody else if you don't get some rest. Besides, Freight Train is there, and they got good doctors and nurses in the hospital."

Mary's daughters are building Lego cities in the living room. They had spent the day there with Beulah watching over them. They stand up shyly when their mother and grandmother and Uncle David open the door. Demurely, they wait to be spoken to. "Girls, this is your uncle," Mary says.

David says, "Hi. Who's who?"

"I'm Patricia," the oldest says. "I'm eleven."

"I'm Rhonda," the younger sister says, "I'm six."

"Well ya'll are just two of the prettiest girls I've ever seen," David says.

"As pretty as Jasmine Jones?" Patricia asks.

"Even prettier," David says.

And Rhonda asks, "Do you know Brad Pitt?"

"No, I never had the honor."

"That's enough pestering your uncle," Mary says.

Stepping into the old house is like entering a dream where everything seems to be the same or is at least hauntingly familiar, but changed into something totally different. The smells are there, the old familiar smells he thought he had forgotten: the cloying odor of mold and mildew, the smell of old leather, of cigarette smoke, of bacon grease and lard, fried chicken and collard greens, and from the open windows the strong smell of the salty sea and all the dead sea creatures it carries. The two big recliners are the same ones he remembers from childhood, as are the pictures on the wall: an oil painting of a sunset over a lake and another of a fly fisherman hip deep in a mountain stream, a portrait of Pop before he grew his goatee, skin tones painted in deep burnt sienna, and a matching portrait of Shelly with a Jackie Kennedy hairdo and pillbox hat. Newly added to the wall art are framed movie posters from *The Witness,*

Travlin' Light and *Cold Justice*. Everywhere I go, David thinks, there I am; first at Little Don's and then here. I'll bet they've even got these posters up in the high school.

In his monologue he described the house as being like an old farmhouse, with all the furnishings and decorative touches well worn, homey and comforting. He remembers the dull orange shag carpet and the stained white walls and the floral patterned curtains. Ugly, ugly pea green linoleum in the kitchen. Now there are hardwood floors with burgundy area rugs and cream colored walls. The wall between the kitchen and living room has been taken down to make one large family room with conversation and television areas demarcated by the rugs and furniture placement and a large, granite-topped island counter in the kitchen. The old back porch and sunroom are no longer there, but have been replaced with a redwood deck that sweeps across the back of the house and is accessed by sliding glass doors. Just inside those doors sits Shelly's grand piano with the two porcelain figures sitting on top, a man and woman in evening dress, the toe of one of his shoes broken off—one of the few remnants of the many knick knacks he so fondly remembers from his childhood.

"Supper's ready," Beulah says. "Y'all get on in here and get washed up and I'll put it on the table." To Mary she says, "Mister Buddy called and said to tell you he has to work late." David takes in Beulah's appearance in a brief glance—short and pudgy with light chocolate skin and braided hair—and immediately tags her as a college student. He is tickled by the old fashioned "Mister Buddy," and he thinks the expression "get on in here" is delightfully quaint considering that there are no divisions in the front room. She's using carryover words from when the dining room was separate, much in the way people still call the refrigerator an ice box. He imagines invisible walls with electric barriers and you have to enter a digital code to get from kitchen to dining room to television room to family-and-entertaining-company room, and he pictures Beulah in a French maid uniform right out of some fifties romantic comedy, bowing as she ushers people from "room to room."

Rather than bringing them food from his own café, Little Don had given Beulah money for dinner from a take-out restaurant. She picked up two family-pack fried chicken dinners—chicken, potato salad, coleslaw and biscuits—and just to be sure there was enough food, because she never knew how many people might show up for supper, she cooked up a few side dishes to go along with the chicken. She sets the food on the table. Mary says, "Let me give you a hand," and gets up and heads for the stove, ignoring Beulah's protest that she doesn't need any help. They have two kinds of potatoes—yams roasted with a topping of marshmallows and raisins (the girls' favorite) and lyonnaise potatoes with caramelized onions swimming in a hot butter sauce. There are also fat butter beans, steamed corn on the cob, cornbread and tossed salad.

Beulah pours ice tea all around.

"It's enough to feed an army," David says.

Mary's girls fight over the yams.

Mary says, "Beulah, sit down and eat with us."

"Oh no, I can't."

"Sure you can."

"Well I don't know."

David says, "You can't just stand there like some kind of serving girl," and then figures, well I guess she is, but still... and she says, "I was going to sit over there and study for my algebra test." (He knew it, she *is* a college student.)

"Aw come on," David says. "You can study later. A girl's got to eat."

He has just then met Beulah for the first time, but he knows she's Little Don's granddaughter and that she's been working for his parents for three or four years.

Her hesitation to join the family at the dinner table is habitual. She is, after all, the domestic help, and her mama and daddy have taught her to treat her employers with diffidence. After much insistence from them all she finally says, "Well okay. Thank you."

Rhonda and Patricia both say, "Sit by me." "By me." "Me, me!" They are excited to be able to sit at the grownup table, a rare treat when they have company, and they think of David as company even though he's family. If he hadn't already sat down between his mother and his sister they'd be clamoring for him, not Beulah, to sit by them. David is much more than just company to them, he's extra special company. He's the glamorous hero of *The Witness*. Patricia has saved copies of every movie magazine she's been able to locate with any mention of their famous uncle. The girls can't wait to tell their friends about eating dinner with him. They didn't understand much of his monologue, but they got to watch *The Witness* on television, and they loved it. They had not yet been allowed to see *Travlin' Light* or *Cold Justice* because they were R-rated (nudity and violence in one and some very explicit sex and violence in the other, this according to some of Patricia's eleven-year-old school chums who had seen all of them). Mary had told Patricia "You're probably mature enough to watch them—with parental guidance, of course—even if R-rated is supposed to be for seventeen or older. But Rhonda's not old enough yet, and it wouldn't be fair to her to let you watch it and not let her." Patricia knew that this meant eventually her mama would give in and let them watch. She also knew that there was nothing to keep them from playing the DVDs when they were home alone, but so far they had been good about minding their mother even when there were no grownups at home. Patricia was proud of that and wouldn't want to slip up. Her inner parent was working overtime.

The table is old scarred oak that seats eight with the center leaf inserted. It's a family heirloom passed down from David's grandfather. It rests on ornate legs that end in eagle claws gripping polished spheres the size of billiard balls. David thinks it would fetch a small fortune in a Los Angeles antique store. He wonders if it were sold as an antique would his name carved on the underside of the top increase or decrease its value.

Shelly has spread the blue silk table cloth from Spain that Pop gave her for their silver anniversary. She had quickly darted upstairs to freshen up and change clothes as soon as they got home, and now she's dressed in her Sunday best for this meal with her prodigal son. She feels giddy. Perhaps, she thinks, it's sheer relief from escaping the hospital and the constant worry about Earl Ray. And, of course, the joy of being with her son after so many years—both children at home, and her grandchildren; and, as much as she hates to admit it, freedom from Earl Ray's constantly looming and judgmental presence. She takes her place at the head of the table. David and Mary are seated on one side and Beulah and the girls on the other. Shelly glances around the table to see that everybody seems settled, and then she says, "David, would you care to say the blessing?"

"Mama, you know I don't really..." he's about to say he doesn't really believe in God, but he sees the disappointment on her face and stops short and then says, "Sure."

He's an actor; he can fake it.

They hold hands around the table. Shelly and Mary each give David's hands an extra loving squeeze. He stumbles through a kind of generic blessing, carefully avoiding any mention of God or Lord or Father. He'd just as soon not mention to his mother that he's an atheist. He knows that she would be horrified. He's not too sure how Mary would react either. He suspects she might be somewhat agnostic herself, but he'd rather avoid any talk of religion with either of them.

After he mutters "amen," they noisily pass platters around and help their plates. Beulah puts dainty helpings on her plate, and Shelly scolds her. "That's not enough food for a bird. Now you help yourself to some more of those sweet taters and don't be stingy with the chicken."

"Yes ma'am."

Shelly says, "Thank God for Murabbi. That man is a saint. I don't know how he does it, but he hasn't left Earl Ray's side."

"Who is Murabbi?" Rhonda wants to know.

Mary explains, "You know who Murabbi is. He's Freight Train. Murabbi's his real name, but grandma's the only one that calls him that."

"If that's his real name why do they call him Freight Train?"

"Because he's so big and strong like a big ol' train."

The television is playing in the background, but nobody pays any attention to it until they hear David's name. An announcer on some celebrity news show is saying, "Are David Lawrence and Jasmine Jones about to break up? And what hot British rocker is Jasmine seeing in London?"

There's a film clip of Jasmine exiting a club and climbing into a limo with British rock star Spike Love. The announcer says they have been dating while Jasmine is filming in London. "It's the usual crap," David says. "We both know Spike. Big deal if they go to a club together. What's she supposed to do, stay locked away in a hotel room while she's in London?"

He's relieved that there's no speculation about him having a love affair with an old girlfriend from back home. Apparently the local reporter kept his word on that one. So far.

*

After supper David and Mary help Beulah clear the table and load the dishes in the washer. Shelly runs upstairs and comes back down wearing an old pinafore nightgown. "Are you ready for bed, mama?" David asks.

"Oh no. I just wanted to get comfy."

Soon Mary and her kids head for home, and so does Beulah. David is left alone with his mother, who despite the nightgown shows no evidence of being ready for bed. David is not sure, but he thinks the nightgown his mother is wearing is the same one she wore when he was in high school, white cotton with tiny blue and pink flowers, buttons down the front and two large pockets, from which he remembers her pulling a seemingly endless stash of tissues. After giving it a little more thought he realizes that it couldn't possibly be the same one. Maybe she'd had a succession of almost identical gowns so this one would simply be the latest in a long line. He finds that comforting.

She says, "Come sit with me on the deck a bit."

They walk out and settle in the wicker rockers. It's still quite warm out, even though the sun has been down for a couple of hours. But they can smell rain in the air. The night is loud with croaks and whistles. The bayou, barely visible across the slope of the yard, is slick and black, and across the water by the Moss's house there is a dull, almost rust colored glow in the night sky. Pollutants from God knows what source, David thinks, trapped by low hanging clouds, and lights from buildings clear down on the coast reflecting off the underside of those clouds. There are no stars and no moon visible in the night sky. A breeze kicks up, the steely taste of approaching autumn in the air, and after a while heavy splats of rain move up onto the lawn and then machinegun splatters on the overhanging roof that protects their half of the deck. "Storm's a coming," Shelly says. "This here's just the start of it. Weatherman says there's a hurricane brewing down in the Caribbean."

"The ubiquitous Weatherman Donny, I presume."

"Yep."

"Well, it's that time of year."

"At least the wind's drove the mosquitoes off."

David rocks quietly and savors the smell of the rain. The rocker creaks. He pulls out a pack of cigarettes and lights one up.

"I didn't know you smoked," his mother comments. "We been together practically all day, and this is the first time I seen you light one up."

"Yeah, well. I've been trying to quit. Can't quite do it, but I managed to cut down to just two or three a day."

"Damn. I couldn't a done that for nothing when I was smoking. It was either two packs a day or nothing."

"How'd you quit, then?"

"Cold turkey. Flushed a whole pack down the toilet one day and never picked up another'un."

After a while he asks about Mary. "How's her marriage?"

"Lord, don't ask."

"That's what I was afraid of."

"I imagine you heard about that gal from Pascagoula."

"No, I never did."

"Oh. Well, she was a sales gal for a boat dealer over there. She'uz posed to be selling him a boat and they got to messing around."

"You mean right in the showroom?"

"Oh no. Worse than that. I mean in his office in the back of the store. Going at it like ruttin' dogs right there in his office. Poor Mary walked in on them."

"Godamighty. That probably woulda been real funny if it weren't so sad."

"It sure wasn't funny to Mary."

"I guess not. If I'd of been Mary I'd of left him right then and there."

"Maybe you would and maybe you wouldn't. If you was Mary you'd understand how maybe living alone might be scarier than having to put up with his crap. She's always had some man to take care of her. First her daddy then Buddy. He's the only man she's ever been with. You know how it is with them. They was sweethearts since the eighth grade or thereabouts. Except there was the time she was in love with Randy. Thank the good lord that didn't last. But anyway, she wouldn't know what to do on her own. You know what they say. You got to make the bed you sleep in or sleep in the bed you... well, you know what I mean."

"Yeah, well he sleeps in everybody else's bed."

"That may well be, but their private lives are none of your business. Now what about you? What about that Jasmine Jones? The gossip rags say you're going to marry her. I'd think you'd tell your mama before you told some reporter."

"That's why they call them gossip rags, mama," David laughs. "There's not an ounce of truth in those stories. Jasmine and I are friends. That's all. She's a nice girl." He knows what she's probably thinking, even though she doesn't say it: cohabiting is not something *just friends* do—in Hollywood maybe, she would surely think the worst of Hollywood, but not where regular Americans live. He knows that his mother is proud to think of her family as regular Americans.

From somewhere off to the south they hear the peal of a bell from a buoy rocking to the wake of a boat, and they hear the distant chug of an old engine. David wonders who could be out on the water this time of night. Shelly pushes herself up from her chair. "I'm gonna get me a nightcap. You want something?"

"I'll take whatever you're having." He knows what she'll be having. As far back as he can remember she has always had the same nightcap at about the same time of night and always right there in the same rocking chair on what was the porch back then, unless the weather was perfectly horrible, which it's not—yet. The only thing different is this time she's going to sip her nightcap with her son instead of her husband. She's been sleeping at the hospital since the old man's wreck. He wonders if she's ever once slept alone in their bed.

Watching her go in he notices that her shoulder blades seem bonier than he remembers but that she still has a seductive girlie sway to her hips. He mentally voices the phrase, "Not bad for an old gal."

He flips his cigarette out into the dark and watches the glowing tip quickly blink out into nothingness in the rain. The downpour is steady but not hard. The temperature has dropped to the upper-sixties. If it gets any cooler they'll have to go in. There's no more insect chatter, and he enjoys the quiet, rocking gently and almost falling asleep until the scrape of the screen door startles him. Shelly comes back out on the deck and hands him a Bourbon and Coke. "It's turned out to be a pleasant night," she says. "Maybe the big bad storm ain't coming after all."

"Oh, I bet it's coming all right. It's just trying to lull us to sleep. Then when we're completely off guard it's going to slam into us like Freight Train Taylor sacking a quarterback. Besides, I just saw lightning way off to the south."

She sits down and immediately asks the question he's been dreading: "I want to know how come you hate your father so much. I want to know why you never want to speak to him. What did he ever do to you to make you hate him so?" He doesn't respond at first and she continues, "I know he can be really gruff, and he was tough on you kids growing up. Especially you. He was easier on Mary because she was a girl. But all he ever did was work his fingers to the bones trying to give us a good life and love you best he could in his own way. And you repay him by treating him like he was the devil himself."

"He never loved me, mama. He never loved anybody."

"He loved me. I like to think he still does."

"Well maybe. Okay. And maybe he loved Mary too, but if he loved me, he sure had a funny way of showing it."

"He did the best he could."

David's at a loss for words. Surely she must know better. She's been pressing for this conversation ever since he left home, in letters and on the telephone, and he has always managed to avoid engaging her. He knows it's useless. The old man was a tyrant. He was abusive to David and Mary and to their mother, if not physically, than certainly psychologically. But both Shelly and Mary had been making excuses for him as far back as he can remember. He can understand that his mother was probably blinded by the old man's charm. Maybe Mary too. He'd seen how Pop could turn it on, and yes, he had to admit the old bastard could be funny, a real riot when he took to kidding around. But he was also quick to lose his temper, and the least little thing would set him off on a verbal tirade. The insults he lashed all of them with, especially David, were downright vicious. It was a common saying about mean tempered men that you wouldn't treat a dog the way they treat the people they love. That was the way Earl Ray Lawrence was with his family. But Shelly was from the old school, dependent and subservient. She had been taught by her father that the man of the house was the absolute ruler, and Mary had learned the same lesson from her.

David was willing to grant the old man this much: he was a product of a culture in which men were expected to be lord and master in the home. Probably his father had been even worse. What man could have come out of that environment any different? David also understood that the war had changed him, too. He had been gentler and more understanding before going off to war, but by the time he came home from Vietnam with a bullet wound and psychological scars he had developed a hair-trigger temper, and he had no patience with a son who could be just as hardheaded as he was.

Excusable or not, it had been David who bore the brunt of the old man's moods for eighteen years, and that was not easily forgotten. As for the notion that the old man had worked his fingers to the bone, David finds that laughable. The old man was a wheeler-dealer, not a worker.

David changes the subject. He says, "We had lunch at Little Don's before coming out to the hospital."

"I know. Beulah told me."

"Little Don entertained us with stories about when you and Pop first met."

"The Jump 'N' Jive, huh? That old story."

"Yeah."

"How many times have you heard it?"

"Probably about a hundred," he laughs. "But I never heard what happened after Sheriff Moss hauled you out of the car and took you home."

"Well nothing really," Shelly says. "He just took me home. That's all."

There's not much light on the deck, but David doesn't need much light to see the pain on his mother's face. A lifetime of memories is etched in the fine lines around her eyes that come in and out of view as she rocks back and forth. There are surely memories she loves to revisit and memories that must be unbearably sad, memories of herself as a young woman singing her heart out and memories of the first meeting with a man whom she has loved for half a century—the memory of what must have been the most wondrous night of her young life, a fairy tale night that ended in... what? Horror? Bitterness? Or just confusion and disappointment?

*

Sheriff Moss was alone in his marked sheriff's department car that night. Shelly was fearful when he pulled them over. She tried to assure herself that her fear was unreasonable. He was probably stopping them for some minor infraction, although she couldn't imagine what that might be.

They were not speeding, and Luther wasn't drunkenly wavering about the road. He had had only two or three drinks all night. Maybe they had a burnt out taillight or something like that and the sheriff was just stopping them to give them a warning. But she had a bad feeling about Sheriff Moss. She had had a bad feeling about him in the Jump 'N' Jive, and she remembered how Earl Ray had sassed him, and she knew something bad was bound to come of that. And it didn't seem right that two other cars were riding along with the sheriff and that they pulled off the road and stopped a few feet from them.

As she watched the sheriff crawl out of his patrol car and walk toward them with a gait something like a duck's waddle, Shelly told herself it would be all right.

Lucy, said, "Aw shit. This ain't gonna be good."

Luther didn't say a word. He knew the sheriff better than either one of the girls. He knew what happened in the South when a pissed-off law enforcement officer stopped a black man on a quiet back road. He knew this sheriff was pissed off at him for bringing Colonel Barbour's daughter to the Jump 'N' Jive. Still fresh on the minds of Southerners of both races was the murder of Emmett Till, and his would naturally be the first picture to form in Luther's mind. It hadn't been all that long since that young boy's naked and severely-beaten body had been tossed in the Tallahatchie River because he dared to flirt with a white woman. And Luther knew that there had been other more recent if less well known instances of vigilante law enforcement in the dark of night. His only hope was that the sheriff would have the good sense to be scared of the consequences if he did anything to hurt him or his passengers. After all, he worked for Colonel Barbour and Shelly was the Colonel's only daughter. It was generally known that Sheriff Moss did Colonel Barbour's bidding. Luther thought: I wouldn't be a bit surprised if he sent his goons out to hang my black ass, but he'd never do it in front of Shelly. Not even Randy Moss is that stupid.

Besides (he hoped, he prayed) he had another ace up his sleeve. Earl Ray Lawrence. Earl Ray hated Randy Moss. Everybody knew that.

And Earl Ray had connections with people who could end the sheriff's career—namely Riley Rogers, who was even more dreaded than Colonel Barbour. Wasn't it Earl Ray's son, Earl Ray Junior, that had stood up to Sheriff Moss not two hours ago in the Jump 'N' Jive and told him to bug off? Earl Ray Junior was not someone the sheriff was likely to mess with. Not only was he his father's son, he was also best friends with Riley Roger's son, Sugar. The Rogers and the Lawrences were as tight as ticks on a dog's ass.

That was what desperately ran through Luther's head, but none of it stopped him from trembling with fear. No amount of rationalizing could ease his fears about what a hot headed lawman might do in the dark of night.

The sheriff sidled up to the window like he owned it and stuck his head in and said, "Miss Barbour, I need to ask you to get out of the car, please ma'am."

Luther watched the big lawman escort Shelly to his patrol car, and he watched her get in on the passenger side front seat—how odd, he thought, when the cops arrested someone they never put them in the front seat. But then maybe she wasn't being arrested. He knew the sheriff would probably not want to piss her off.

With a sinking feeling, Luther watched the sheriff drive Shelly away. And from the sheriff's car Shelly saw the four men from the other cars approach Luther and Lucy as Sheriff Moss pulled around a bend and out of sight.

The other four men, only two of whom were law enforcement officers, were in civilian cars, unremarkable black sedans. Eugene Close was a deputy sheriff. He was in his early thirties, a knobby-kneed, towheaded country boy with the beginnings of a beer gut. With him was Jimmy Greely, a mechanic who moonlighted as a part-time deputy sheriff. Big Jim, they called him. Six-foot-three, two-hundred and forty pounds, prematurely bald, married to a waitress at Strickland's Café and the father of five children, all under the age of ten. The other two men were Ku Klux Klanners from Jones County who had come down to the coast to go fishing and were staying in an area motel as Sheriff Moss's guest. They were the ones who took Luther away while Greely and Close forced Lucy into Greely's car.

*

Shelly sniffles and reaches in her pocket and draws out a handful of the ever present tissues. She blows her nose. She says, "Poor Lucy. She was never the same after that. She was so beautiful, so vibrant. And unafraid. She'd do anything on a dare, like swimming all the way across Long Bay down at the tip of East Freedom or like flashing her tits at the whole damn town at a Booker T football game. Can you imagine that? That was like in 1956 or '57. Nowadays, the way I hear it, girls do stuff like that all the time. They flash their tits for beads at Mardi Gras. But back then something like that was so daring you just can't imagine. Lucy was a cheerleader. On a ten dollar bet she faced the stadium and yanked up her top and showed that she wasn't wearing a thing underneath. Her parents were in the crowd. They like to died. Oh that Lucy. She was so much fun, just a joy to be around. A Christian girl too, despite all her wild ways. Happy-go-lucky they called her. But then she had that horrible accident when she lost her leg, and then she got dumped by her boyfriend. It seemed like it was just one thing after another with her. And then after that night when those deputies hauled her away I never again heard her laugh. Something happened to her that night that shriveled her into a fearful ghost of her former self. I hardly ever even talked to her after that. Maybe three times at most, and then never again. Eventually she moved out of town."

"That's really a shame," David says. "What about Luther? The rumors are that those Klan guys killed old Luther?"

"That's what everybody said. Luther went missing, that much I know. The rumors were that the Klan guys lynched Luther and weighted him down and tossed him in the bay, and that Sugar Rogers took care of those Klan guys. The law wouldn't or couldn't catch them or prove anything, but they said the Negro Mafia answered to a different law and that Riley Rogers and Sugar were judge and jury. That's just what people said. I don't know anything about that."

It's pretty obvious to David that there's still a lot his mother is not telling. When it came to wheeling and dealing on the coast, nobody had any more of an inside track than Earl Ray and his father, and David can't imagine his father wouldn't have known and eventually told his mother. For a long, long time they are silent. He wants to challenge her, but he's never in his whole life called his mother a liar, and the resistance to it is pretty strong. But finally David says, "Mama, you're not being truthful. You're protecting somebody or you're ashamed of something."

"You're right," she says. "I was holding back. Out of habit, I guess, and just because it's painful to talk about. But there's no reason not to tell you the whole story now, or at least as much as I know of it. That poor Lucy, it just breaks my heart what they did to her."

He waits while she clears her throat. "Lucy had a job working at a drive-in hamburger joint on the beach. You probably remember it. It was that place where they had the speakers like in a drive-in movie and you ordered from your car and girls on roller skates brought your food. Down by where the Golden Eagle is now. Well, Lucy was at work that next Monday afternoon acting like nothing at all ever happened. I went down there with Bonnie Van Slyke, a girl I'd gone to school with, and we ordered milkshakes. We had to order something, see, because the only way to get to talk to Lucy was to order something from her. We didn't want to get her fired. When she brought our shakes out to the car I asked her about what happened that night. She said they just drove her home, that didn't nothing happen.

"It wasn't till years later, after neither one of them guys Greely and Close lived in the area any more, that she finally told me what really happened. That was after me and your daddy got married and were living here in Freedom. Lucy called me one day. She said 'Shelly, I got to talk to you.' We planned to get together the next day. She picked me up and we went to lunch at Little Don's and then drove to the beach. We sat on towels in the sand and talked all afternoon. It was in the winter, too, and it was cold out there on the beach.

"She told me that after the sheriff hauled me off in his car that night the deputies took her to their car and opened the back door and told her to get in. They hauled her off to the county jail. They weren't any other officers there. They took her down to the basement and put her in a cell, and they went in there with her, and they told her to take off all her clothes."

"They raped her."

"Yeah, sorta. At least I'd call it rape, what they did to her. They made her take off ever bit of clothing she had on and sit on the cot. There was only the one cot in there. It was a special holding cell, the only jail cell in the basement. She said it felt damp down there and smelled like old piss. They told her to scream all she wanted because they weren't nobody there to hear her except for prisoners locked up upstairs. They didn't really rape her—this is embarrassing to talk about—because couldn't neither one of them get an erection, but they got naked and they sat down next to her on the cot and they made her take them one after the other in her hands, but they finally gave up since, like I said, neither of them could get hard. I don't know if they were too drunk or if it was because they were scared or maybe because she was crying so sadly and deep down inside of them there was just enough of a smidgen of decency to not let them go through with it. Like maybe their bodies were telling them to behave even when their nasty little minds were thinking dirty thoughts. But anyway after a while they just quit trying. And then the big one, Big Jim, he told her that if she ever told a living soul what they did they would bring her back and lock her up and never let her out.

"The whole time she was telling me that she was shaking something fierce so I put my arms around her and hugged her real tight to warm her up, but it wasn't the cold she was shaking from."

"What about Luther?"

"They don't anybody claim to know for certain what happened, but it was pretty much common knowledge. Those two Ku Klux Klanners took him off and beat him to death and threw him in the bayou. They never found his body. They never even looked for a body because he was never reported missing. Now here's the part nobody knows about. Your daddy, he found out what really happened. Heck, it wasn't ever really that big a secret. In certain circles, everybody knew. Well your daddy told Sugar Rogers. He told Sugar about the two Klan guys, who they were and where they lived, and he told him as much as he knew about what Jimmy and Eugene did to Lucy. He actually thought at the time that they raped her. Sugar put the word out to take care of them—not just those two Klanners, but Big Jim and Deputy Eugene Close as well."

*

The Negro Mafia was an open secret. The name came about when a reporter asked Sugar Rogers about it. "Word has it organized crime on the Gulf Coast is run by black folk in Freedom and that you are the leader," the reporter supposedly asked Rogers.

As the tale has it, Sugar replied with a Stepin Fetchit imitation: "Yassuh, boss man, we's what white folks call the Negro Mafia"—dragging it way out like neee-grow.

They say that Sugar followed that little bit of theater with a booming laugh that shook the wall, and then he gave the reporter a threatening look and said, "Word also has it that nosy reporters been known to end up on the bottom of Long Bay."

Since the reporter's story was never published, what they said is pure hearsay. Nobody knew if Sugar had ties to the actual Mafia, but he definitely had underworld connections of some sort. Word on the street was that Sugar's father, Riley Rogers, a funeral parlor owner in Freedom, ran the local crime syndicate that answered to a boss in Detroit. Ask anyone in the know on the coast and they'd tell you that all the liquor, prostitution, gambling, juke boxes, pinball machines and slot machines in juke joints from Pensacola to New Orleans were run out of a back room of Riley's funeral parlor in Freedom and the little makeshift office in the storeroom in the back of the Lawrence store. Riley was a successful businessman and a deacon in the Holy Redeemer Baptist Church. A

dapper little man never seen without his black suit and bowtie, Riley
Rogers was known and loved by everybody. Sheriff Moss stayed in power
at the whim of Riley Rogers, to whom he gifted an annual Christmas check
in an amount reputed to be in the thousand dollar range, and it was
common knowledge that Colonel Barbour would never get a seat on any of
the more powerful committees in the state legislature and would never
realize his dream of being elected to the U.S. House because Riley found
him personally distasteful. But go into a barbershop or a pool hall and ask
about Riley Rogers and his son, Sugar, and the answer you'll get will be,
"They're good men. Honorable men. Either one of them, father or son,
would give you the shirt off his back if you really needed it." Ask around
the mostly poor and black neighborhoods in the north of Freedom across
Bujold Bayou and you'll get story after story of Riley helping people out,
from no-interest loans to helping promising poor kids get into college.

But it is also commonly said: Don't ever cross Riley Rogers. Not if
you know what's good for you. It was even whispered about that the arson
that destroyed a reputed house of prostitution and the unsolved murders
of two minor crime figures had both happened at the direction of Riley
Rogers. If he was really responsible for those things, the good citizens of
Freedom said the victims had it coming. The sleazeballs Riley was credited
with knocking off were running an insurance scam that was ripping off
elderly people, and the girls working the whorehouse were being held
against their will. That's what people said anyway.

Earl Ray Jr. called on Sugar Rogers on the day after he met Shelly
Barbour in the Jump 'N' Jive. He told him about meeting Shelly and said,
"I'm gonna marry that gal," and he told him that Sheriff Moss had harassed
them in the club and about what had happened later. "His goons made off
with Luther Smith. I'm pretty sure his body is on the bottom of the bayou
now, but they'll never find it. And he sicced Greely and Close on poor Lucy
Kirby. God knows what all they done to her. The poor girl is too scared to
talk."

It didn't take Sugar Rogers long to find out what had happened
that night. Big Jim Greely and Eugene Close were stupid enough to brag to

some cronies in a pool hall about what they had done to Lucy. "We took turns on her," Greely said. "Not just once, neither. And it weren't rape. She let us do it. Eugene done it first and then me, and then we each took another turn. And she acted like she enjoyed it, too. I think she did."

A day after Greely and Close shot off their lying mouths, Sheriff Moss called them in. "I told you to take that girl home," he said. "I didn't tell you to rape her, and I sure as hell didn't tell you to go bragging about it in a fucking pool hall."

"We didn't rape her," Greely said. "We'uz just bullshitting the guys in the pool hall."

"Did you take her straight home?"

"Naw," Close said, "We brought her down here first. We wanted to put the fear of God in her so she wouldn't go talking to nobody."

"So you locked her in a cell and you threatened her, is that it?"

"Yessir."

He grilled them as relentlessly as he would have grilled any crime suspect, and eventually they confessed to everything, including the embarrassing fact that neither one of them had been able to get an erection. Sheriff Moss made them go down into the basement of the jailhouse. He put them in the same jail cell where they had taken Lucy. He slid the door shut and locked it. He hung the keys on a hook ten feet away from the door, in plain view but out of reach, and he went back upstairs and outside and got into his patrol car and drove away. Six men were standing on the corner watching the jailhouse. Sheriff Moss halted his car on the corner and talked to them for a minute, then he drove off, turned the next corner and was immediately out of sight. The men crossed the street and went into the jail and went downstairs to the basement where they took the keys off the wall and opened the cell door, and they beat Close and Greely until they were both unconscious.

The sheriff kept them both locked up until their injuries healed, then he told them to get out of town and never come back. "But I got a wife and five youngun's," Greely said.

"Not any more you ain't," the sheriff said. "She knows what you done and she don't never want to see you again. Betty and the kids been well taken care of. She's set up with a good job somewheres else and you ain't never gonna find out where she's at."

One day shortly after that a man driving a black sedan showed up where Lucy was working and ordered a hamburger and a Coke. She brought his meal in a paper sack and handed it through his open window. He took it and thanked her and handed her an envelope saying, "There's a message for you from a friend."

He slowly ate the hamburger while listening to music on the outside speakers. It was Elvis Presley singing "Heartbreak Hotel." Inside the restaurant Lucy peeked in the envelope. Inside was a hundred-dollar tip and a note telling her that the men who had hurt her had been taken care of and that she would never have to worry about them hurting her again. It was signed, *a friend*.

*

"What about Luther?" David asks. "Did they really kill him?"

"Yes they did. It was a Klan lynching just like countless others. A year later it was the Klansmen's time to be hanging at the end of a rope. Two white men were found hanging by their necks from an oak tree up in Jones County. They were wearing white robes and hoods. Far as I know it was the first and only case of Klansmen being lynched. Just as in the case of all the lynchings of black men, the people responsible for it were never found. But there's no doubt that Sugar Rogers or his daddy one or the other gave the order."

Shelly stands up. She says, "Wait right here." She goes in the house and a couple of minutes later comes back out and hands David an envelope. He opens it. It's the note that was given to Lucy half a century ago. He recognizes the handwriting. Pop Lawrence has an unmistakable way of looping his Os.

"Lucy gave this to you?"

"Yes she did, right before she moved to... I think it was Chicago. I never again heard from her."

*

When they open the door to Pop's hospital room the next morning, David once again smells cigarette smoke. He bursts in like an avenging angel intent on clearing the air of demon smoke. Completely oblivious to Freight Train standing with his hands on the window sill, and anybody else in the room, he shouts at his father, "You've been smoking again!"

"That's none of your bees wax," the old man says.

"That's right, it's not. Go ahead and kill yourself. See if I care."

Shelly, having stepped in practically on David's heel, shoots her son a look of pure exasperation, which he shrugs off. What her look says to him is you smoke, too, to which he mentally replies, yeah but I'm not dying from a damaged heart. But underneath the arrows of exasperation in her look is the satisfaction of knowing that his anger at the old man shows he cares. Shelly steps up to her husband and gives him a perfunctory kiss on the forehead. "Good morning, sweetie," she says. She also sniffs audibly. "He's right," she says, "you have been smoking." Her tone is chiding but much gentler than David's.

That's when Melissa speaks up. She says, "How do you know it wasn't me, Big Boy?"

He's struck again with Melissa's beauty. Quite obviously she has not allowed her hospital stay to be an excuse for letting herself go. She's wearing dark lipstick, rouge and eye liner, and a robe brought from home and thrown on over her blue hospital gown. More than just proud and beautiful, Melissa is defiant. While he's ranting about smoking, she's holding an unlit cigarette between her fingers, tapping it on the edge of the ashtray by her chair.

"Do you know the term enabler?" he asks.

"Do you know the term mind your own fucking business?" she responds.

Her biting retort is quickly followed by a loving smile, and it draws a boisterous laugh from Freight Train.

Steering the conversation away from accusations about smoking and back to her favorite subject, her appearance, Melissa says, "I guess I'm going to have to get my nose fixed unless I want to go through the rest of my life looking like a boxer that's taken one too many hits to the schnoz."

"Maybe you ought to come out to Hollywood with me. We got the best plastic surgeons in the world out there."

"Actually, I have a good one in Atlanta. He fixed me up once before."

"Really? When?" This is news to David.

"It was before you even knew me" she explains. "Before I moved in with y'all. You never knew it, but I was born with a misshaped jaw. It looked like a boulder jutting out on one side only. I was all lopsided. God, I was one butt-ugly kid. Never would have figured it, would you?"

"No, I wouldn't," and he assumes she must be exaggerating now.

"I had plastic surgery when I was fifteen and I came out looking gorgeous."

"You certainly did. You still look gorgeous. But damn, girl, why did you never tell us that?"

The big mystery about Melissa had always been who she was before. Where had she come from? What had her life been like pre-Lawrence? She was orphaned and adopted by Earl Ray when she was sixteen years old, and whatever baggage she came with had been carefully hidden away. She seldom talked about her past life, and when she did, her stories sometimes seemed contradictory. She never showed them any childhood pictures. It had been as if she had not existed before moving in with the Lawrence family. David remembers wanting to ask her about her past, but so soon after the death of her parents he had been hesitant to bring it up. Now David thinks that in the many years since their high school days she must have surely opened up to the rest of the family. Now he figures that if he's in the dark about her history it's his own fault.

Something else that's been sticking in his craw is the thought that the old man was probably stupidly and thoughtlessly responsible for the accident that put them both in the hospital. He'd like to be able to stick the blame squarely on his father.

"Was Pop drunk when he ran off the damn building?" he asks Melissa.

"Sure. Of course he was. Ain't he always?" Melissa winks at Pop. "But that's not what caused it. It was the heart attack that caused the accident, not the other way around." She doesn't mention that he was driving straight for the edge at 60 miles per hour when the logjam in his aorta knocked him out.

"Well that's good to know. I was afraid he was showing off by driving like he was in a Demolition Derby."

Pop says, "You coulda asked me. I was there too, you know." He hates being spoken of in the third person. "I'm right over here, you know. Laid up in this fucking hospital bed." He kicks at the sheets with his one good leg. The sheets are all tangled up, and the more he kicks at them the worse they get. "God! Can't somebody get a nurse in here to straighten these sheets up?"

"I'll do it, honey," Shelly says.

She starts to fiddle with the sheets, but he slaps her hands away. "Get the nurse to do it. I need new sheets. These are all sweaty."

It is too hot in the room. They can all feel it.

David says, "You've been drinking, too. I can smell it."

"So what if I have?"

"What kind of idiot brings a dying man whiskey?"

"A good friend. Not like a idiot son who never bothers to call or anything. How come you even bothered to come now? Trying to make sure you get your share of my money?"

That elicits a sardonic snort from David. "You may not know it old man, but I make a lot more money than you ever dreamed of." (He's not really sure if that's true.)

Melissa says, "Why don't you give him a break?"

"Yeah. Okay. Sure. Sorry, honey. I don't mean to be so nasty. It's just that the old man brings out the nasty in me."

Since leaving home almost two decades ago David has tried to avoid thinking about his father, but he's never been able to completely shut him out of his mind. There must have been ten thousand imaginary conversations between them, and in every one of those conversations David got to slap the old man down with all the witty and nasty insults he'd never had the nerve to say or the quick wit to think of when he was younger.

Their last lengthy argument had been over his choice of a major in college. When he said he wanted to major in theater his father called him an idiot and a dreamer, and told him the theater was for queers, and he finally said, "If you do that, you're on your own. I'm not going to pay good money for you to throw your life away like that."

Working his way through college after the old man withdrew his support had been tough. David had had to find a job, something he'd never done. He had no idea how to go about searching for a job, and he quickly discovered that he had few skills or marketable experience or training. With the help of a classmate who had a brother who ran a small roofing outfit he finally found a job. He carried heavy packages of shingles up a ladder to roofers on top of houses and carried hot roofing compound in steaming buckets under the blazing sun in ninety-to one-hundred degree temperatures. Steaming, sultry work that melted pounds off his body. That was the first summer after he lost parental support (except for the little money Shelly sent him without Pop's knowledge). In the fall of that year he got a job with a carpenter and learned the trade, skills that came in handy backstage in the theater department.

Despite exhausting work and study and long hours in the theater department building sets and rehearsing, he never got discouraged throughout his college years. Going without sleep was no big deal. Cracking the books had never been difficult, and as an actor he seemed to naturally fall into good roles as if it were his due. He was the star of the drama department. But in the years following graduation when he tried and tried to get acting jobs that always went to someone who looked more the part or who had a friend who knew the director or (he often suspected but never could prove) was sleeping with the director or the producer, he began to reluctantly grant that his old man might have been right after all. Maybe he was a dreamer and a fool. But when he got his first big fat check from his first starring role in Hollywood, he felt totally vindicated. He sent his father a letter. It included a photo copy of the check and a note that read "This is from the kid who threw his life away studying acting."

*

He had been sixteen years old when Melissa first came into their lives. It was in the fall. Football season. Late in the afternoon. David had just walked home from practice kicking clouds of fallen leaves all the way home. He tossed his jacket at the hall coat tree and watched it miss the hook and fall to the floor, as happened more often than not. He kicked the jacket into a corner and then kicked off his shoes and hopped on first one leg and then the other to pull his sweaty and stinky socks off.

"Is that you, David?" his mother hollered from the kitchen.

"Yes ma'am."

"You better not be strewing your stinky stuff all over the hallway."

Jesus, she must have x-ray vision, he thought. He pulled his shirt over his head. He was standing there bare-chested and sweaty, his dirty blond hair looking like sea grass after a hurricane, clothes strewn like the leaves in the yard, exactly as his mother had just said they shouldn't be, when the front door opened and his father came in with a girl whose beauty made him gasp. His first impression was that she must be a South Sea Islander. Her skin was tanned, creamy and smooth with an inner rosy glow. Large black eyes looked incredibly sad. Flaming hair swirled with coiled ringlets and a two-tone dye job, coal black streaked with bright orange. Tall enough to meet him eye-to-eye, she stood slump shouldered at the moment, wearing a bulky sweater that covered her all the way past her hips, with only her fingertips showing out of the tattered sleeves. He did not at first notice what a voluptuous body she had, a body he would later describe to his buddies as a wet dream walking.

His father and the girl both halted in the doorway as if taken aback by running into a half-naked David in the foyer standing slack-jawed amidst discarded clothing. The old man said, "God, David. You look like shit warmed over."

The girl smiled a deeply dimpled smile at that. She stifled a giggle and sweetly said, "Hi, I'm Melissa," and offered her hand in greeting.

"Hi." He waved away the handshake saying, "You probably ought not touch me. I'm all sweaty. Just came from football practice."

Shelly stepped into the hall from the kitchen, and at the same time Mary came in from her room, the jazzy strains of Dire Straits' "Sultans of Swing" coming from her CD player. Pop said, "Everybody, this is Melissa Baker."

Mary and Melissa greeted each other shyly.

Shelly said, "Hi, honey. Would you like something to drink? Maybe you'd like some cookies."

To David, Pop said, "You need to get yourself cleaned up. Go on, get to it. We can wait for you."

Shelly added, "And pick up those nasty clothes and put them in the hamper."

David grabbed up his dirty clothes and carried them to the bathroom where he dropped them in the hamper. He showered and brushed his teeth, put on clean jeans and a white shirt, and brushed his hair.

Everyone was seated at the kitchen table when David came in looking spruced and fresh. Pop said, "That's better. You look halfway decent."

David turned a kitchen chair backwards and slung his legs across the seat and crossed his arms over the back. Pop said, "I know y'all are wondering what's going on. I'll get right to it. I hope this ain't too abrupt. Melissa here lost her parents recently. It was very tragic. I don't want to talk about it now. She can tell you more when she's ready. But the thing is, she's all alone. She don't have anybody to take care of her. No relatives or nothing. So she's gonna come stay with us." To David and Mary he added, "She's gonna be your new sister."

There was silence for the longest time. Melissa looked down at her hands. Finally Pop said, "Well? Is anybody gonna say anything?"

Shelly said, "Welcome to the family, honey."

"Is she gonna sleep in my room?" Mary asked her parents.

"Yes. We'll have to put another bed in there," Pop said. "It might be a little crowded, but..."

"Oh no, it'll be fine," Mary said. To Melissa she said, "It'll be fun. I always wanted a sister."

Somewhat later Pop managed to corral his wife and children one at a time and tell them individually that they should not ask Melissa anything about her folks or where she came from or, in fact, anything at all about her past. "She's been through a lot. She's been hurt. And we don't want to remind her or hurt her no more." Shelly, Mary and David each got the unsaid message loud and clear. There was something dark and dangerous about Melissa's past, and they were never to question her about it.

*

In the hospital David takes a long look at Melissa, trying to reconcile this beautiful but damaged forty-two-year-old woman with his memory of the sixteen-year-old girl who unexpectedly became a part of the family in the fall of his junior year in high school. She looks the same except for the nose, of course, and she's given up the flamboyant hair color for a more natural looking dark auburn, and she must have been spending a lot of time in the gym because her body is harder than he remembers. She also looks much more self-assured.

"I was just remembering when the old man brought you home for the first time," David says.

"You were all sweaty and half naked, and you smelled like a locker room."

"Yeah, and you flat dab knocked me out with your beauty. You looked so terribly vulnerable. And then when you smiled, those dimples lit up the world. You probably still don't have any idea how you affect men."

"This coming from the hot shot movie star." She flashes those same dimples at him and says, "But oh yeah, I think I have a pretty good idea how I affect men. They have a way of letting me know."

"I thought you might, but you never know. Especially considering that you just now revealed that you had had plastic surgery as a child, I figured you might need a little reassuring that you're not half bad looking."

"And you gave it to me in spades. Thanks, honey."

When Earl Ray brought her home to meet his wife and their children—her new mother and brother and sister—it had been less than a year since the surgery to fix her jaw, and she still looked in the mirror and wondered who the face staring back at her belonged to. Reason told her it was a lovely face, a face she could compare favorably to faces seen in the fashion magazines she constantly perused, but she had a hard time believing others would see her that way. At first anyway. But even then she was beginning to get used to her new looks, and now that she had a new brother who was tall and handsome and who constantly raved about how beautiful she was, her confidence was beginning to grow. And, as if David's constant gushing about her beauty were not enough, the boys in her new school melted into globs of sexual desire in her presence.

Reminded of those days, she winks roguishly and flashes her dimples. "Lord knows you never tried to hide the way you lusted after me."

"What did you expect? I was sixteen and horny."

"Ripe and randy. Yeah, that's how I'd put it."

Shelly is shaking her head as if to say will these kids ever grow up!

David says, "If I remember correctly, there was a thick fog of pheromones in the house throughout the next two years."

And Shelly says, "I was scared that the two of you might do something you'd regret."

"Yeah, well I think we were both pretty much aware of the temptation," Melissa says. "He was always wandering into our room without knocking. I was scared he was gonna catch me with my pants down."

"I tried my best," David confesses.

"Yeah, and you were always staring at my tits."

"Damn right. And you loved it too, didn't you? It wasn't any accident that you forgot to shut the door all the way, and you went around twitching your ass like some kind of hoochie koochie girl making me all hot and bothered all the time."

"I did not!"

"Did too, and you know it."

She laughs and winks and then grimaces because winking hurts her injured nose, and then she says, "You're right. I confess. But geeze, you were so easy."

Coming in on the conversation late, Pop says, "Amos and Andy."

"What!?" they all ask at once.

"She said something that sounded like Amos and Andy. What was it she said?"

"Ripe and Randy."

"Oh, I never heard of them."

David thinks that his old man's messed up hearing is going to be the one thing that softens the hatred he's been nurturing for such a long time.

*

Simply moving another bed into Mary's room was not good enough for Pop. He brought in carpenters and had the room remodeled and expanded, knocking out the outer wall and extending the room out another ten feet. He bought matching beds and dressers and put in a new carpet. The girls painted the walls a soft purple called Fresh Heather with Wild Bamboo trim. The remodel was completed in a week, during which time the girls bunked together in David's room and David slept on the pullout couch in the sunroom. The first thing the girls did after moving back into their remodeled bedroom was to scoot the beds together, and late night gab fests after dates or parties became a frequent ritual. They'd sit on their scrunched-together beds and tell delicious tales about how a bunch of Booker T cheerleaders stumbled on Mary Ann Wilson making out with Brian Smith under the bleachers or what James Buford Martin said he was going to do to Randy Moss. Sue Ellen often spent the night with them, and the three of them would gossip late into the night, and more often than not David was asked to join them, although they would usually reserve some of their juicier bits of gossip for after they kicked him out and he went to sleep in his own room.

Years later David and Jasmine watched a video about the comedian Richard Pryor, which included a segment about him growing up in a brothel. "That's what it was like in my house," he told Jasmine. "Not that I grew up in a whore house, but I had two sexy sisters and they were always having friends over to spend the night, and it was like half naked chicks and constant sex talk. It was hard on a teenage boy, I'll tell you."

"Literally hard, I imagine," she giggled.

And he said, "Like a fence post."

"And I bet I know what you did after you went back to your room, and I bet your sisters and their friends had it figured out, too, and were probably snickering at your expense while you were getting yourself off."

"Oh God, that's too embarrassing to think about."

In the hospital he tells Melissa, "You girls had no idea what torture you put me through," and she coos, "Poor baby."

The sun is now high and the room is heating up. Freight Train closes the drapes. Melissa and Pop have started a poker hand. The cards are on his rolling lunch tray. Pop picks up the deck and deals. His hands shake. David sees him spasm and grimace as he tries to stifle a cough. Shelly places her hand on his chest. Melissa looks at her cards and then at Pop. She waits until she sees him relax out of the pain, and then she discards a single card. He deals her a card and takes three for himself. She lays her cards down, a full house, sixes and eights.

"If them sixes was aces it'd be a dead man's hand," Pop says.

Shelly says, "Let's not even think about dead men."

Pop folds his hand back into the deck without even showing it. "Not even a pair," he says. He palms the deck and shuffles the cards absent-mindedly. He says, "You're cleaning my clock today." He closes his eyes for a few moments and then opens them and asks, "Did I drift off?"

"A little bit," Shelly says.

Sue Ellen peeks her head through the open door. "Is it all right if I come in?"

"Hi," David says. "Yeah, come on in."

She asks Pop how he's doing. He says he's not doing bad considering. "Triple bypass," he says as if that's something to brag about. "Hurt like a sumbitch. They say you can't feel anything when they put you under, but I swear to God I felt it when they broke my chest open. And then when they yanked a tube out it was like a damn fence post jabbed in there and then pulled out." He can't see the tiny prick of festered skin where they inserted a tube into his chest. If he could see the actual tube he'd be amazed at how small it was. It felt as big around as one of his fingers.

"That sounds terrible," Sue Ellen says, "but I'm glad to see you're doing okay now."

The room is crowded. Shelly is seated on the edge of the bed, Freight Train leaning by the window, Melissa in the one chair, David standing by the foot of the bed. There are flowers and Mylar balloons printed with get well wishes, and one apparently sent to the wrong room that says "It's a boy."

Shelly pats the bed and says to Sue Ellen, "You can sit down here, honey."

And Melissa copies her gesture, but instead of patting the bed she pats her lap and says, winking, to David, "And you can sit here."

"I think I better not," he says.

Sue Ellen sits down on the bed. She's wearing tight blue jeans and a loose button-up man's shirt with the top two buttons undone. Her hair is piled high on her head and tied with a bandana. She asks David if he's coming to the game Friday night.

"What game?"

"Listen to him," she says to the room at large. "Pretending like he doesn't remember what happens every year at this time."

"Oh, *that* game," David says.

She doesn't have to explain that she is talking about the annual pre-season scrimmage between Booker T and Freedom High. Called the Shrimp Bowl locally, it's a game with no official conference standing, but to the residents of Freedom it might as well be the Rose Bowl.

Sue Ellen says, "My boys are playing for Booker T."

Pop says, "I gotta see if they'll let me out of this prison in time for the game."

"Don't you be ridiculous," Shelly says. "You're not going to any football game in your condition."

A few minutes later another visitor pops in. Randy Moss. David immediately notices that Randy has gained a lot of weight. He looks like his father. His complexion is even worse than it was in high school and his buzz cut barely hides that he's almost completely bald. His uniform stretches taut across a prominent beer belly.

As soon as Randy walks in Melissa pushes herself out of her chair, leans over to kiss Pop on the cheek, and darts out of the room without saying a word, leaving an icy contrail behind.

*

"What gives with Randy and Melissa?" David asks Sue Ellen. The two of them plus Mary are having coffee in the hospital cafeteria, having escaped the room and Randy Moss's uncomfortable visit, and Melissa— still a patient and perhaps not so spry as she acts—has gone back to her room. "Let mama and the old man put up with him, they're used to it," David said as they were taking the elevator. Now he says, "I know nobody's exactly crazy about Randy, but we always kind of put up with him, and the two of them were pretty hot and heavy the last I knew."

Sue Ellen says, "Nobody knows for sure what's going on with them. I guess they musta had a lovers' spat. Not too long after you headed out west. She never talked about it, and they haven't said a word to each other since."

"Musta been some spat."

"Tell me 'bout it. You know Melissa. She never holds anything back. But this... wow!"

He reminds her that, in fact, there are many things Melissa has held back, such as her entire childhood. But they both know that's not what she's talking about. Melissa may have been silent about her past, but she freely talked to David and Sue Ellen, and most especially to Mary, about her emotions and her love life and anything else that was current in her life.

"She never even talked to Mary about Randy?"

"I don't think so."

"Damn."

Sue Ellen remembers Melissa's first day in school. "We were all hanging out in front of the school the way we all did, with the kids from Freedom High across the street and everybody smoking. Mary Ann Wilson and Beverly Duncan were doing their Valley Girl imitations and Jimmy Dale was there in his punk get-up. Thank God he finally outgrew that. And y'all came walking up, and the boys all went ga-ga over Melissa. Not that I blame them. She was one hot looking babe. And then in homeroom, remember? Miss Whitaker had this whole welcoming speech all prepared."

"She read it like from cue cards," David says.

"Yeah, she said, 'We want to welcome a new girl, Melissa Baker. She comes from the island of Hawaii, our fiftieth state.'"

David clarifies that Melissa actually came from a little town on the coast no more than forty miles away where she had lived all her life, but her parents were Hawaiian and she did say she had visited the islands a few times.

Sue Ellen says, "Remember what happened at lunch that first day? One of the boys—who was it?"

"Bo Bergeron."

"Yeah, Bo Bergeron. He asked her if she could do the hula. And man, did she ever put him in his place. She did a really wild and sexy hula with her hips all swaying and stuff, and then she said, 'You're looking at my ass. You're supposed to watch my hands. The story is all in the hands.' And he smarted off, 'Yeah? So what are your hands saying?' And she said,

'They're saying you ain't gonna get none a my ass, not in your wildest dreams.'"

*

The first time Melissa dated Randy, it was on a bet. They had known each other for about a year at the time, and Randy had asked her out almost a dozen times. He had asked her shyly and politely, and he had asked her as a challenge and as a joke and as a tease, trying every approach he could think of. When she turned him down for about the tenth time he asked, "Why the hell not. Ya think I got rabies or something?"

The next time she turned him down he said, "Goddamn, I seen some of who you've dated, and there ain't no way they're better looking than me. I think you're just playing hard to get. I gotcha. All right, I'm willing to play that game. I know you really want me."

Her response to that was, "Eeeyuch!"

It wasn't much of a stretch for him to assume she was playing him like a fish on a hook. Her body language gave him all the clues he needed.

After moving in with the Lawrences, it had not taken her long to notice the burly boy across the bayou. She saw him zoom cross the bridge from East Freedom to Freedom on his Harley, black leather jacket gleaming in the morning sun, no helmet, long hair blowing. Later that same day she spotted him across the water building what looked like a barbeque pit in his back yard. He was shirtless despite a chill in the air, wearing jeans and sneakers. Bricks were piled in a wheelbarrow. He was spreading mortar with a trowel and stacking bricks. Maybe it was a wall he was building and not a barbeque pit. She couldn't tell. He was too far away to see clearly, but that was an easily remedied problem. She was sitting on a lawn chair in the back yard, and sitting on the table next to her chair was a binocular that Shelly used for spotting birds. She picked it up and brought him into focus. She noted his muscular build, the winding snake tattoo on his upper arm encircling a big bicep. Maybe he had other tattoos hidden away somewhere just out of sight. Where might they be? She loved the look of his golden hair in the sun, flopping back and forth as he picked up bricks and set them on the wall. Periodically he would reach up to brush hair from his eyes. He's got a bit of a gut, she thought, not flabby but like hard rubber stretched over boulders. His skin looked like it had blistered and peeled, yet he was shirtless in the sun, a sure sign that he was a risk taker.

"Who's that boy across the bayou?" she asked Mary and David later that evening.

"That's Randy Moss," David said. "You don't want to know him."

"Why not? He looked kind of cute to me."

"Cute? Him? You've got to be kidding," David said.

Mary concurred that Randy was "kinda cute," but added, "He's a first class asshole,"

Melissa said, "I bet he's good in bed."

"Jesus!" David said. "I hope the hell he never finds out you said that. He already thinks he's God's gift to women."

"Your mama said y'all were all good friends."

"Sometimes. Yeah, maybe." David chuckled. Mary made silly gestures that could mean almost anything as they hemmed and hawed about their relationship with Randy Moss.

It was late at night, a week before Halloween. Everyone had gone to bed, the three of them piled onto Mary and Melissa's pulled-together beds. An almost full moon washed their room with a milky glow.

Mary said, "Everything is a contest to Randy. He and David compete at swimming and running and wrestling and everything else you can think of. Don't you, David?"

"Guess so. That's about the size of it."

Melissa said, "I could imagine wrestling with him" with the same proud-to-be-naughty tone she had used when saying she bet he was good in bed. Mary and David had not yet learned how much of Melissa's bad girl banter to take seriously.

"Well you'd better watch out," Mary said. "He's a real pussy hound."

"So maybe I'm a pussy cat."

"I'm not kidding. He's the kind of guy that'll do anything to get in your pants, but once you let him in he loses interest. You know what I mean? I mean he'll tell you he loves you and that you're beautiful, and never call you again."

"Sounds like you've been there."

"No, not me."

"Never?"

"No."

"Then how do you know?"

"I just do. You can tell by the way he talks."

David challenged, "That's not what I heard."

"Oh yeah? What did you hear?"

"He told me y'all almost went all the way."

"Did not."

"He said you let him play with your tits."

"So what? That's nothing."

Variations of that conversation were repeated throughout the weeks between Halloween and Thanksgiving, but sometime before Christmas they all got bored with it. There were never any new revelations to keep the conversation hot. During that time Melissa did finally get to meet Randy and the four of them spent some time together—not a lot of time then because Randy went to a different school, but come summertime they would become almost inseparable. That was also the year in which David started dating Sue Ellen and when Mary started getting serious about Buddy Boudreau. Outdoor cookouts in the spring and swimming in the summer often saw the six of them together as a group: two couples plus the two, Melissa and Randy, who were not yet a couple.

David and Mary had been across-the-water neighbors with Randy from birth and the three of them had started playing with each other as soon as they were old enough to cross the water. They had teased, fought, bullied, loved and hated each other. They had tested one another with every imaginable version of I'm bigger, stronger, faster, smarter, and played all the variations of I'll show you mine if you show me yours that boys and girls can come up with.

David and Randy loved to hate each other. They were athletes at rival high schools competing in swimming and football and baseball. Randy was a linebacker for Freedom High. David was a wide receiver for Booker T. On their respective baseball teams David played second base and Randy was an outfielder and Freedom's best hitter. Both were distance swimmers. And then there were the boys-only contests: who could piss the farthest and shoot off the farthest, and who had the biggest dick. The boys' friendship was laced with spite and anger and envy. Randy and Mary's friendship was competitive in similar ways but with a boy-girl twist instead of the various forms of pissing contests that Randy and David engaged in—meaning a bigger heaping of unconsummated sex. It seemed like the more Randy and Mary grew to despise each other the more they wanted each other and the more they wanted each other the less likely it became that they would ever touch one another. And the older they got the more they found to despise in one another. She hated his arrogance and the crude sex jokes he was always cracking; he hated that she made better grades; she developed a love of literature and he had no interest in reading; she flirted with liberal politics and suspected he was ultra conservative and bigoted, even though she could never get him to seriously talk about politics.

In the seventh grade Randy was madly in love with Mary, but she couldn't stand him. That lasted about a month. In the tenth grade they loved each other for three whole days and then got in a big fight because he told her she had a big butt and she spent the next few weeks glancing over her shoulder whenever she came close to a mirror or reflective glass. For a month or so they wouldn't speak to each other, and then they started dating again. And then broke up for good. They probably would have drifted apart for good, David included, if Melissa hadn't entered the picture.

*

In his monologue David talked about the big bet between Randy and Melissa. "The steaming days of summer found us all swimming and skiing in Little Bay. All except Buddy, 'cause he had a summer job clerking in Pop's store. We spent nearly every waking moment together on the water, even though half the time Randy and Mary weren't speaking to each other. Randy had a fourteen-foot runabout with a big ol' Mercury outboard, and his dad had set up a small ski jump anchored twenty feet out from their dock. We took turns skiing. Randy and I competed to see who could jump the farthest. Those were contests I easily won because I was smaller and lighter. Randy was a blob of muscle and fat. The girls teased me about skiing, saying I loved it mainly because it was one of the few things I could best Randy at. What the hell? There was a lot of truth in that.

"The diving platform floated on empty oil barrels, same as the ski jump. It was secured to the Moss's dock by a length of nylon rope. It was about ten feet square with a low diving board. The board didn't have much spring to it, but the platform was a floating paradise for our small group of teenage boys and girls. It was our cabana in Hawaii, complete with a big beach umbrella. It was the last weekend before school started and six days before the annual football game between Freedom and Booker T, almost a year since Melissa's arrival. We were lounging on the diving platform, Mary and Melissa lying on air mattresses in their bikinis, Randy seated next to Melissa, and Sue Ellen and I in the water hanging on to the platform and lazily scissoring our feet out behind us. The movement of water below and clouds above created a sensation of drifting even though we were held in place by the rope—the platform itself like a dog straining at its leash, only gently with no barking, trying to follow the ebb of the tide.

"Randy said to Melissa, 'If you're real good I might take you out after the game Friday night.'

"'Are you talking to me?' Melissa knew good and well he was talking to her.

"'Who else?'

"'Thanks but no thanks,' she snorted.

"'Come on. You know you wanna.'

"And then she said, 'Maybe, just maybe, if you're really super nice I'll go out with you sometime. But not after the game.'

"They were going at it like wildcats. Randy complained, 'You been saying that for a year.'

"'I know, and I mean it. Really. Sometime. But not after the game.'

"'You just said that. Why not after the game?'

"She said, 'Because everybody knows you've been after me all year. If y'all win the game and then we go out together it'll be like you won me or something. I don't want to be a football trophy. And if you lose the game... well I guess that would make me like the booby prize. That'd seem weird. Besides, there's the dance after the game. Everybody goes, and I don't like to dance.'

"'You do too. I know you do. I seen ya.'

"She just flat out ignored that. She said, 'All the football players are going to get drunk. You'll be sneaking out to get a snort of whiskey and hanging out with your buddies, and I'll be left standing around with a bunch of Freedom High girls that I hardly even know, and I'll be like the Booker T bitch to them.'

"Mary sat up and dangled her legs in the water. We all looked at each other wondering where the hell Randy and Melissa were going.

"Randy said, 'All right, then we won't go to the dance. I don't care about the silly dance anyway. I'll take you to the coast. We'll go to some really nice club.'

"'And do what?' She shot right back.

Randy laughed. He said, 'And get snockered, and then just do what comes naturally.'

"'You mean get in my pants.'

"'Like I said, you know you wanna.'

"That was when she really got pissed. She said, 'Yeah? Well screw you, Bub, and the horse you rode in on.' And she got all puffy and pushed herself up and dove off the platform, her splash a door slammed in Randy's face.

"Randy stood up as if to dive in after her, but then he just stood there and waited to see what she would do next. In a few seconds she surfaced and blew water out of her mouth and treaded in place and said, 'You are so fucking stupid. If you really wanted to date me, you just blew it. You had me ready to say yes and then you had to go and screw it up.'

She sounded like she was about to cry.

Randy said, 'What do you mean? What'd I say that was so bad?'

"'Making it all about sex. (In a sing-song whine she mimicked him.) You *know* you wanna.'

"Then Randy said, 'I was just playing around,' and he thought about that for a moment and then corrected himself. 'No I wasn't. I was telling the truth. It *is* all about sex. Ain't it? Ain't it always? Dating I mean.' He quickly glanced eye to eye at me, Sue Ellen and Mary, seeking confirmation. Nobody responded. He said, 'We talk about dating as if it's all about going out for dinner and going to a movie or a dance and stuff like that, but what dating's really all about is testing each other out to see if we want to do it and then either doing it or breaking it off. I mean that's the whole of it when you come down to it. So why can't we just skip the bullshit and get it on?'

"'Man, you are crass,' Melissa shot back, still treading water a few feet away and spouting streams of water Randy's way (falling far short of her target).

"'Hey, don't give me that shit. Like I'm all nasty just for telling the truth. I know you're not some lily white virgin yourself. You come across like some kind of world class slut, and I can name at least three boys you've done it with and probably guess one or two more.'

He was rocking the platform with his leg-pumping movement, two hundred pounds of agitated meat and muscle. She was treading water furiously.

"'That's right,' she said. 'And don't that just chap your ass? Can't stand the thought of me giving it to somebody else and not to you, can you? God damn you, Randy Moss.'

"Man, she was on fire! Finally I just had to jump into the argument. I said, 'Why don't y'all just go ahead and get it on? You know you're dying to.'

"'Oh yeah?' Melissa splashed me and then took a couple of strokes to get back to the platform and climb up. Slipping and grasping with clawlike hands, she crabbed onto the platform and grabbed a towel and furiously dried her face, shook water out of her hair, took a deep breath and said, 'Get it on with shit for brains, huh? Okay, so maybe I will. Think I'm chicken? I'll show you. I'm up to the challenge. But only if Randy wins the bet, only if Freedom wins the big game Friday night. If I'm gonna be a trophy date, I might as well be a trophy date. Like there's a chance in hell they're going to win.'

"'Oh yeah? Randy said, 'So the bet is on?'

"'Sure,' Melissa said. 'I'm willing. But just to be sure we're all clear on this, let's spell out exactly what the wager is, okay?'

"'What you just said, that's the bet. You and me. We go out on a date after the game. And yeah, okay, you go to the dance with me. You be my trophy, since you put it that way. What happens after that? ... hmm, we'll just have to wait and see about that now, won't we?'"

Proving his acting skill, David did that last bit as if imitating Randy imitating Nicholson in *The Shining*.

He continued: "Melissa sat down next to Mary on one of our air mattresses. She glanced around to see what the rest of us might be thinking about that. Our reaction was anticipation. We were all poised to hear her response to Randy, and it looked like nobody was going to make a move until they finalized the wager with a handshake. 'All right,' Melissa finally said, 'I'll go out with you if Freedom wins. But it's just a date. I'm not promising anything more.'

"'All right. You're on. You're all witnesses.'

"Melissa said, 'What if I win?'"

"That was about when I climbed back up on the platform. I had to get clear of the water to think that one out. I reached down for Sue Ellen and helped her scramble up. We grabbed towels to dry off, and I fished a cigarette out of the communal Marlboro pack we were all sharing—Randy's. And then I reached for the beer stringer. That was a neat device if there ever was one, a rigged-up fish stringer tied to the diving platform and holding beer cans in the water to keep them cool. I popped a can, took a swig and passed it around.

"For a long time nobody could think of anything Randy could bet that Melissa might want or that he'd hate to give up, nothing worthy of her going to the dance with him. Mary suggested his Harley, but that was too extreme. Melissa said she didn't want it anyway, and Randy wasn't willing to bet it. After a long time I came up with the perfect bet. I said, 'If you lose, you've got to transfer to Booker T.'

"Randy detested Booker T. We all knew that. Freedom was, in many ways, a much better school. They had smaller classes and better equipment. Even their textbooks were much newer. Randy liked the kids there, and they seemed to like him, at least more so than a lot of the kids at Freedom that he knew. The school districts were divided north and south with Booker T to the north and Freedom to the south. Families in the southern district, which included the island of East Freedom where Randy lived, were on average much wealthier than the families on the north side—not counting us, of course—and since school funding was based in large part on the tax base there was more money for their school. There were class distinctions that the upward-striving Freedom families were happy to embrace even while denying that any such class differences existed. But the biggest difference between the two schools was that Booker T was predominantly black and Freedom predominantly white. Not that anyone would admit that had anything to do with anything. They'd say it was pure coincidence that they lived here and the other ones lived over there and that there just happened to be more people with money over here where all the white folks lived. You know, the ones who were accidentally white.

"It hadn't always been that way. Old timers had vivid memories of the way it used to be when Freedom was truly integrated and about as color blind as a place could be. But then after they built the private Christian school that later became Freedom High a new kind of sneaky racism reared its head.

"But anyway, Randy—guess where he fit in all that—he thought my idea was pretty damn extreme, and he said so. But Melissa thought it was a cool idea.

"Randy said, 'That's a hell of a lot to stake on one football game.'

"'Yeah, but I'm worth it,' Melissa teased, and she reached down and splashed water at Randy.

"'All right,' Randy finally conceded, 'It's a bet.' They shook hands, and then we all shook hands to confirm we had witnessed the deal. Since Melissa was seated and he was standing, Randy had to bend forward to shake her hand. When he did, she grabbed his arm with both of her hands and jerked him off the platform and into the water. But he was fast. He hooked onto her and pulled her into the water after him. They splashed around for a while, pushing each other under, tousling each other's hair and laughing gleefully, and then we all decided it was time to get out of the water and go to Little Don's for burgers and shakes."

*

David went on to talk about the big football game. This came earlier in his monologue, before the part about the flood. He said, "It was a high scoring game and close all the way. Freedom scored first. Their kick returner took the opening kickoff on the five yard line and got behind a wall of blockers clinging to the right sideline. Freight Train Taylor broke through the blockers and had a clear shot at the runner, but a Freedom player dove at him from behind, catching him sideways on the back of his knees in a blatantly illegal clip. Freight Train crumbled like scrap metal in the jaws of a bulldozer. The referee didn't see the illegal block, but almost everyone on our side in the stands did, and loud boos rained down on the field. Meanwhile, the runner was still galloping down the field. He sidestepped the clump of meat that was Freight Train on the ground and sped toward the goal line. The only player on our side that had a decent shot at him was our kicker, Jimmy Dale Patterson, who I don't think had ever made a tackle in his life. Ol' Jimmy Dale wasn't very big and he wasn't very strong, but you had to hand it to him, he had lots of heart. He took a mighty dive at the runner and knocked him out of bounds on our thirty-five, preventing the humiliation of letting them run the opening kickoff back for a touchdown.

"A lot of good that did us. For a minute after that things were starting to look pretty good. On their very first play from scrimmage we sacked their quarterback, but then it all fell apart. On the next play their quarterback connected on a pass to the end zone for their first touchdown. Again, Booker T fans complained of a missed call. Their right tackle had his hands all over one of our guys who otherwise would have had a good shot at sacking their quarterback again. All of our fans started shouting that the referee was on Freedom's side, which was like, yeah, right. Of course he was. And the other one was on our side. That's the way it always was. There were two referees. They were parents of players, one from each team. If there was a hall of shame for bad refereeing, not to mention bad sportsmanship, our two schools would have shared the honor.

"So they scored first, but we came right back on our first possession with a sustained drive into Freedom territory, grinding out turf in three- and four-yard bites—trench warfare as retaliation for their blazing air bombardment. And then, having established a grinding up-the-middle ground attack, we surprised the Freedom defenders with an air bombardment of our own. Check out all the metaphors. We don't need war; we got football.

"It was third and long from the Freedom thirty, and it was my time to shine. I ran a long stop-and-go pattern along the left sideline, and Randy Moss ran with me stride for stride, bumping me as much as he could get away with. The quarterback faded back and threw me a long pass. I had gained a step on Randy. It was a picture perfect pass. I stretched to pull it in, but in the second before the ball touched my hands that asshole grabbed my arm and jerked it down, and I missed the catch. This time both referees saw the obvious interference and called a penalty that gave us a first and goal inside the five, and I gave Randy the raspberry going back to the huddle. Ragging him was fun, but making a touchdown would have been better. And I would have made one, too, if he hadn't grabbed my freakin' arm.

"Deep in their territory, it was now time for what we liked to call our secret weapon, which was no secret to anyone—Freight Train Taylor at fullback. His sheer bulk guaranteed at least two yards on every run no matter how much the other team stacked the middle. He got three yards on his first run and pushed it in for the tying score on the next.

"The teams took turns scoring. It was an ugly game with a lot of penalties. Tempers were raw among players and fans alike. A fight broke out in the third quarter, and one of the referees announced that if it happened again they were going to call the game off. With less than a minute to go in the fourth quarter and Freedom ahead by a field goal, we mounted a final drive. It was third and long and we were a good five to ten yards outside of Jimmy Dale's field goal range, so we went for a desperation pass. We sent both wide receivers to the end zone, me and Johnny Lambert, and our quarterback faded deep. Randy blitzed from his linebacker position, leaving me wide open in the secondary but giving Randy a shot at our quarterback. Our fullback saw him coming and blocked him out. Randy grabbed the fullback's shoulder pads and threw him down. The quarterback, feeling pressure, rushed his throw. It was meant for me again, but it sailed incomplete well over my outstretched arms. The play was over, but Randy in his headlong rush to get the QB didn't know it was over. He didn't see that the pass had gone incomplete, but there was no way he failed to hear the referee's whistle. He was out for blood. He saw that he had a clear shot at the quarterback, and he couldn't resist. He plowed into him with a solid hit squarely in the chest a good three or four seconds after he had already thrown the ball. The quarterback went down and the referee—this time the ref who had a kid on the Booker T team—tagged Randy for unnecessary roughness. Freedom fans erupted in complaint. Randy's father, who had been prowling the sidelines and loudly complaining throughout the game, rushed onto the field and tackled the referee. Bedlam broke loose. Players and coaches from both sides ran out to break up the fight. Fans threw soda cups and shouted, and a lot of students and a few parents rushed onto the field to join in the melee. Randy's father the sheriff had his own freakin' whistle, and he blew it wildly while swinging fists at anyone and everyone, confusing everyone on the field. The referees blew their whistles, too, and the announcer's voice pleading for calm went unheeded. One of the school bands in the stands started playing 'Another One Bites the Dust.'

"At least the stupid sheriff kept his gun in his holster and didn't pull out his nightstick and take a whack at somebody. It took the referees ten minutes to clear the field and resume play. They did not call the game off as promised, but they penalized Freedom and ejected Randy from the game. When everyone finally settled down and the ref blew his whistle one more time as a signal to restart the game, we were trailing by one point and had possession in excellent position for what should have easily been the winning field goal. The field clock showed thirty-three seconds to go. After getting a gift first down on the penalty, we ran it up the middle for two yards and watched the clock tick down to five seconds before calling timeout. Then we went for the easy field goal. But the snap from center was high and the holder wasn't able to get it in position, and Jimmy Dale chipped it. The ball hit the right upright and bounced off, and the Freedom fans went wild.

"Randy Moss had been sent to the locker room early, but he won his date with Melissa. It was no wonder that he resorted to pass interference and kamikaze attacks on the quarterback. With a date with Melissa as the payoff he was willing to do anything to win.

"Both schools held dances in their gymnasiums after the game. Since the schools were right across the street from each other, there was always a lot of intermingling. Typically boys from one school dated girls from the other, each thinking it was a badge of honor to walk into the school dance with a date from the rival school—an odd kind of rivalry to say the least considering that more than likely the dates from rival schools were next door neighbors; the town was way too small for two high schools.

"There was a ceremonial placement of a trophy ball with the winning team, and traditionally kids from the losing school would try and steal it back, often with disastrous results such as when Randy Moss punched his fist through the Booker T trophy case and ended up with six stitches in his hand. That was the year before. Often there were eggs thrown or graffiti sprayed on the school walls, and sometimes the teachers-cum-security had to break up fights, but for the most part the rivalry was good natured. After that particular game Randy Moss marched into the Booker T gymnasium like a conquering hero. Melissa was waiting for him. She turned her head along with half the Booker T students to watch him make his way through the hostile crowd of kids, which parted in a wave. She stood proudly. He halted in front of her and slung his red and black Gators jacket over her purple and gold Pirates sweater. He took her hand and they walked out of the gym as a couple, and he proudly escorted her across the street to the Freedom dance.

"After dancing a few dances and talking with groups of students, Randy bought Cokes from the vending machine and they snuck out to his car and mixed whiskey in their Cokes and sipped them and smoked cigarettes, and Randy wanted to make out but she fended him off.

"Naturally we heard two versions of what went on in Randy's car. You can pretty much figure it out. After she fought him off for no telling how long he finally got all exasperated and said, 'Not even a little hand job?'

"'God, you're crude.' She pushed him against the driver's side door and scooted to the other side. He slipped over right back against her side.

"'Well how 'bout a kiss? Just one little kiss.'

"So okay, she was willing to give him a little kiss. Dying to, to tell the truth, although she never would have admitted that. They kissed for a long time, but when he tried to shove his hand inside her top she pushed him away.

"While they were at it, we were at it too. Across the street in the back seat of my old Nash Rambler, the first car I ever owned, parked under an oak tree on the outer edges of the Booker T parking lot. Sue Ellen and I were making out in pretty much the same way that Randy was making out with Melissa, but not so crudely, I'll have you know, and with less resistance on Sue Ellen's part. And not far away in Pop's car, which Mary was using for the night but which Buddy would be driving later because she didn't want to subject him to the indignity of being escorted by his girlfriend, Mary was using her hand to relieve Buddy of unbearable tension—an act for which he was so grateful he was crying. And in yet another car in the same parking lot, James Littleton and George Matthews, the only openly gay couple at Booker T High School, were exchanging their first tender and tentative kisses."

When the whole family watched the DVD, Buddy went berserk at this point, saying, "This is way too much. I refuse to watch any more."

"What's he talking about, daddy?" Patricia asked. "I don't get it."

"Just never you mind, young lady."

Even Melissa and Mary and Sue Ellen were beginning to react more like Buddy, drowning each other out with their shouted protests. Sue Ellen said, "Oh my God, I can't believe he's telling this!" and Mary said, "If I ever get my hands on him I'll rip his heart out."

But they didn't shut it off. David continued: "Inside the two gymnasiums very few couples were dancing and the teacher-chaperones were saying to each other that the young folks seemed to be calling it a night awfully early. How dense can you get? They thought we'd all gone home early, and I don't think it ever dawned on them that half the kids were sneaking smokes and booze and making out in the parking lot. Had they no memory at all? Hadn't they all, at our ages, done the same things? How much imagination would it have taken for them to figure out there was a group grope going on right outside?"

He segued into how after the dance they all met up at Little Don's—Mary and Buddy, David and Sue Ellen, and Melissa with Randy—and devoured burgers and shakes, and how he and Randy congratulated each other on a good game (and Randy apologized for the pass interference, and David countered, "Meaning you're sorry you got caught," and Randy acknowledged that he was right). And then he talked about how back at home they all piled onto Mary's bed as usual to talk about the evening.

He said, "Mary and I were really anxious to hear how Melissa's date with Randy went. 'Not too bad,' Melissa said, as casual as could be. 'He's really a good dancer. That surprised me.'

"He's really a good dancer? That was all she had to say? Mary wouldn't let it go at that. She asked, 'Did you kiss him good night?'

"'Oh gross. No way. I'd rather kiss a monkey's butt.'

"'Bullshit,' Mary said. 'Don't pretend that you think he's gross. I know better.'

"'Yeah, y'all made out some, didn't you?' I asked her. And Melissa admitted that yeah, they made out a little. But she said it was no big deal.

"And so we ended up with this little bit of conversation. Mary: 'You gotta admit he's a pretty good kisser.'

"Me: 'Gross!'

"A few days later she told us she was going out with him again. That time they went nightclubbing along the coast highway.

"'How 'bout this time?' Mary asked her after the second date, 'Any hot loving this time?'

"'Maybe a little bit.' Melissa giggled.

"'Details. We want all the details.'

"'Not me. I don't want to hear it.' I said I thought I was gonna puke.

"Mary kept pressing for particulars, but Melissa said, 'That's for me to know and you to find out.' We knew they must have got it on or come pretty freakin' close for her to tease us like that.

"Melissa played the drama for all it was worth, and at last she said, 'Okay, are y'all ready for this?'

"'Yes.'

"'I gave him a hand job.'

"'You didn't!'

"'I did. And guess what? He's got a thing on his dick.'

"'A thing?'

"'Yeah. Like a wart or a mole or something. It was kind of gross at first.'

"'Did you see it or just feel it?'

"'Just felt it. I was scared to look.'

"'I've seen it,' I said (a lie). 'It's a big old ugly thing. I think it's some kind of rare venereal disease or something. You'll probably get it now.'"

*

The cardiac floor of the hospital is noisy and busy. Pop's room and the area around the nurse's station right outside his door are humming. Friends and relatives and friends of friends constantly flow in and out of Pop's room, along with Pop's doctor, nurses, orderlies. Maintenance staff and technicians push equipment and food and bedding and cleaning supplies. In his room and gathered at the nurse's station they talk about his condition and speculate on his chances of survival. They've cleared his arteries for now, but there was another partial blockage that may or may not need attention. The damage to his heart was significant. His cholesterol is sky high and his blood pressure is unsteady. The consensus opinion is that if Pop gets through the next few days he can live another ten to twenty years—*if* he slows down and quits smoking and cuts down on the booze and keeps on his medication, but that ten to twenty years could be shortened to that many days, or even minutes, if he doesn't start taking better care of himself.

The people crowding Pop's room talk a lot about politics and football and the weather. David notices that they have divergent opinions about football, but on politics and even the weather everyone quotes the same two apparently infallible sources: Weatherman Donny and right wing radio talk show celebrity J.J. Jackson. Weatherman Donny is convinced that they are experiencing the beginnings of a worldwide weather disaster that will ultimately lead to the end of life on earth, and they all agree. What they don't agree on is whether the worldwide weather disaster is a natural phenomenon, the result of overcrowding and industrialization, or the wrath of God. Most are of the mind that it's a natural phenomenon aided by the worldwide idiocy of overdevelopment. Even J.J. Jackson agrees that the end of the world is eminent, and most likely by way of some catastrophic global weather phenomena, but he also believes that before that calamity comes to pass America's social and political structures will collapse because of illegal immigrants, welfare, soft-on-crime liberals, African-Americans (but only inner-city, drug dealing, gang-related African-Americans not the good kind of colored people), high taxes, rampant so-called political correctness, and the homosexual agenda. And he believes that anti-Israeli/American Muslim nations will supplant the United States as world leaders.

David attempts to rationally argue against the gospel according to J.J. Jackson, and the majority team up to shoot down his arguments. He has a hard time defending his position because he doesn't have a firm understanding of many of the issues. He doesn't pay close attention to the news. No one else seems to have much knowledge either, but they're able to beat him down by repeatedly quoting J.J. When quoting J.J. doesn't seem sufficient, they turn to the Bible and to so-called indisputable proof that we're living out the final days as outlined in the Book of Revelation. Only Sue Ellen and Freight Train take David's side, but her grasp of the issues is not any better than David's and Freight Train has better debating skills but trips himself up trying to tippy-toe down the yellow line in the middle of the road.

Football is a much safer subject for discussion. They fight good naturedly over Southeastern Conference teams (Ole Miss is number one, Mississippi State should stick to playing in cow pastures, and LSU is the devil's college) and over the rival high schools (Yeah Booker T!), but they have no arguments about professional football teams. Everybody loves the New Orleans Saints and despises the Dallas Cowboys. Other pro teams matter only in so far as they have former SEC players on their rosters.

Pop says he'll put up a hundred dollars on Booker T against anyone in the upcoming game with Freedom High. Nobody's willing to take his bet.

Pop's doctor comes in for a consultation and everyone focuses their attention on him. He says, "You're not doing well at all, Pop. I hate to tell you, but I think we need to go back in and take another look."

"You mean crack my damn chest open again. No fucking way."

"No, no. I wouldn't dare do that now. I'm thinking about angioplasty."

"Well that's a twenty dollar word if I ever heard one. What's it mean?"

He explains: "We take a look at your heart by inserting a tube that runs up from your groin. We inject iodine, it's harmless, but we can see it as it flows through your veins and arteries, and if there's any blockage we'll be able to see it."

"Jesus! That sounds like sci-fi shit."

"Not long ago it was, but now it's been done millions of times. Don't worry, it won't hurt. You'll hardly feel it at all, but it'll give us a good look at what's going on up in there. I suspect there's probably another blocked artery, hopefully not so severe as what we already repaired. If there is, we can fix it. You'll be good for another ten to twenty years unless somebody takes a notion to shoot you."

"I don't think so," Pop says. "I'm tired of y'all fucking with me."

Shelly says, "You really need to do this, honey. I don't want you dying on me."

"Another blocked artery, if we don't catch it soon enough, could kill you," the doctor warns.

But Pop is obstinate. He says he's not going to allow any more poking or prodding or cutting on his body. "I don't mean to insult you or your hospital, doc, but this ain't exactly the Mayo Clinic. If a goddamn triple bypass didn't fix my ticker, then maybe we need some kind of specialist."

"We could do that," the doctor says. "We could take you to New Orleans. But the trip would probably kill you."

Pop is playing with the doctor and they all know it, because everybody knows that Doctor Duvall is, in fact, a heart specialist and probably as good as any they could find in New Orleans or any big city hospital. Even though he grew up in Freedom, he studied in New Orleans and later in Boston, worked Beth Israel Deaconess and in private practice in Boston, and came back to Freedom to enjoy what he called semi-retirement as a family doctor. He has known Pop for almost fifty years. He knows how to talk to him, verbally poking and prodding with a mixture of humor and logic. "You're blind and bullheaded," he says.

"And you're in love with your scalpel."

He first has to convince Pop that he really is in danger of dying and that the procedure can save his life. Then he has to not so much convince him but make a show of convincing him that he is competent to perform the procedure. He has to go through this charade because Pop wants everyone to hear that his doctor is one of the best. So he prods him. "How many of these procedures have you done, Doc?"

"More than a thousand."

"And how many people have you kilt thataway?"

"None that I know of."

"Not none of 'em died?"

"Not during the procedure. One guy got run over by a truck a week later while he was jogging."

Finally Freight Train realizes what's going on and decides to put an end to it. He says, "Boss, you got to do what the doctor tells you. It's the only sensible thing to do, and if you need to hear it, I have an irrefutable argument." He can barely stifle his laughter.

Pop decides to play along. "Oh yeah? What's that?"

"It's this here: If you don't, I'm gonna kick your scrawny ass halfway to Sunday."

They all laugh at that and Pop says, "Well crap. Nobody put it thataway before. All right, let's do the angio-whatchamacallit."

The doctor says, "We'll do it first thing tomorrow."

David listens to all of this and then says, "I thought I was the only actor around here."

Doctor Duval is as serious as can be, despite this little vaudeville act with Pop and Freight Train. He says, "Yeah, I could do your job, but God help us if you ever try to do mine."

On that note the doctor leaves, and soon after that they wheel in Pop's dinner. At the same time a nurse comes in to check his vitals. The nurse says, "Some of y'all have got to clear out. There's too many of y'all up in here." Mary, Sue Ellen, Shelly, David, and Freight Train are all crowded into the room— along with Melissa, who was discharged from the hospital an hour earlier but dropped in to stay with the family in Pop's room instead of going home.

Shelly tries to tell everyone to go home and get some rest. She can stay with Pop, she says. But Pop tells her she has to leave as well. "I'll be fine," he says. "I don't need none a y'all hovering over me. I need to rest too, and I can get more rest if I'm left alone." Since he's dropped his smart-alecky tone, everyone knows that he really does want to be left alone. Shelly tells him she'll be back bright and early in the morning, and she kisses him good night.

*

The hospital is fifteen miles from Freedom as the crow flies, but closer to thirty miles on a road that crawls around the bayous. Shelly suggests that they all meet at Capt. John's for dinner. It's only ten minutes away. In the restaurant a waitress pulls two tables together to seat the six of them. It's all you can eat seafood night at Capt. John's. They pile their plates with shrimp, oysters, crab, and rock bass—all breaded and deep fried and served with coleslaw and French fries. David quips, "I can't tell Freight Train's plate from the serving platter."

"The serving platter's the little one," Sue Ellen says.

Freight Train would be disappointed if they didn't joke about the huge quantities of food he consumes. But after a while he notices that

David has managed to eat almost as much; he just doesn't pile it all on his plate at once.

They linger for an hour and a half. At long last Shelly says, "I've really got to get home and get some sleep. Somebody's got to take me."

"I will," say Mary and Freight Train together. It's less out of the way for Freight Train, so she goes with him. Melissa drives herself home, as does Mary. Both of them have been unusually quite during dinner, Melissa because she is worn out from her ordeal and Mary because she's worried about Buddy, who hasn't called all day. She assumes the girls are still at their grandparent's house being taken care of by Beulah, because if Buddy had picked them up he would have called her. She thinks that maybe she should have offered to take her mother home and gone ahead and picked up the girls. But since Buddy's agreed to be responsible for the girls while Pop is in the hospital, she figures she'll let him do it. Or else they can just sleep over at grandma's.

David and Sue Ellen are left at the table and are not ready to part company. David picks up the tab, and the two of them go to the lounge and order drinks. There's a country band playing. They're playing sad songs. The drummer is dragging the beat and the singer sounds bored to tears. David and Sue Ellen leave their half full drinks on the table along with a pretty good tip, and walk outside and get in her car. It's not the same van she had driven him from the airport in, but it's another Honda, smaller, the same forest green color. They drive down to the beach highway and then head east along the coast.

They're cruising along at the speed limit when a not-too-new Jaguar passes them on the right and then cuts in sharply, forcing Sue Ellen to brake. "Damn fool," she mutters, then, "Oh crap, that's Buddy."

"Buddy Boudreau?"

"Yeah."

"Wonder what he's up to."

"No telling."

It's a warm night but not so warm as to need the air on in the car. David sails his hand out the open window in the wind. Sue Ellen presses down on the accelerator again but holds steady at fifty-five and pulls into the right lane to let other cars zip past them.

The Jag speeds up. He's almost out of sight, and then they see him pull into a left turn lane far ahead and slow down, and they both glance over as they pass by to confirm that yes, it is Buddy. He guns it to make a left turn cutting across two lanes of oncoming traffic.

"Damn fool," Sue Ellen mutters again. "He's gonna make a widow out of Mary if he doesn't watch out."

"She might be better off."

Sue Ellen says, "You don't really mean that."

"No, of course not. I don't want her to be a widow, just a happy divorcee. She'd definitely be better off if she divorced his sorry ass."

The Jag heads inland for half a mile and makes a right-hand turn. Buddy knows where he's going but he tries to tell himself he's just riding, going nowhere, killing time, not wanting to go home. Not quite yet. He might drive around aimlessly for half an hour or so, but he's not fooling himself one little bit; he's going to end up at the Rough Rider. He's pissed at himself because he can't fool himself. He knows damn good and well what he's up to even while trying to fool himself into thinking otherwise. Round and round his dissembling goes and where it stops only Buddy knows. It's an old story. Whether it's picking up somebody in the Rough Rider or Clancy's or some street walker on the strip, once he gets it in his mind that he's got to get laid, his more rational self hasn't a chance against the devilish self that keeps egging him on.

He turns onto Parker Avenue. It's a four-lane road through a light industrial area a mile north of the beach. The stretch of Parker that runs from First to Eighth is known as the strip. Traffic crawls, cars cruising, tops down on convertibles, windows rolled down, drivers and passengers rubbernecking. Buddy's going forty-five in a thirty-mph zone. He eases off the gas and slows down. He has a bottle of Budweiser propped between his thighs. He's steering one-handed. He reaches for the bottle and turns it up for one last swig, wipes his mouth with his sleeve and tosses the bottle on the floor. He's talking to himself. "Maybe I'll stop in at Clancy's. One beer and that's it, then straight home. Right on home to the little lady. Just one beer. Maybe something to eat. Probly oughta get something to eat. Maybe some nachos." He's not hungry, but he knows he shouldn't drink too much on an empty stomach.

He crosses First Avenue and starts looking for a parking space. A block ahead he spots one across the street from Bob's Burger Barn. He backs in to a parallel parking spot, runs a wheel up on the curb, pulls up a bit and gives it another shot. Getting out and stepping onto the sidewalk, he surveys his parking job. "Not bad," he says. "Seen a helluva lotta sober people couldn't do that. Like to see a woman do any better drunk or sober."

He strikes up a cigarette and starts walking. He passes Payday Loans and Rent-to-Own and a video arcade and an adult book and movie store. Music blares from a passing car, a throbbing bass that rattles his bones. He looks at his watch: ten o'clock. The night air is still warm and sticky. There are a lot of pedestrians on the sidewalk and men of all ages prowling the street by car. Airmen from the base in Biloxi and students from the junior college. Whores lounge on the corner of Third and Parker. He stops on the sidewalk in front of Melvin's Hideaway, reads the notices on the door about coming bands, then walks on down the street to the Rough Rider.

Inside the Rough Rider ceiling fans barely stir the stale air. It's a good ten degrees warmer than outside in the night air. He grabs a seat at the bar and orders a Bud. "Y'all need to air condition this joint," he says to the bartender.

"No shit," a woman at the end of the bar says.

"See? The lady agrees." He looks her up and down. Probably in her mid-forties, maybe even older, skinny, wearing a red split skirt. Long legs open on the bar stool, flesh showing practically to her crotch. Strong legs in mesh stockings. Another man takes the stool next to Buddy. He murmurs under his breath, "That one looks pretty damn skanky to me."

"Yeah, that's 'bout what I was thinking."

"She's probably got ever damn STD known to man."

"Yeah, well, it's not like I was planning on taking her home, you know what I mean?" He rolls his eyes to indicate anybody that would try and pick up such a skanky old bitch would have to be half crazy or drunk, one or the other.

His new companion looks like someone Buddy could be friends with. He looks to be about the same age, dressed in the same stylishly casual manner. Buddy figures he must be a businessman, married more than likely, bored with his job and his home life. "Buddy Boudreau," he says, offering a hand.

"Jimmy Smith. Pleased to meet you." He grasps Buddy's hand with a strong two-hand grip and holds it for quite some time.

Buddy says, "I heard of a Jimmy Smith that was somehow related to me, or actually to my wife's daddy way back during the Civil War. An ancestor. Maybe we's related somehow."

"Could be. But it's a damn common name. Lots of us around."

He offers to buy Buddy another beer. Buddy says, "I probly shouldn't. Oughta get on home."

"Okay."

"But, hey, what the heck. One more can't hurt. Hellfire, it won't kill the old lady if I'm a little late. Sometimes it seems like she's my jailer, you know what I mean?"

"I know. I surely do. But what the heck, it ain't gonna kill her if you're half an hour later getting home.

"Right. You married?"

"Nah." He is a nice looking man. Brushcut hair and beard to match. He swivels slightly on his barstool as if rocking to some tune in his head. Every time he swings to the left his knee brushes against Buddy. He doesn't seem to notice.

"How do you trim your beard like that?" Buddy asks. "I always wondered about that ever since I first seen Sonny Crockett on <u>Miami Vice</u>."

"They make special shavers for it."

"Really? I always wondered about that. Maybe I oughta get me one of them. How you think I'd look with a short beard like that?"

"I think you'd look really nice."

After another beer Buddy says, "You know, I really oughta get on home. I don't want my wife worrying about me."

"Why'oncha give her a call? Tell her you got hung up. I got a cell phone if you wanna use it."

"Yeah. I could do that."

He calls home on Jimmy's phone. He gets the answering machine and leaves a message— "Hey, it's me. Uh, yeah, I got tied up. Don't wait up."—hands him back his phone and then surveys the rest of the joint. The décor, if you can call it that, is a cowboy theme. Rodeo posters on the walls, brown leather barstools. As bars go, it is pretty well lighted with wall scones and fluorescents over the pool tables and swathes of colored light provided by neon beer signs and a jukebox with cycling tubes of rainbow neon. The concrete slab floor is littered with peanut shells. Bowls of peanuts sit on all the tables and on the bar. The two pool tables are in an alcove at the back. There are few customers in the bar. Two men at a corner table look like a young hustler and his uncle, the older man looking like a throwback from an earlier decade in Polo shirt and light blue double-knit pants, and the younger man blanketed with tattoos and wearing a ripped muscle shirt. There are also two men shooting pool. The woman in the red dress is the only female in the joint.

A mile to the south, Sue Ellen parks in one of the many pullout parking places along the beach. It could very well be the spot where they first made love, but neither of them mentions that. They get out of her car and she steps around to the trunk and opens it and pulls out a couple of folded blankets. "I'm always prepared," she says.

There are a few strollers along the beach. The nightclubs, the casinos, the hotels and restaurants all along the beach are brightly lighted as far as they can see. A man walks his dog by the water's edge. There is phosphorescence where the water laps the beach. It is very quiet but for the gentle lapping of waves and the hiss of passing cars on the highway.

Sue Ellen spreads the blanket on the sand and they sit down. She slips her feet out of her shoes and digs her bare toes in the sand. "Look up there," she says, nodding her head in the direction of one of the few old houses still standing on the beachfront. It's a barnlike silhouette of a two-story house with a spindly-legged pier running out over the water's edge. "Remember that?"

"How could I not? Randy Moss's beach house. The hurricane."

"What a night!" She picks up a handful of sand and lets it run between her fingers. "Whatever happened to us, David? Why did we never call or get together again?"

After the night of the hurricane they had said they would call, but they never did. Once they returned to their respective colleges, they immersed themselves back into their various activities—his fraternity, her sorority, the drama department for him, the Young Democrats for her. He was going to invite her to the opening of *Cat on a Hot Tin Roof* (he played Brick) but he heard from a friend that her sorority was having some kind of big to-do what week, and he knew she would not be free. During the run-up to the play, especially during tech rehearsals, he worked late every night—doubling up as a stage hand, lighting technician and errand boy, as many of the cast did. After the run of the play he was so far behind on his studies that he had to buckle down with the books. Time went by, and they never got together again.

"I think we really were in love," she says. "It wasn't just some school girl crush for me."

"But you must have started dating Jimmy Dale not long after that, didn't you?"

"Yeah. But that was because you weren't around. It wasn't serious with us. He was just someone to go to parties with, to go to movies with. Besides, didn't you date other people too?"

"Uh huh. Yeah, but I didn't marry them. You married Jimmy Dale."

He's sitting up now and she lays her head in his lap. "Tell me all about your life," she says. "What's it like being you?"

He laughs. He says, "It's not half bad, if you want to know the truth."

The college production of *Cat on a Hot Tin Roof* was the first play David ever tried out for. Before that he had no desire to act. The only reason he even tried out was because his fraternity brothers talked him into it. They thought he would be perfect for the role of Brick. So did the play's director. He cast David not because of any demonstrated acting ability, but because of his smoldering good looks. As it turned out, he had a natural talent for acting. He fell in love with theater. But he never again got to play such a juicy role. He was too handsome. He was always cast as the romantic lead, the young lover of the ingénue. Those might be the leading roles, but they were not the best roles. He wanted roles with character, but what he got was a lot of opportunities to smile and kiss the girls. Not bad work, he often said, but not real acting either.

After graduating college he went to New York.

"I wanted to do serious theater, but what few roles I could get were pretty shitty. Pretty boys were a dime a dozen. I didn't want to go to Hollywood. People kept telling me I could make it in the movie business, but that wasn't the kind of acting I wanted to do."

He stayed in New York for ten years. He got small parts in Off-Off-Broadway plays that nobody saw. Makeshift theaters that sat twenty people on folding chairs where the cast shared a single closet-size dressing room. He did commercials and picked up odd jobs between acting gigs, more odd jobs than acting gigs. He finally got noticed in a touring production of *The Glass Menagerie*.

"It kind of worried me for a while," he says to Sue Ellen. "It seemed like the only decent roles I could get were in Tennessee Williams' plays. There's this kind of hidden homosexual undercurrent in all of his plays, sometimes not so hidden, so I couldn't help but wonder why directors kept picking me for those roles. Did they see something in me I couldn't see in myself?"

"You wondered if you might be gay?"

"Nah, I'm just kidding. But it was kinda weird what plays I got cast in."

"Never dawned on you that it might be the Southern accent, huh?"

"Naw, never," he drawls and guffaws, but then, as if to prove his point, he drops the accent, which he can easily do when he puts his mind to it. Minus the drawl he says, "Sam Rogers was a young film director highly influenced by popular television drama who was beginning to make his mark in Hollywood. He saw me in *Menagerie* and asked if I'd like to play the lawyer in a courtroom drama he was making, *The Witness*. He described the role as a Southern version of the Jack Nicholson role in *Easy Rider* (It had been described to him with analogies from TV, but he was sharp enough to figure a stage actor would be more impressed with Nicholson than with Magnum P.I.). That sounded pretty good to me, and the money was fabulous. I decided it was time to give up on the legitimate stage and become a movie star, and I figured *The Witness* might be my last good shot at it." She remembers that in his monologue he called it his "get real" moment.

He doesn't have to tell her that the public went wild over the lawyer, Raymond Moon, and that *The Witness* was followed by two highly successful spinoffs, *Travlin' Light* and *Cold Justice*.

They are now lying side by side on the blanket. David's fingers are intertwined behind his head. She rests her head in the hollow between his shoulder and chest. The sky above is filled with stars. The night has finally begun to cool off. She says, "And now you're a famous movie star, and in every film you make I get to watch you make love to a different glamorous woman."

"Hey, it's just acting. It's all make believe."

"You expect me to believe that making out with all those beautiful woman doesn't turn you on?"

"Really. It's just acting. If you ever tried it you'd know. There's nothing sexy about shooting a love scene."

"Maybe." She begins to absently trace figure-eights on his chest. "But from what I've heard you've been in a lot of sex scenes when there weren't any cameras around."

He says, "Don't believe anything you read in the tabloids."

She unfolds the extra blanket and drapes it over their shoulders.

He says, "That's enough about me. What about you?"

"All right. What about me?"

"What have you done since that night we made love in the middle of a hurricane? Which, by the way, was better than anything I've known since."

"Well," she says, "I got pregnant. That kind of tells the story. I got pregnant. Honorable man that he was, the father of my children married me and gave me a good home, and we stayed together for the kids' sake until about a year ago."

"You didn't love him?"

"Not with any burning passion, no."

"And now?"

"And now, well, we're doing okay."

He notices the plural pronoun and thinks for just a second that the other half of that *we* is her husband, but then he realizes that she must be referring to her children. Having never had children, he can't quite grasp what it must be like to be the parent half of a child-parent relationship. For sixteen or seventeen years now that has been the reality of her life, and that is truly beyond his comprehension. He thinks that this is what life is like for people in the real world. He assumes that life outside of his narrow little world is all about couples coming together to create a family. And family becomes their identity. He always thought of people with families as being somehow other—mom and dad and two kids living in the suburbs somewhere in Kansas, not in any kind of real world that he can identify with. But maybe he's the one who is out of whack with reality. People with families always have other people there at breakfast. When they're sick they don't suffer alone, and they don't even have to tell anyone they're sick because the people in their lives know them so well they can

read signs that are invisible to outsiders. People with families never watch
TV or movies alone. They never dine alone. When their teenage sons and
daughters rebel and say they don't want to go to church or to dinner at
Aunt Mabel's, or when they take to wearing outlandish clothes and hair
styles, they know that that rebellion is the end result of thousands of little
things that began with nasty diapers and spit-up and escalated through
scraped knees and elbows and first dates and learning to drive, and will
end with them going off to Hollywood to become movie stars or moving to
New York and becoming investment bankers and forgetting all about their
parents back home.

Suddenly she pushes herself up off the blanket. "Let's hit the
water," she says. She pulls her pants down and steps out of them, standing
in her panties and unbuttoning her blouse.

"Are you kidding me?" David says. He's thinking what is this, some
kind of freakin' romantic comedy? Next thing you know we're going to be
tripping through the surf hand-in-hand, riding Ferris wheels and eating
cotton candy, all to a Fleetwood Mac soundtrack. Just when he is
beginning to think that people like Sue Ellen with her family ties are the
only ones in touch with reality she wants to play out a romantic movie
montage in her undies. And it's starting to get cold. He watches her,
dumbfounded, as she starts running toward the surf. Reluctantly he
follows her lead. He pulls off his shoes and socks, takes off his pants and
shirt, leaving his T-shirt and underpants on, and heads for the waves. The
water is tepid and calm. They wade in up to their knees and splash each
other. The breaking surf laps the shore like lazily licking tongues.

*

In the Rough Rider the woman in the red dress is still nursing her
drink. She keeps looking over at Buddy. His new friend on the adjacent
barstool laughs at him. He says, "Hey man, you better get your mind off
that skank."

"Nah, I wasn't paying any attention to her. I was thinking about
my wife, you know? She don't really deserve me treating her like this.

Staying out all hours. I mean what kind of way is that to treat a woman? I can't remember. Did I ask you if you're married?"

"I think you did." He can't remember either, since they're both a little drunk. "I was, once. Big mistake. But I came out to her a long time ago."

Came out? *Came out?* It's out in the open now. The man is gay. Of course he is, they're in a gay bar. Buddy does not consider himself gay, not even bisexual, but he has messed around a little with other men. The term is men who have sex with men. He's read about it. As weird as it might seem, it has nothing to do with sexual orientation, at least not according to what he's read on the subject. It's more about compulsive sexual experimentation.

Buddy says, "Coming out to your wife must have been scary."

"It was scary before I did it, but once I made up my mind it was surprisingly easy. Oh sure, the wife was hurt. Her expectations were dashed. She had wanted children but we never had any. But, you know, she really suspected all along that I was gay. I think it might have been a relief to her. At least she knew it wasn't her fault that I didn't want to have sex with her."

Buddy nods in affirmation, but doesn't say anything. The conversation is beginning to dampen his ardor. He doesn't like to get all mushy and feely with other guys. Just get it on and get it off is the way he puts it to himself. Intimacy puts him off, and the conversation with this guy Jimmy in the Rough Rider is getting to be too intimate. His waning interest communicates itself nonverbally, and soon they both realize that nothing is going to happen between them. With growing discomfort they continue to make small talk for a few minutes and then, when someone new comes in, Jimmy says, "That's an old friend. I think I'd better go say hello. D'ya mind?"

"No, go ahead. Hey, it was nice talking to you."

It's getting late now. On the beach, David and Sue Ellen trudge back across the sand to plop back down on their blanket. They towel each other off and then lie down and snuggle under the cover, she with her head on his chest. In the bar, Buddy turns on his stool and lifts a glass to the woman in the red dress, who had given up flirting with him and turned away. Now she swivels on her barstool to face him. She leans back with elbows on the bar and shoots him a Sharon Stone impersonation. The blatant come-on shakes him, and what she exposes to him shakes him even more. This is entirely new territory for him, and he doesn't know how or whether to respond. While he's trying to sort it out in his mind she stands up and moves down to his end of the bar and grabs the vacated stool next to him. "Buy you a beer, honey?"

"Okay, uh yeah, thanks."

She sticks out her hand. "Beverly Swan."

"Hi, Beverly. I'm Buddy Boudreau. What's your pleasure?"

"I'll have a Bud, same as you. A Bud from Buddy."

"That's cute. It's about the millionth time I've heard it, but it's cute."

He tells the bartender to bring her a Budweiser.

She dispenses with all shilly-shallying. She says, "Never been with a shemale before, huh?"

"No, I... uh."

"Like they say, don't knock it if you ain't tried it. You might like it. It's the best of both worlds."

David and Sue Ellen drift gently to sleep on the blanket on the beach under the stars. When they wake the sun is up. They can't see the actual orb of the sun, which would be just behind some buildings to the east, but they can see how its light has washed over the surf like a flow of transparent watercolor.

"Good morning," Sue Ellen says. She reaches over and musses his already mussed hair.

"Good morning." He pushes himself up to a sitting position, shivers in the early morning chill, and says, "I gotta piss like a race horse."

"Oh yeah?" she smirks. "And exactly how does a race horse piss?"

"Same as us but in great gushing gallons."

"Well I reckon we better high-tail it to the nearest restroom. There's a McDonald's just a few blocks away."

He was thinking of just cutting loose in the sand, but realizing she would think that uncool, he says, "Aaah, coffee. Egg McMuffins. Bathroom. Let's go."

*

They come for Pop early in the morning. A cheery young man wearing flower-print hospital scrubs, with a shaved head, earring and tattoo-covered arms wheels a gurney into the room and parks it next to his bed. "Are you ready for this?" he asks.

"I guess so."

"All right. Let's get you onto this rolling bed."

He unhooks Pop's IV and oxygen and lowers the rail, and Pop slides over onto the gurney, and then the perky technician spreads a blanket over Pop, saying, "Don't want you to get cold," and wheels him out into the hallway. They go fast. Ceilings and upper walls fly by. Past the nurses' station and a quick turn in front of the elevator, wait a minute for the elevator to arrive and the door to slide open, into the elevator and down three floors. Ding, ding, ding and the door opens and out they go and down another corridor to the cath lab. Pop is on his back looking up at moveable things on big crane-like arms wrapped in clear plastic. He's chilly and feels woozy. Did they give him something to help him relax? He can't remember.

The young man says, "I'm going to shave you now," and then Pop feels a damp washcloth on his groin and the young man's hand lifting his testicles out of the way and the scraping blade, and next Doctor Duval's face is in his face, and he says, "We're ready to go now. You'll feel a cold sensation when we put the iodine in, but there won't be any pain. Try to be as still as you can, and let me know if you feel any discomfort."

The rush of cold liquid is eerie feeling, and he can feel the tube probing his arteries. It's a dull sensation that doesn't exactly hurt but sure as hell isn't pleasant. And on the monitor above his head he can see the tube worming its way through his body.

"Are you okay?" the doctor asks.

"Yeah. I'm fine."

The doctor probes for a good ten or fifteen minutes. Pop has to pee. The pressure gets stronger and stronger. It feels like his eyeballs are swimming. Finally he has to say something. "Doc, I got to pee."

"Okay, I'll have the nurse get you a urinal."

He can urinate while they're doing this? He never would have thought it. A nurse—he hadn't seen her before, but he had sensed more people in the room—gets a urinal and reaches under the covers and guides him into the top. "You can urinate now," she says.

The doctor says, "Let 'er rip."

It's such a relief. But the flow feels like it's going to just keep coming and coming and never stop. He's afraid he'll overflow the urinal, but then he's all empty.

After some time he begins to feel something strange. He can't tell what it is, but it doesn't feel right. He wonders if he should say something. And suddenly it's as if he's experienced something like a jump cut in a movie. He's here and now and then he's still here but it's another now. Doctor Duval is leaning over him. "Are you all right?" he asks.

Pop says, "Yeah, I guess."

"I'm sorry. I wasn't expecting that. It's rare, but it sometimes happens."

Pop hasn't the slightest idea what he's talking about. His heart had stopped. The doctor had shocked him with a defibrillator to bring him back. His body had ceased to function for a few minutes. And now the doctor is inserting a tiny metal object that will hold open the walls of his damaged artery.

Back in his room, Doctor Duval says, "That went well, except for the one scary part. But we found what we needed to find, and we fixed it."

*

David and Sue Ellen stand up and brush the sand off their clothing and out of their hair, and they fold the blankets. Minutes later they're in the restaurant with bladders emptied, breakfast rolls on their plates and steaming hot coffee in cups. The clock on the wall reads 9:45 a.m. "I can't believe we slept so late," Sue Ellen says.

"Me either. Are your kids going to freak out?"

"It's okay. I called them last night from Capt. John's long before we went to the beach. I told them I wouldn't be coming home."

"So you had a hunch all along that we were going to spend the night together?"

"Yes I did, but if you must know, I thought we were going to do a little something more than sleep in the sand." She takes a sip of coffee and then says, "It's funny, isn't it? When we were kids we went to all night parties and were scared to death of what our parents might think. Your sister used to cover for me. She'd tell my folks I was staying at your house and I'd tell your folks she was staying with me."

"I remember. For me it was usually sneaking in just before daybreak hoping they wouldn't hear me."

"Uh-huh. And now we're all grown up and I'm making excuses to my kids."

They finish their breakfast and he goes up to the counter to get coffee refills—his black with one sugar packet and hers filled with cream and two sugars, just as they had taken their coffee back in high school. He comes back and sets the two cups on the table. "Which one of your kids did you talk to?"

"Jeri."

"Jerry. Is that one of the twins?"

"No, Jeri's my daughter. The twins are James and David."

"Oh yeah." He thinks she must have told him that before.

When they get to the hospital an hour later they see that Pop seems to be recovering nicely from his procedure. His face is less pasty and he seems to be feeling better, although he complains about not being able to move. "That lying sack of shit Doctor said it wouldn't hurt. The whatchamacallit didn't hurt much, but he forgot to mention how agonizing the fucking recovery was gonna be." The insertion site in his groin is painful, and his back hurts from having to be perfectly still for hours. "They won't let me move for another three or... what time is it?"

"Twelve-thirty."

"Yeah, that's one, two three... four more hours. Jesus, my back is killing me. Might 'swell take me out and shoot me."

The usual people are there: Mary and Shelly and Freight Train and Melissa. David smells the cloying odor of air freshener. At least it's better than stale smoke. He wonders if the old man has actually, finally, heeded the doctor's warning and laid off the cigarettes. If he doesn't quit now, he thinks, he never will. And the old man's not the only one. David hasn't had a smoke in over twenty-four hours. Maybe it's his time to quit too.

Visibly relieved to be no longer wearing a hospital gown and robe, Melissa is dressed in pants and a scoop neck blouse. Her nose is still bandaged, but she's no longer wearing the pained expression from the day before. To David and Sue Ellen she says, "You two look like you've been up to something. I smell sex in the air. A hot romance a-brewing in the bayou. What y'all been up to, huh? I heard nobody came home last night."

"Well maybe it's none of your bees wax," Sue Ellen says.

"Oh honey, everything's my business, don't ya know?"

Pop says, "Don Ho? Is he playing in one of the clubs? Damn. I'd like to get out of this hospital and go see that."

"No, no," Melissa say, "I didn't say Don Ho. I said don't you know."

"Well speak up next time, girl. You know I can't hear too good. Tell me again what y'all were talking about."

"We were talking about David and Sue Ellen doing the nasty."

David says, "I'm glad to see everybody's in a good mood, even if you are sticking your noses in where they don't belong." For a moment he seems to have forgotten that he can't stand his old man. That's the way it's always been. Despite it all, when Pop is in a good mood everybody around him seems nicer. And Pop is in a wonderful mood despite the pain. The angioplasty had revealed a clogged artery that Doctor Duval had missed during the bypass. "We see the big stuff, the widow makers, and we fix those first. Sometimes we miss smaller blockages," he had explained. He told them that this time he had inserted a stent to open the flow of blood. Pop came out of it feeling better than he had in years. The doctor also told Shelly that Pop's heart had stopped beating. "It was touch and go there for a while, but we got him all patched up." But he warned, sternly, "His heart is far from being good as new. It's like patching a tire. Only in this case it's more like patching a patch, and it can't stand up to the kind of reckless living you're used to. Smoking can kill you, and so can too much booze, and if you get all pissed off at somebody and start in hollering like I know you can, it could explode."

Pop continues to complain about his aching back, but he's relieved that a more distressing pain he's put up with for ages is gone. He's almost in tears, yet everyone can hear in his voice a softening of the edges indicating that a great weight has been lifted. "I didn't even notice the tightness until it wasn't there anymore, but there was this almost constant pressure. It was like the skin was pulling and stretching across my chest, and my arm, my left arm, it felt sorta like that darn blood pressure machine when they pump it up. And I just generally felt like crap all over. And now... oh boy, I feel free. If only I could move my leg."

When the doctor comes back for his afternoon rounds, he says, "I think we'll be able to let you go home in the morning."

"Why wait?" Pop asks.

"Because we need to monitor you overnight. And don't think you can go home and just get back to doing what you used to do. There's a very specific recovery routine you have to follow."

"Yeah, yeah. You told me. No smoking and no drinking and no hollering."

"The nurse will fill you in on that. We're going to send you home with written instructions for after care."

"Instructions for Africa?"

Everybody laughs, including Pop, who knows he must have misheard something again but can't imagine what until the doctor repeats it more distinctly.

There's a tap on the door and Buddy sticks his nose in. "Is there room for one more in here?" he asks.

Buddy steps in. He gives Mary a kiss. He says, "Sorry about last night, honey. I met up with Johnny Simpson. He tried to sell me on a big promotion deal for a new line of weight loss products, a front counter display that oughta go over big. I think there might be some real money in it. But anyway, we had a few too many drinks, and I guess it dragged on longer than it should have."

"I'll say," Mary answers. To the room at large she says, "He staggered in about two in the morning smelling like he'd been swimming in whiskey. Cheap whiskey at that."

"I'll have you know I had nothing but the finest Tennessee sipping whiskey."

"Well hooray for you and Jack Daniels."

*

"So how's the picture coming along?" David asks Jasmine. He's just finished off a heaping plate of roast beef cooked by Beulah and he's relaxing on the deck with his first cigarette in almost two days. It's made him a little dizzy. Inside the house Shelly and Mary are watching Weatherman Donny talk about a couple of tropical storms brewing in the Caribbean. There's a big one swirling over the hot seas between the Cayman Islands and Cuba, and a baby storm building strength south of Puerto Rico.

"It's a bitch," Jasmine says. "We did the eating scene today. We must have done forty takes. If I never taste barbeque sauce again it will be too soon."

The film, called *The Adventures of Tammy Jones*, is a revision of the classic *Tom Jones* but with a feminist twist. In and out of horribly uncomfortable eighteenth-century costumes faster than bunnies can mate, Jasmine romps through one sexual escapade after another.

"I can't wait to see it," David says.

"And I can't wait to see you again."

They talk about nothing for a few minutes and then she asks, "What about this old girlfriend I hear you're bonking in the bayous?"

"You know how they blow things out of proportion."

"Uh huh. So is there or isn't there an old girlfriend?"

"Yes, there is. And she's really nice. You'd like her. But there hasn't been any bonking going on."

A warm gust of wind off the water reminds David of the Santa Ana winds out west, only this breeze is loaded with moisture. In London it's daybreak. A hard, cold rain splatters Jasmine's hotel room window. She's not worried about rumors of David's new/old girlfriend. What she does wonder about is whether or not he's seen or heard any of the scuttlebutt about her and Spike Love. Surely he must have, but he hasn't said anything.

"Did you read the story in the *Enquirer*?" she asks.

"What? The one where they said you're having an affair with Spike Love? You know I don't read those things."

So now she knows that he's heard the rumors. She figures as much, but it's no great concern to her. Neither of them has ever been particularly possessive. What they do when the other one is not around has never been a big issue so long as it remains casual.

*

The football gods must know it's the day of the annual game between Booker T and Freedom, because they ring in the dawn with the first chill of autumn. Wives and mothers fill their family's bowls with steaming oatmeal for breakfast instead of the usual mushy cold cereal. Or they fry eggs with sausage or bacon with heaping mounds of buttered grits on the side, or make stacks of pancakes slathered in butter and syrup. Kids pull light sweaters out of drawers for the first time since early April, and everyone leaves home for work or school with a renewed spring in their step.

Sue Ellen drives Pop home from the hospital in her big van. She and Shelly bring pillows and blankets from the bedroom and spread them on the couch in front of the television and set a folding snack table next to the couch. Once Pop is comfortably settled down, David and Sue Ellen leave the room, ostensibly to let his parents have some time alone but really for more alone time for themselves.

Shelly fluffs Pop's pillows, fiddles with his covers. He shoves her hands away. "Leave me alone, woman. For God's sake. Quit hovering."

He stretches out with his head propped on pillows on one end of the couch and his big feet on the armrest on the other end. Trying to comfortably situate the covers, he grimaces with pain and his eyes water, but he refuses to let her help him. The doctor had sent him home with what they called a heart pillow. Pop calls it a silly girly pillow. His instructions are to hold the pillow to his chest whenever he stands up, and to stand up slowly—to take it easy and remain on his back as much as possible, but to walk around the house ten minutes twice a day and gradually build that up until he's walking at least a brisk thirty minutes every day. He picks at the sticky residue of tape that is all over his body. All that crap they stuck on him. Now he feels like he'll never be able to get it all off. There are big red circles on his chest and the sides of his ribcage and stomach and other places he can't see, all where he was hooked up to the EKG. And they itch.

"Would you like something to eat?" Shelly asks. It's lunchtime.

"Yeah, I would."

She makes ham and cheese sandwiches. She helps him sit up enough to eat. This time he doesn't object to her fussing over him. He's at home alone with Shelly; he can let his guard down. Halfway through his sandwich he drops it on his plate and begins to sob, not so much out of pain or fear but simply to let all the tension go. Since the accident he has struggled to maintain the stoic front that has been his face to the world throughout his whole life. Only when he is alone with Shelly can he let himself go. She holds him and lets him sob knowing that if he did not have this outlet his head would surely explode.

The only other time he had given in to emotion so strongly had been right after he came home from 'Nam.

Earl Ray was no starry eyed kid rushing off to war in a fit of patriotic zeal. He was long since out of school and had been married four years already. But like many of his younger compatriots, he was outraged when President Johnson told the country that the North Vietnamese Communists had attacked American ships. He felt it was his duty as an American to join the battle. And there was another reason he was glad to go off to war. It was an escape from problems at home.

The problem was they had been trying for years to get pregnant, ever since they got married. He insisted that it had to be her fault. Using biblical language, he called her a barren woman and reminded her that in olden days being barren was grounds for divorce. She countered that it takes two to tango. She suspected the problem might be his. Fertility tests showed there was no reason she should not be able to conceive, but when Shelly and the doctor asked Earl Ray to get himself tested, he said, "There's no damn reason for me to get tested. I know I'm fertile."

"How do you know?" Shelly asked.

"I just do."

She said, "That's no answer, Earl Ray," and the doctor told him that a medical test was the only way to know for sure.

Shelly kept pressuring him. He said, "Get off it, woman. I'm telling you, I don't need to take no tests. I know I'm fertile."

"How do you know? How could you possibly know?"

And he said, "I know because I already fathered one baby."

Shelly was shocked. "How could you not tell me? I'm your wife. I deserve to know these things."

"It was before I even knew you."

Once she recovered from the initial shock, Shelly wanted to know who the woman was and all about the baby. "Was it a boy or a girl?" (A boy.) "What's his name?" (I don't even know.) How could you not know? Where does he live?" (I don't know.) "Did you even see him?" (No, I never have.)

He said that the woman, the mother of his baby, was "a nobody, really, just a one night fling when I was younger. It didn't mean a thing, not to neither one of us. She moved away. I set up a fund for her through the bank. She gets a big check every month to support the baby. She's happy enough with that. Sure, I could find out where they are and all if I wanted to, but I don't. That's all in the past, and that's where it oughta stay."

They never discussed it again, but after the revelation that he had fathered a son—a son he didn't even care enough about to ask his name—there was constant tension in the Lawrence home. Shelly then felt that she could never again fully trust her husband and that perhaps she had never really known him the way she thought she did.

That was not the first monkey wrench tossed into the gears of Shelly and Earl Ray's marriage. The first had been when Earl Ray talked her into quitting singing at the Jump 'N' Jive. He loved listening to her sing, but he didn't like the way other men looked at her when she was on stage. That first night when he saw her sing for the first time, it was her innocence that attracted him to her. But when she became a regular entertainer at the Jump 'N' Jive she started dressing the way she thought a torch singer ought to dress. Sleek dresses that hugged her hips and thighs, dark lipstick, lots of gunky mascara. She flirted with the audience and made love to the microphone. "You're just trying to make them men horny," he accused.

"No I'm not. It's just show biz, honey."

But he didn't like it. He didn't want her going to the Jump 'N' Jive when he couldn't be there to keep an eye on her. She didn't want to give it up, but she thought her marriage was more important than her singing career, and when she wasn't peeved with him for being so damn controlling she thought it was sweet of him to be protective of her virtue.

Earl Ray and Shelly were living in a rental house on the west side of Bujold Bayou at the time. Left childless and alone when Earl Ray was deployed to Vietnam, Shelly went back home to her parents to wait it out. But she was even more miserable living with her parents than she had been living alone, so she moved back into the apartment. With her father-in-law's help, she went shopping for a car and found a red and white 1956

Chevrolet that was perfect for running around Freedom. She got a part-time job clerking in a fabric store in Gulfport—a short commute three days a week in her new Chevy. Twice she drove herself, all alone, out to the Jump 'N' Jive. But as much as she loved singing, she did not feel comfortable going out there alone. The drive out along the narrow road canopied with mossy oaks was spooky, and once there she worried about drunks trying to put the make on her. She was also afraid of what Earl Ray would do if he found out when he came home, so she quit singing after only two nights.

She tried taking up quilting, and then knitting, and then cross stitch, but none of those hobbies were satisfying. She volunteered for a while in a day care center, but being with children made her sad because she didn't have children of her own. She ended up spending time home alone, cleaning up an already clean apartment, reading and watching television.

It wasn't long before Earl Ray was sent back home to her, wounded and sullen and disillusioned. The bullet was easily removed from his stomach, and there was no permanent physical damage, but inside his head was a kaleidoscope of nightmare visions: jungles aflame, burning villages, dead and wounded soldiers. He was skittish of sudden movements and loud noises. He had night sweats. He snapped at Shelly. He didn't trust her. He was sure she must have been with other men when he was gone. When she got pregnant, he wanted to know who the father was. She swore he was the father. "I've never been with another man. Not once."

When the twins were born he renewed his suspicions, because he didn't think they looked anything like him. "Beside, there's never been any twins in my family. Don't it run in the family?"

"It's passed down from the mother's side. That's what I've heard. And there are twins on my side of the family. My grandmother was a twin."

There were no psychological breakthroughs. There was no moment when she finally convinced him to trust her. But Earl Ray did become a little easier to live with over time. He gradually accepted that yes, he was the father of the twins, and no, Shelly had never been untrue to him, not during the war and not since. His nightmares didn't go away completely, but their frequency and violence did slack off a little, and gradually he got to where he did not startle so easily.

He put the war behind him and refused to talk about it. When news of the war came on TV, he shut it off. When opposition to the war began to grow, he shut his mind to that as well. When Daniel Ellsberg released the Pentagon Papers he said they were fake, and then many years later when Secretary of Defense Robert S. Macnamara said that the attack in the Gulf of Tonkin—the government's justification for the war—had never happened, Earl Ray unplugged their television set and tossed it in the bayou (and Shelly made him go out and buy a bigger one).

*

Memories wash over David as they approach the football stadium. He's in Buddy's car, riding shotgun. Buddy's driving and Mary's on the back seat. The schools face one another at the intersection of Freedom Loop and Liberty Street. One red brick and the other whitewashed concrete. Mary always said the two schools were "like us, fraternal twins who love each other but constantly fight as only siblings can." David had always thought of the twin schools as the Lawrences and the Mosses, generations of family feuds. Randy's dad and David's dad hated each other, and held each other at arm's length. The clash between the two of them had been most vehement in their young adult years when Shelly and Earl Ray were first married. When Randy's father retired, young Randy was chosen by the party machine to take his place and was ushered in virtually without an election. Earl Ray was convinced that the election had been rigged, but he couldn't prove it. When Randy came up for reelection Earl Ray made it his mission in life to find a worthy opponent to run against him. He was prepared to jump into the campaign with six-shooters blasting, and if he couldn't find a suitable candidate to challenge Randy, he was going to run for sheriff himself, despite having no law enforcement experience. But his father convinced him not to. "It's better to keep your enemy close by your side where you can keep an eye on him. Look, as long as that fat bastard is in the sheriff's office he can't take a crap without Riley Rogers telling him it's okay, and Riley is in our corner."

With David's generation, the feud was much friendlier. And now, David realizes—how odd—he is on his way to a replay of the old rivalry on the old field of battle, but with another generation of Mosses and this time no Lawrence on the field.

Buddy pulls into the muddy parking lot that is shared by the two schools. "All these years and they still haven't paved this lot," David says. "I can't believe it."

The shared football field sits kitty-corner from the two schools at the crossroads. Next to the stadium is a baseball diamond used for P.E. and for practice; actual games are played in the football stadium. David remembers how often baseballs rolled into the creek behind the field, and he remembers pulling off his shoes and rolling up his pant legs to search for those lost balls. He remembers kissing Melinda Jensen underneath the bleachers, the unexpected shock of pain when their teeth clanked together. He looks for the sweet gum tree they used to climb to get on the roof of the concession stand, but it's been chopped down. The children's swing set is still there, and a single child about ten years old has put a football helmet in the swing seat and is pushing it as if it's his baby. The old wooden bleachers have been replaced with aluminum (why didn't they fix the parking lot at the same time, he wonders).

Families are pouring in with their blankets and folding seats and pom poms and "We're Number One" foam fingers, those on the left side all dressed in purple and yellow (Booker T) and those on the right in red and black (Freedom). A gauze of low lying clouds shrouds the floodlights that encircle the field. Families trudge to the upper rows of the bleachers and students gather together closer to the field where the cheerleaders are already leaping and shouting. Among the cheerleaders is Jeri Patterson, Sue Ellen's daughter. David has never met her but he has no trouble spotting which one she is. She looks that much like her mother. The amount of déjà vu he's encountered on this trip home has been eerie, but Jeri Patterson's resemblance to Sue Ellen seems only natural.

Atop the bleachers on the Freedom side there is a new, glass-fronted press box and on top of it the sign: Martin Luther King Jr. Stadium (newly named since David left home).

David, Mary and Buddy merge with the entering crowds. Everyone greets David, the few he remembers and the many he doesn't know. They all tell him how good it is to see him and how much they loved him in *The Witness*. For reasons he's never understood, that's the one movie everybody seems to mention. He thinks *Cold Justice* was the best of the three films, but it was the least successful because it had a downer ending. (His character, the defense lawyer, found the evidence he had been looking for that would free his client, but too late; his client hung himself in his jail cell.)

Half a dozen people or more ask him for his autograph before they can make it to their seats—top row on the fifty yard line on the Booker T side. The same row of seats has been reserved for the Lawrence family since David was in high school. David and Sue Ellen get the seats that are normally held for Pop and Shelly. Sue Ellen is already there waiting for them. She's wearing a plaid skirt and a white sweater, a hot drink in a paper cup on her lap. "Is that coffee?" David asks as he takes a seat next to her.

"Hot chocolate. But they got coffee too, if you want some."

"Nah, not now. Maybe at halftime."

"Turned off cold, didn't it?" Sue Ellen says.

"Yeah. Sure did."

"Got a blanket right here," she says, pointing with her free hand at the folded blanket at her feet.

David spreads the red and black plaid blanket over their laps. "It's the wrong color," he points out (red and black are Freedom High colors).

"Shhhh. Don't tell anybody." Under the blanket she squeezes his hand.

Buddy reaches in his jacket pocket and pulls out a silver whiskey flask. He takes a swig, caps it and reaches across Mary to offer David a drink. (Buddy is by the aisle, Mary next to him, and then David and Sue Ellen. Empty spaces to Sue Ellen's left await Mary's two girls and Melissa.

"No thanks." David declines the flask.

Melissa shows up and they all have to stand up to let her get to her seat. On a cardboard tray she balances hot dogs, chips and sodas for her and for Rhonda and Patricia, who are down near the field with their friends. Presumably they will climb up to their seats before the game begins. The bandage on Melissa's nose has been removed, and David notices that her nose doesn't look so bad. Slightly discolored, but the swelling is hardly noticeable. She edges past David and Sue Ellen and sits down. Soon the girls squeeze in and immediately grab for their hot dogs. "What do you say?" Mary asks the girls.

"Thank you, Aunt Melissa," they chirrup in unison.

The Freedom band marches onto the field on the north end, headed by leaping and cartwheeling cheerleaders. The band starts playing "Dixie," and across the way a sea of mostly white faces in red and black garb stand for what they call the Southern Anthem. For the so many thousands of times he heard it when he was growing up, David never thought of "Dixie" as being racist or divisive, but now he feels like he should be embarrassed for sitting there listening to it. He remembers that his mother had often commented on how obvious the racial divide in Freedom was, in stark contrast to the community's history of harmony. Since that history went back before his time, he had never been very aware of it; but like many expatriate Southerners he studied the region after leaving home, and now it is very noticeable.

The Booker T band marches in under purple and gold streamers on the south goal and drowns out the Freedom band with a rousing rendition of Queen's "Another One Bites the Dust," and the Booker T fans go crazy. David remembers them playing the same song when he was playing for Booker T. He wonders if today's teens have ever heard the original. Do they even know who Freddy Mercury was?

When the music stops, David asks Sue Ellen, "Are the Pirates favored this year?"

"Are you kidding? By about three touchdowns is all. We got the best quarterback in the whole state. He made the all-state team last year, and he was just a sophomore. Not bad for a town that's not really big enough for two high schools. Major colleges are already courting him. And with Abdul heading up the defensive line, Freedom doesn't stand a chance."

Booker T has dominated the series since the founding of Freedom School in 1966, having won thirty-three of the forty-two games. Most recently they've carried home the trophy six years running, and everybody is excited about this year's Pirates, even Freedom fans. They all want to see Marcus Campbell in action again after his exciting sophomore season. He has an arm like a rocket, and he's a scrambling quarterback who can run as well as he throws. Plus they have a six-foot-five wide receiver by the name of Frankie Owens who can run the 100 meter dash in 10.6 seconds, and Abdul Taylor is almost as big as, and faster than, his father when he played for Booker T. He holds the state record for sacks and can double up as a blocker in the offensive line, which he is often called upon to do in short-yardage situations. His father had been put in as a power running back in those situations, David recalls, but this Pirate team has a strong fullback and needs Abdul's strength more in front of the ball carrier. On the other side, Randy Moss's son, Gerald, will be guarding the Pirate's leading receiver. At six-feet even he can't match Frankie Owens' reach, but he has great leaping ability and is a ferocious tackler (and like his father, Sue Ellen says, he gets away with a lot of grabbing and holding). The Gators also have a running back who is supposed to be one of the best in the state.

"What do your boys play?" David asks Sue Ellen.

"They're both corner backs, and dual return men on the kicking teams."

There's a strong wind blowing in from the southwest, strong enough that when the teams line up for the kickoff the ball keeps blowing off the tee. The Freedom High Gators are kicking off. After two attempts to settle the ball on the tee, they finally get a lineman to hold it. "This wind's gonna play hell with the kicking game," Buddy says.

"That'll be to our advantage because we'll be facing south in the fourth quarter," Mary says. Mary is not one of those wives who put up with the games out of duty. She can recite statistics and makes better play calls from the stands than the coaches on the field. She's also a rabid, one-person cheering squad.

It's a short kick. Jimmy Patterson takes it on his own thirty. He angles for the center of the field and his brother, David, takes up position to block for him. He blocks out one Gator defender but Gerald Moss slips past him and hits Jimmy with a crushing chest-high tackle that spends him sprawling to the turf and sends the ball bounding across the sideline. Sue Ellen hides her eyes for a second but looks back to the field in time to see her boy climb to his feet, apparently unshaken. "Was that an illegal tackle?" she asks.

"Nope, just a hard tackle," David says.

"Oh God, sometimes I hate this game."

Marcus Campbell connects with Frankie Owens for a touchdown on the first play from scrimmage. The Pirates miss the extra point attempt. The Gators mount a methodical drive downfield on their first possession culminating in a fifteen-yard field goal. Then, on the Pirates' next possession, Gerald Moss intercepts a Marcus Campbell pass.

"You gotta give him credit," Davis says. "The Moss kid ain't half bad."

"Yeah, he's the best player they have," Mary says.

The Pirates score again late in the second quarter and are leading by two touchdowns at halftime. In the second half, Abdul Taylor sacks the Gator quarterback on his own twenty and forces a fumble, and the Pirates turn that into another touchdown. They're ahead 20-3.

A mile away from the stadium Pop and Shelly are listening to the game. Shelly, having lately taken up the quilting hobby she had first tried when Earl Ray was in Vietnam, has an almost finished quilt tossed over her lap and is lazily hand-sewing a border to her Victorian crazy quilt pattern. Pop is stretched out on the couch with his head propped up on two pillows. He sits up and shouts "Go! Go!" when the announcer shouts,

"Owens is going deep! He's got two steps on Moss. Campbell passes. He's reaching! He's got it! Down on the Gator five yard line. That was an amazing diving tackle by Gerald Moss, folks. But the Pirates are in scoring position once again. It looks like they're about to put this one away for good."

Pop sinks back down on his pillows and grabs at his chest. "What's the matter?" Shelly asks, frantically dropping her quilt and rushing to his side. "Is it your heart?"

"No. No, I don't think so. I think it's just..." He pauses in obvious pain. His eyes water.

"Do you need one of your pills?" The doctor has sent him home with nitro pills for chest pain.

He says, "I don't know. I don't think it's my heart. I think it's the bone or the... I don't know, where they cut me open. Oh God! It's so hard to tell. Maybe it's just indigestion."

His eyes water. She hands him a tissue, and he wipes his eyes. He says, "I'm just so fucking tired of being in pain. Is it always gonna be like this?"

"No, honey, no. You're going to get better." She's confused because the day before he seemed much better.

"Like hell I am. Doc Duval says you never really recover from heart disease. Sooner or later it's going to get me. I don't care. I ain't scared of dying. It's the pain I can't stand to live with."

"It'll get better, honey. I know it will. Doc Duval said it would."

Back at the football field Sue Ellen asks David if he wants to sneak out and beat the traffic. The game is almost over and Booker T has it sewn up. No need to hang around. David laughs. "Traffic! Jesus. There aren't enough cars in the whole county to cause a traffic jam."

"Well maybe not like a L.A. traffic jam, but I'd still like to beat the crowd out."

He starts to say, "You call this a crowd," but decides he's belittled Freedom enough for one night.

Time remaining: 1:48; Booker T has the ball. They can run the clock out. No sense in watching any more. David says, "All right, let's go." Turning to Mary he says, "Sue Ellen's going to take me home."

Sue Ellen gathers up her blanket and they stand up and are making their way down and out of the bleachers when they are distracted by a disturbance on the sideline. There's a blur of movement and a pile of bodies. Both referees frantically blowing their whistles. A fight has broken out. Sheriff Moss comes bounding out of the lower bleachers with his nightstick waving to break up the melee. Football players and coaches and fans are all pushing each other and fists are being thrown (knuckles cracking against helmets and shoulder pads doing more harm to the people throwing punches than to the people being hit). The sheriff pushes two of the fighting players apart and cracks another across the back with his baton. Someone tackles him. Two adults from the stands leap on the sheriff's back. He pulls out his gun and fires it into the air. Everyone freezes when they hear the gunshot. "Jesus!" Sue Ellen exclaims. "Did he shoot somebody?"

"Nah, I don't think so. I think he shot the scoreboard."

Sure enough, they look up at the scoreboard and see that the LED display has gone dark.

"This is like when we were in high school, only bigger," Sue Ellen says.

"Yeah, I know. I just had this weird thought that like years from now generation after generation of Sheriff Mosses are going to be starting fights at Booker T and Freedom games. In the year 2121 he'll be shooting out the scoreboard with a laser pistol."

An announcement is broadcast over the public address system: "Ladies and gentlemen, the game is called off due to the fight on the field. Please separate and go home. No official winner will be announced. The Liberty Bowl trophy will be removed and stored in the district school office until the series can be reinstated next year. Please separate and go home, ladies and gentlemen."

The announcer repeats his message until the mingled masses of fighters on the field break up and people start heading for the exits, some, itching to get one more punch in but being physically restrained by friends. The crowd from the bleachers heads down and out to the parking lot. David and Sue Ellen, having lost their chance to get out ahead of the crowd, are caught up in the stampede across the muddy parking lot. But the snarl of traffic pulling out is small, and soon she inches her Honda out onto Freedom Loop and heads south. "Where are we going?" David asks.

"I don't know. Are you hungry? Want to get a drink?"

"Actually I am a little hungry."

"Little Don's?"

"No, it'll be too crowded."

They find a family style restaurant about five miles south of Freedom. There are few cars parked out front. When they step out of the car they're hit with a chill wind. "Wow! It's really starting to blow," David says.

"Sure is, and it's getting cold."

David heads around the front of the Honda and puts his arm around her shoulder. Cool blue light like that from a television screen softens her facial features. The source is a neon sign that commands them to EAT. She leans into him and they rush with heads ducked forward into the restaurant. The hostess leads them past the upfront counter to a corner booth—dark wood, padded with purple, and a Formica top, a window seat looking out on the parking lot. On the television behind the counter Weatherman Donny is saying, "High tomorrow in the low seventies with a chance of scattered thunder showers. In the Caribbean, the tropical storm that started over the Caymans has now made landfall on the western tip of Cuba causing massive flood damage. Thousands are homeless in Havana and in farm communities to the west. Three deaths have been reported. The other storm south of Puerto Rico has been upgraded to hurricane strength."

The hostess seats them, plops down menus and says, "Your server will be Janine."

She waddles off.

David looks at the list of beers. There's nothing but the standard domestic brews. The wine list consists of house red and house white. Janine shows up, asks if they want anything to drink. They order the house red.

"Did you see what started the fight?" David asks.

"No."

"Me either."

"It's probably a safe bet that Gerald Moss had something to do with it."

When Janine brings their wine and stands with order pad in hand, they order a fish platter to share. Near their table is yet another overhead television mounted on metal brackets and angled in their direction. They're subjected to Weatherman Donny in stereo. He says, "... category two and gathering strength. If it follows its current projected path it will skirt the Bahamas and make landfall on the southern tip of Florida sometime Sunday morning as possibly a category three or maybe even a four."

Their fish dinner is served in a plastic basket. They eat leisurely, picking at their fish platter and dawdling over their wine. The fish and shrimp are breaded and deep fried and come with little paper cups of tarter sauce and a shrimp dip heavy on the ketchup and Tabasco. The wine is heavy on the tannins, but drinkable. They glance up at Weatherman Donny and look out the window where wind is whipping through trees on the outer edge of the parking lot, and then they look back at each other. Sue Ellen picks up a French fry and pops it in her puckered mouth. He picks one up and dangles it in his hand; she picks up another and copies him. They're silently competing to see who has the longest French fry. He's reminded of the eating scene in *Tom Jones* (or *Tammy* as described by Jasmine over the phone). They smile at each other as if to say, how silly can you get. Finally Sue Ellen says, "What are we going to do?"

"In general?"

"About us."

"I don't know. Is there an us?"

"I think so. What do you think?"

"Yeah, I think there might be an us."

He pours the last of the wine into their glasses. He says, "I shouldn't have ever let you go. I should have married you right out of college. What went wrong? Why didn't we?"

"What happened back then doesn't really matter."

"No, but we can't just take up where we left off, can we? We have lives and careers and children and... you know, it's just not that simple. Maybe. Is it?"

"I don't know either. Maybe it is that simple."

"Are we talking about marriage?"

"Or living together. Maybe marriage. Maybe we're just trying to decide if it would be practical."

He laughs ahead of what he says next, knowing how silly it sounds. "We could shack up."

"Aren't you already shacked up with Jasmine Jones?"

"Oh God."

They nibble on their shared seafood sampler awhile, and then he says, "I don't think our careers would be a problem. From the way you described it, you could do your job anywhere. It'd just be a matter of whether or not you'd be willing to move to L.A."

"Or if I'd want to, or whether the boys would be willing to move. That's a pretty big decision."

"You wouldn't have to work if you didn't want to. Lord knows I've got enough money for us both."

They discuss the pros and cons of moving in together as if it's a business arrangement, avoiding any talk about how they feel in their hearts, although that is heavy on both of their minds. They love each other, there's no doubt of that. As soon as they met on the flight from Atlanta they knew it. It came rushing back like a tsunami. But is it a romantic love or something more familial? Is it all wrapped up in memories of their teenage romance? Are they being seduced by nostalgia? David knows that he feels something wonderful every time she speaks. He thinks she is more beautiful than any woman he's ever known other than Melissa, who doesn't really count in that way—more beautiful by far than Jasmine Jones, whose beauty is manufactured and predictable at best. He knows that he feels an electric current whenever she touches him. Yet they have spent a lot of time together since his return to Freedom, and so far he hasn't felt an overwhelming urge to make love with her.

Sue Ellen has no doubt whatsoever that she's in love with him. And yes, it is romantic love, not some kind of familial feeling or feel-good agape type of love. And it doesn't bother her that there's been no electricity. She knows that will change. They'll be there again, not every minute of every day as when they were seventeen but in rare and unexpected moments. She'll grab it and hug it to her chest when it comes. But for now it's a more comforting relationship she hopes to ease into.

But looming in the distance with the insistence of Weatherman Donny's predictions is the question of Jasmine Jones. Aren't they lovers? That's what the celebrity magazines say. She knows they're living together. Aren't they? Now that she asks herself point blank she can't recall if he ever actually said he was living with her, but he certainly never disputed the implication. If David and Jasmine are romantically linked he'd have to break up with her. Is he willing to do that? Does he want to? And—oh my god, this is the weirdest thought of all—what if I'm expected to just accept that he has a mistress? Does anybody even use the word *mistress* any more? What was that seventies term? Open marriage? It wouldn't be out of the question. After all, they are movie stars. What do I know about life among the stars in Hollywood? Don't they have wholly different values and beliefs than the rest of America? Certainly different than those in Sue Ellen's little corner of the world. She is forgetting for a moment that she's actually a pretty worldly traveler whose liberal value system would probably fit in much better in Hollywood than in Freedom. But she's not so liberal as to accept the kind of free love arrangement she imagines might be common out there.

"Your boys are seniors in high school," he says. "They shouldn't have to leave their school or their friends." He pours the last of the wine.

"They could stay with their father. At least temporarily."

"And come out to visit as often as they want. They'd love it there."

"They probably would."

"Just wait until you see my house." He's beginning to talk like it's already decided. "You're gonna love it. It's right on the beach in Malibu. Let's face it, being rich is pretty nice. There's a big deck and a huge family room and a TV room with a giant screen that fills one whole wall. And you oughta see the kitchen. And the bedroom. A king size bed and his-and-hers closets you could live in."

He sloshes his wine in a slow whirlpool and thinks about Jasmine, how hard it will be to break up with her. Jasmine is truly sweet. She's also fun-loving, and she shares David's taste in music and movies, and she's used to all of David's quirks and bad habits, which Sue Ellen doesn't even know about. At least not about the quirks and bad habits he's developed over the past twenty years. Like sleeping with the lights on. Glaring overhead light, not merely a bedside lamp. David reads in bed and falls asleep with his book still open. If he has to get up and turn the light off, then he's fully awake and can't go back to sleep. Jasmine sleeps with a mask to shut out the light. He also takes baths twice a day and shuts her out of the bathroom. There are other bathrooms in the house that she can use if she has to, and he doesn't like to be disturbed. Baths are to him escape and meditation. The screenplay he's been working on for the past ten years is all being written in his head, in the bathtub.

And if he and Sue Ellen got married it would not be like a wedding in Freedom with family and friends in attendance. It would have to be huge. In his world, every social occasion is an audition, if not for a particular film, then for some possible future project. He would have to invite his agent and his publicist and directors and producers and critics and screenwriters and anyone else who, if slighted, might come back to stab him in the back. Would she be up for schmoozing with all the artsy pretenders?

They've finished their meal and the wine, and taken the conversation as far as either of them wants to at the moment. They sit quietly for a while, even as the restaurant is loud with the clatter of dishes and overlapping conversations and the drone of the television. And then David's cell phone plays "Dixie." Quickly he grabs for the phone, anxious to silence it before disturbing the whole restaurant. He's embarrassed that he hadn't thought to put it on vibrate. He's even more embarrassed about the ring tone and surprised that everybody in the restaurant didn't suddenly come to attention and salute the Confederate flag.

"It's Mary," he says.

"Better answer it."

He's full of dread, expecting her to say the old man's had another heart attack. He's surprised when a giggling Mary says, "I'm calling for Knockers Jamison."

"Oh sweet Jesus." He hands the phone to Sue Ellen. "She wants to talk to you."

She scrunches up her face in a puzzled look and takes the phone from him. "Hi," she says.

"Hey girl," Mary's perky voice shoots back. "Did you get in my brother's pants yet?"

"What? Are you drunk?"

"Not quite, but we're working on it."

"We?"

"Melissa's here. We've been captured by aliens and whisked away—back in time. We're seventeen years old again and having a spend-the-night party, and we need you and David here to make it just like old times."

Sue Ellen gives David the old finger circling the ear signal to say she's crazy, and then asks Mary, "Where's here? Are you at home?"

"Yeah. My folks' home, not my house."

*

It's midnight when they pull into the Lawrence's driveway. Through the slashing rain Sue Ellen's headlights pick up the back of a red

Corvette, a match to the one Pop demolished. David reads the bumper sticker: IMPEACH EVERYONE. He says, "That's gotta be Melissa's."

"Yep. None other."

Inside, they pile onto the pulled-together queen size beds that were Mary and Melissa's when they were teenagers. They have already kicked their shoes off. Mary is under the covers on her bed, her head propped up on a pile of pillows. She's wearing baby blue cotton Winnie the Pooh pajamas.

"I didn't exactly come prepared for sleeping over," Sue Ellen says.

"Me either," from David.

"And you think I did?" Melissa pulls back the covers to reveal that she's wearing nothing but an extra large T-shirt."

"You got anything under there?" David asks.

And Melissa teases, "You mean anything other than the sexiest body east of the Mississippi?" and briefly flips up the hem of her shirt to briefly reveal cotton panties.

"Old lady panties!" David snorts.

"Yeah, but on me they look good."

Ignoring them, Mary says to Sue Ellen, "We can probably find you something to sleep in."

The girls figure David can stay dressed or strip down to his underwear like he always did when they were younger. Mary and Sue Ellen tip-toe to the laundry room. David crawls under the cover still fully dressed except for his shoes. When Mary and Sue Ellen come back, Sue Ellen has donned one of Pop's T-shirts, which hangs down almost to her knees to make a perfect night shirt. She's still wearing pants but steps out of them and then reaches under the T-shirt to shrug out of her bra.

"Okay, kiddies, now that we're all gathered here, what do we talk about?" Mary chirps.

"What did we always talk about?" Sue Ellen laughs, already anticipating the answer. They all blurt out as in a well rehearsed chant: "S E X!"

But Melissa laughingly says, "We can't talk about that."

"Why not?"

"Because ain't none of y'all getting any." Pleased that they stepped right into her set-up. Of course they all know she doesn't really think that's true. Actually, Melissa and Mary assume that Sue Ellen and David are now lovers. Certainly they did it the night they slept together on the beach. They can't imagine that they didn't.

Deciding she can play this game as well as Melissa, Sue Ellen punts to David: "Maybe I ain't been getting any lately, but I imagine our movie star here has been getting more than his share. There's probably forty twenty-year-olds camped on the beach behind his house waiting for him to come home."

Mary says, "Yeah, I'm sure he's got his pick of the bimbos. God knows most of the girls around here would give anything to get in bed with him."

They all start in teasing David much as they used to when they were young, but taking into account his new fame as a movie star, saying the girls wouldn't be so hot for him "if they knew what we know"—with disparaging references to firecrackers that fizzle out and soldiers that can't stand at attention and, from Melissa, "the little engine that couldn't."

"Go ahead, gang up on me," David says.

Melissa says, "I want to hear about Jasmine Jones. What's up with you and Jasmine?" She's fairly bouncing on the bed.

"She's just a friend," David replies—a little too quickly and too defensively they all think.

"Aw come on. You expect us to believe that?"

He looks to Sue Ellen to try and read her face. He says, "Okay, yeah, we have been living together. Y'all know that already. But it's never been real serious between us. We're really just friends."

"I've heard of girls getting knocked up from being that friendly," Mary says.

Melissa says, "All I want to know is, is she as hot as she looks?"

"Oh yeah, she's hot all right." Again he looks at Sue Ellen to make sure she understands. Hyperbole is the game they're playing. Her expression assures him that she gets it.

"All right. If you must know, she's hot as a fire cracker. She's hotter than Maggie the Cat on her hot tin roof. Catch her in the right mood and she could take on the whole Booker T football team and wear them down and go out looking for more. Of course that doesn't quite put her in the same league with you," he says, pointedly looking at Melissa. He's giving just the response they were hoping for and has managed to bring it right back home to Melissa, who has had a reputation for getting off on just such banter as long as they've known her.

Melissa has always flaunted her supposed promiscuity, which was downright legendary in high school. And David and Mary and Sue Ellen always played along, knowing that Melissa enjoyed the play acting and also knowing that she was never half the harlot she pretended to be. Did she play along because she was that brazen or was it a way of hiding how much it hurt her when all her classmates called her a slut and a whore? They never knew and she never gave a hint. She proudly embraced her reputation, shoved it right back in their faces, dared them to make anything of it. Truthfully, she may have been a little bit sexually adventurous. Just enough, combined with her sultry good looks, to seal her reputation. But she was no more promiscuous than a good half of the girls at Booker T, and if you could believe the scuttlebutt, nearly all the girls at Freedom. She was at least choosy about who she went out with. As brazen as she pretended to be, the fact was that up until the time she started dating Randy Moss she had sex with only three boys, and after she started dating Randy she never went out with anyone else—not until she suddenly broke off with him and refused to speak to him or talk about him ever again. That was after they had graduated high school and half their crew had gone off to college.

Whatever had happened to cause her to turn so vehemently against Randy, Sue Ellen and David never knew. David assumed that surely Mary must know, but he had never asked her about it. After all, he had had little or no contact with any of them since going off to college.

Now that they're in their forties, nostalgia and juvenile sex banter doesn't keep them entertained for long. They're not comfortable with some of the old stories, and it's hard for them to kid about sex when, of the four of them, only one is married and the others have little or no romance in their lives.

Melissa still plays the game with dramatic flair and bravado, but when she goes out on the town it's usually with Pop, and she goes home alone more often than anyone suspects. As for David, his love life is played out in the tabloids where it is blown all out of proportion, and none of them yet know what's going on between him and Sue Ellen. And Mary? Her marriage is on shaky ground, but it's been teetering there on the precipice for decades, and they all know she's going to stick it out until Buddy kicks the bucket.

Mary says, "Doesn't it seem weird that I'm the only one of us that's married?"

"I don't know," Sue Ellen says. "With the frequency of divorce nowadays, maybe it's not weird at all."

"But doesn't it get lonely not having anyone to come home to?" Mary responds.

"I have my kids. But that's not what you're talking about, is it? Sure, I miss having a man to cuddle up with."

"Not me, honey," Melissa quips. "I got me someone. Oh yeah. Of course it might be someone different every night, but at least it's someone."

They ignore Melissa's retort. Sue Ellen says to Mary, "Are you thinking of leaving Buddy?"

"Oh no, not really. I've thought about it, but the idea of being single with two kids to take care of scares the crap out of me."

"You're talking to a single woman with three kids," Sue Ellen says, "and I've managed all right so far. It was tough at first, but they're almost grown now, and we're all pretty happy with the way things are."

"Seriously, what about you?" Sue Ellen asks Melissa, "Wouldn't you like to settle down?"

"Well yeah, I guess it would be nice if I found some wonderful guy and fell in love and lived happy ever after, but I don't think it's ever gonna happen."

This is as close as they've ever seen Melissa come to opening her heart. Usually nothing fazes her. Mary and Sue Ellen have always thought of her as being untouchable; they've assumed her slutty facade has been a way of keeping the world at bay. But they've noticed that she's been quieter than usual lately. They've noticed that sometimes she stares off into nothingness and seems startled to find herself in the middle of a conversation. It's understandable. Surely her nerves are frazzled, what with the wreck and Pop almost dying. Despite not being blood kin, or perhaps because of it, she has always been closer to Pop than either Mary or David. They all know that he's probably going to die soon, and they understand that it might hit her the hardest.

Her lip quivers. Her hands are unsteady. She looks like she is going to start crying. Mary reaches out and puts a hand on her shoulder, gently. She says, "What is it? Hon?"

That touch breaks the dam. Melissa begins to bawl. Mary reaches across David for a tissue and hands it to Melissa. She wipes the tears from her cheeks. She puts her arms around her and they hold each other for a long time. Melissa says, "I'm sorry."

"It's all right."

"What's the matter?" Sue Ellen asks.

Melissa lets out a pained little laugh. She says, "Y'all are going to think this is strange. I feel funny telling you. I... okay, I'll just come right out and say it."

She takes a deep breath. She says, "I just found out that my father died."

They're stunned. Confused. Nobody says a word. Melissa's real parents were killed twenty-six years ago, and they know she can't mean Pop. They wait for her to explain. She starts hesitantly, sniffling, blotting her eyes, blowing her nose. "I told you it was going to sound strange. Y'all thought my parents were killed when I was a kid. We made that up, me and Pop. I'm not even *who* I said I was. My name is not Melissa. At least it wasn't then. When Pop brought me home to live with you, we made up a story about me. My real name is Tashee Rogers. My father was Melvin Rogers."

"Melvin? You mean *Sugar* Rogers?"

"Yes."

Again there is a long silence. Outside rain keeps pounding against the window. Wind howls. Inside they are cozy but subdued, sitting up on the beds mummified in covers. Melissa says, "Y'all know about him. Heck, you probably know more about him in some ways than I ever did. I know he was somehow involved in organized crime, but I never knew that until near the end. I mean the end back then. I guess he did some pretty bad stuff, but he never talked about it. That was a whole other part of his life that he kept separate from family. To me he was just the daddy that taught me how to ride a bike and taught me how to dance and scared the holy crap out of the boys that came around the house when I first started dating. He went off to work most days and sometimes was gone overnight, but I never knew what he did. Business, he said. Politics. He was always going off somewhere with some legislator or lobbyist. Whatever he was doing, it seemed to me like he was pretty important, and he obviously made a lot of money. We never wanted for anything. I guess I got him to blame for my love of fancy clothes and jewelry. The one thing that should have seemed strange but never did, because it was all I ever knew, was that daddy never seemed to have to pay for stuff. We went on vacations in Hawaii and France, and somebody else always paid for everything—some organization or something. I remember I kind of picked up on that from snatches of overheard conversations. Once there was mention of something called the Coalition for Family Values. I remember Daddy saying CFV picked up the tab. I never suspected his criminal activities until he turned state's witness. He testified against someone in a murder trial, and he was given immunity and put in the witness protection program. I thought that was just something on TV. I didn't know they really did that. They moved him somewhere far away, I guess, and gave him a whole new identity. They never even let me know where he was. As far as I knew, he might as well have been dead. They said it was too dangerous for me to stay with my daddy—something about they can't get out of you what you don't know. They probably also thought he was an unfit parent, being single and a criminal and all, but they never came right out and said that."

"What about your mother?" David asks.

"Daddy divorced my mother when I was a little girl. I can't remember her. All I know is Daddy said she was in New Orleans. Daddy raised me by himself. And then they took him away too, and then I didn't have anybody. That much was true about what we said when Pop took me home and told y'all I'd lost my parents, that was true. I did lose 'em, just not the way he said. It was his idea for me to pass as a white girl." She lets out a little burp bubble of a self-effacing laugh. "Guess what?" she says, "I'm black. My skin may not be black, but I'm black inside. I never wanted to pretend otherwise. Hell, I was proud of being black. I'd read Eldridge Cleaver and I heard Malcolm X speak, and I wanted to be part of the movement. If I'd had my way I'd of been wearing a big ol' afro and marching in the streets. But Pop said if I passed as white nobody would ever suspect I was Sugar Rogers' girl. He said it was a surefire way to keep me safe. And not just me, I had to do it to protect my daddy."

David says, "But why didn't you ever tell me and Mary? Were you afraid we wouldn't accept you if we knew you were black?"

"No, it wasn't that at all."

"Well good. Because we never would've let something like that keep us from loving you."

Melissa reaches across to pick up the tissue box and pull one out and blow her nose good and hard. Setting back on the bed she says, "That's awful sweet of you. I know you mean it now, but let's face it, y'all didn't even know me then, and I didn't know you."

"It must have been Pop's idea to hide it from us. That was just like him. Goddamn him. He never trusted us. He never thought I could do anything right, so naturally he wouldn't believe I could keep a secret like that."

Mary and Melissa respond simultaneously, Mary with anger saying, "Aw come on, man, it's not about you. Not everything's about you." And Melissa more conciliatory saying, "Don't be mad at Pop. He saved my life. Can't you see that? And it wasn't because he didn't trust you. As a matter of fact, he trusted you so much that he said he knew that even if they tortured you..."

"They? They who?"

"Whoever was looking for my father. I guess he could have meant the cops or rival crime bosses or whatever, but I remember he said it was a real possibility. He said 'This ain't a game and it ain't no TV cop show; this is for real.' He said the only way you two would be safe would be if you didn't know anything at all. So you see, he was trying to protect you as well as me. But it was never ever that he didn't think you'd accept me."

"What were you going to say about torture?" Sue Ellen asks.

"Pop said they couldn't even torture it out of you. He said you'd never knowingly give me up. That's how much he trusted you. Both of you. But he was afraid you might accidentally let something slip that would give me away without you even knowing it. He said it was best to play it safe."

Mary says, "How did your father die? How did you find out?"

"He died of cancer. He'd had it for a while. Pop told me."

"Of course, it would have to be Pop," David says. "He's the only one who would know."

"Him and Randy Moss. Randy knew all along." She pauses. Thrown across her knees now is an old bedspread with pink flowers sewn onto a yellow background, faded and well worn. She swirls a loose thread trying to worry out what she's going to say next: "You want to know the real reason I dated that son of a bitch all through senior year and why I hate him so much now? It's because of what he knew and how he used it against me back then."

*

She knew that he knew. What she didn't know was how it might affect her. Could he be trusted not to tell anyone? His old man, the sheriff, was of course in on the whole deal. He had escorted her father to Jackson, where he handed him off to FBI agents who flew him to God-knows-where. Surely the sheriff knew where he was. But Melissa could not fathom why he would have told his son. Pop had made it amply clear that the more people who knew the more danger she and her father and anyone else associated with them might be in. Knowing that—and surely the dumb redneck sheriff must have at least understood that—then why in the world would he go and shoot off his mouth to his son who had absolutely no need to know? Was he bragging? Showing off what a hotshot lawman he was? Could he possibly be that stupid, and if he was really such an imbecile wouldn't Randy Junior have inherited some little bit of his depleted mental ability? Wasn't it likely that Randy Junior would turn out to be just as stupid or thoughtless or hateful as his old man? She didn't like the thought of that because despite some of his more obvious bad qualities, like the fact that he was just about the crudest boy she had ever known, she found herself awfully attracted to him.

With his flowing hair and azure eyes, he looked to her like a Viking warrior. He was built like a boulder, hard and massive, but Melissa could plainly see that within a few years a lot of that muscle would go flabby. He'd turn into a slovenly fatty just like his father. There was something else about Randy that disturbed her, something she couldn't quite put a finger on. She could feel it whenever he was around. It had something to do with his devil-may-care attitude, the way he drove his souped-up Ford and the way he wrapped his thighs around the belly of that big Harley, the way he was so eager to accept any challenge, the way he looked at her sometimes like he wanted to eat her alive. She had to admit that she was attracted to the bad boy aura. All of the boys she was attracted to were something like that. There was even some of that in her newly adopted brother, David, but she felt certain that David would never turn into an evil or hateful person. She wasn't so sure about Randy Moss.

She confided her feelings about Randy Moss to Mary, who had already confessed that she too was drawn to Randy despite a lot of things about him that she couldn't stand. "I don't get it," she said to Mary, "one minute he makes me want to puke, and the next minute he makes me want to rip my clothes off."

"Or his."

"Oh yeah."

"It's like he appeals to our darkest and most shameful..."

"Yeah, but sometimes he's just the opposite too. Like really kind of vulnerable and cuddly. I want to take him home and mother him."

"Don't I know it," Mary said.

"But there's history between you and Randy, right? I mean, if I was to date him, I wouldn't be..."

"Taking him away? Don't worry, it's definitely over between us."

It was an ongoing conversation. Sometimes the Randy Moss talk took place in bed and sometimes when they were walking together along Freedom Loop or pushing each other on the swings on the school grounds—a childish activity they loved. Sometimes they included David in their discussions, but usually it was private between Mary and Melissa. One thing Melissa knew for sure was that whatever it was that attracted her to Randy Moss, it had not a damn thing to do with love or respect or admiration. It was an animal attraction. Naked lust. He was physically irresistible. He was funny, he was challenging, and he was so, so bad. Like the evil looking snake tattooed on his arm, he was as repulsive as he was attractive. He awoke something primal and delicious in her and scared her half to death, like those horned goat satyrs of Greek mythology. At times he could be courtly in the way of the Old South, but most of the time he treated her like she didn't matter with her clothes on, and she felt like he could see right through whatever she was wearing. He belittled women. He made racist jokes. When she challenged him on those things he managed to twist it all around. If she told him his comment was racist he'd say, "No it wasn't. Geeze, don't you get it? It was a joke *about* racists. It shows how stupid they are."

And yes, she could see the logic of that, but she didn't trust his meaning. Same kind of thing with nasty remarks about girls. "Stupid cunt," he muttered about a girl they both knew, and she blasted him. "I hate that word. It's demeaning. It reduces women to nothing but their vaginas."

"Then what should I call her? A stupid bitch?"

"No, 'cause that's the same thing."

"No it's not. It means she's a dumb dog. That's what a bitch is, a female dog."

"Yeah, with the emphasis on female. There's not even an equivalent for a male dog. Just like there's no masculine equivalent for cunt or whore or slut. Jesus, there's like a million degrading terms for women and none for men."

"Well what if I called some guy a stupid dick? That'd be the same thing, wouldn't it? But nobody'd get upset about that."

She sputtered, "But when you call a girl a cunt you're implying that that's all girls are. You might not be saying it outright, but that's the implication."

"So? Same thing. Call a guy a dick, it means that's all he is. But if you ask me, you getting all upset about it just shows how insecure you are. How come girls are so emotional? How come you can't take a joke?"

"That's a stereotype," she said.

And he shot right back, "It's become a stereotype because it's true."

He told her that scientific studies had shown that women were more emotional and men more rational, and she didn't know how to challenge the validity of such studies, if there actually were any such studies. He told her it was a natural result of the evolutionary process. Primitive men were hunters and had to be sly and rational to find and kill game, and primitive women developed more intense emotional responses because of their role as nurturers. "It's not a put-down of women to say they're more emotional; it's just a statement of fact, and if you get upset about it that just proves the fact."

Their arguments were sexual, a kind of foreplay. He told her once that the two of them were the stuff of romantic comedies. "There's been a million movies about couples like us. They fight like cats and dogs until they end up in bed together and living happily ever after."

"God forbid," she said.

Melissa was seventeen years old and no more immune to romantic notions than any other seventeen-year-old—even more so (yet, at the same time more wary) because of having recently been orphaned. She wanted to be swept off her feet. She believed in Prince Charming. She believed with all her heart that some day she would find the perfect man and they would fall in love and live happily ever after. She whole heartedly believed in all the clichés and dreamed that some day her prince would come. What else was there for a young girl to pin her hopes on when her only models were fairy tales and romantic movies in which all women were damsels in distress? If they were pretty enough or sweet enough, Prince Charming would save them from whatever tower they were imprisoned in. In the films she saw and the few books she read women were utterly dependent on men.

Tashee Rogers, now Melissa Baker, was stunningly beautiful and of this at least she was fairly confident—finally, and becoming more so day by day—a blossoming process that began slowly after her plastic surgery and snowballed between her freshman and sophomore years. She discovered that attracting the opposite sex was a snap. She became a senior high seductress who was easily seduced. And she fully (she would later say stupidly) expected the act of lovemaking to be a transcendent experience. She gave in easily and with grand hopes with first a pimply faced kid in her biology class and then with Jimmy Dale Patterson, who would later marry Sue Ellen, and then with an older boy who worked at Little Don's, and with each of them she was utterly disappointed. How could she not be disappointed when she wanted it to be magic but her adolescent lovers were clumsy and insensitive to her needs and always in too much of a hurry to get it on and too quick to finish when they did? She blamed herself when sex failed to transport her to heavenly realms, never once thinking that at least part of the fault may lie with her sexual partners. She thought she must be doing something wrong; she thought that maybe with practice she'd learn to get it right. She read *The Joy of Sex* and *The G Spot* and all sorts of erotic tales by and for women— most especially Erica Jong's *Fear of Flying* and a paperback *Delta of Venus* by Anais Nin, which she flipped through so often that some of the type became unreadable. She learned a thing or two about how to pleasure herself, but the books didn't tell her what to do about boys who just wanted to hop on and hump.

When Randy won his momentous bet over the football game, she expected him to march into the Booker T gym like a conquering hero, gloating insufferably when he picked her up for their date after the game. She expected him to be all strutting and smiling like he'd just won a gazillion bucks. But he came in surprisingly quiet and subdued. He was wearing his Gator jacket with insignia on the sleeve for baseball, football, swimming and wrestling, three years each. His hair was slicked back and tied in a pony tail, his face pink and scrubbed clean, with a bruise on his check from a stray elbow during the game. He also walked with a slight limp and held his right hip. Some of the Booker T fans booed him and told him to go back across the street where he belonged, but the football players from their own team told them to shut up. You don't dis the other players was the unspoken code.

Rather than shouting down his enemies as might have been expected, Randy lowered his head when faced with the booing crowd and slinked past as if he knew he had it coming and deserved every bit of it. He walked up to Melissa and said, "Hi."

"Hi."

"I guess this is it, huh? Do you want to stay here or go across the street? Or we could just go somewhere else if you'd like."

Melissa said, "We had a bet, Randy. You're entitled to your win."

Her response clearly puzzled him, just as his lack of swagger (calculated to soften her) clearly puzzled her.

She said, "That means you get to carry me as a trophy back to Freedom High." She paused a moment and then added, "Well, not literally, but you know."

He took her arm and turned to escort her out of the gym. She said, "Aren't you going to do the jacket thing?"

It was customary if a player from the winning team had a date with a girl from the rival school for him to drape his letter jacket over her shoulders. "Okay," he said, and he put his jacket around her and they walked out of the gym and across the street to the Freedom victory dance. There they were greeted with shouts of approval and slaps on the back. Everybody told him they thought the roughing penalty was a bad call. "Nah, it wasn't," he confessed. I busted that sumbitch long after the whistle, and I got caught. That's the way the ball bounces."

The band, five Freedom High students who called themselves Rollin' Ripple, went into a lush instrumental version of Barbara Streisand's "The Way We Were," and Randy led Melissa out on the dance floor. How smoothly he danced was her second shock of the evening. She never would have suspected he had taken ballroom dance lessons, something that to her or anyone who knew him would have seemed totally out of character. It was something his football coach had suggested. Any kind of dance, he had said, but ballet is best. It does wonders for your balance and agility. Yeah, right, the players scoffed, you gotta be putting us on. So the coach mentioned it the one time and never again. But Randy decided to give it a try. Ballet, he thought, was too sissified. Picturing himself in leotards was more than he could handle, and he didn't think he could handle tap or jazz or modern dance, either (whatever jazz and modern were), so he opted for ballroom dancing, signing up for a class in a studio on the coast and never letting on to his friends that he was doing it. He was surprised to discover how much he enjoyed it. He seemed to have a natural gift for dancing, and he loved the feel of effortlessly gliding across the floor. He loved the feel of holding women in his arms. The women in his dance class were mostly older women, and they melted more comfortably in his arms than girls his own age. Skillfully guiding them around the dance floor gave him a sense of mastery, which easily compensated for any fear he might have that ballroom dancing was a sissy thing.

He barely touched Melissa, yet smoothly guided her around the floor with simple pressures that she was able to read and react to instinctively. Dancing came easily to her as well. She moved as effortlessly as a fish in still water, and when he pulled her body close against him, his warmth, the hardness of his chest against her breast and the heady smell of sweat mixed with after shave lotion made her feel lightheaded.

Later they went out to his car. It was a Ford Fairlane that had once been a police car, or so he bragged to his buddies. It had a beefed-up engine and all-leather seat covers and a terry cloth steering wheel cover. He mixed whiskey from a flask into their Cokes, and they drank and smoked, and he talked about his mother. "I don't know why I'm telling you this," he said. "Maybe it's because I know you lost your parents. I kinda get it that you can understand. My mama was sick as long back as I can remember. I didn't know what it was she had for the longest time. Daddy said she had spells. He protected her by keeping her away from everybody, even me, when she had her spells. I suppose he was protecting me too, from the hurt of seeing her like that."

Randy flicked his cigarette out the car window. He started to roll the window up, but Melissa asked him to leave it open. "The night air feels good," she said.

So he left the window open and propped an elbow on the door frame, and she sank into the comfort of his encircling arm.

Two decades later she tells David and Mary and Sue Ellen: "It just felt right, you know what I mean? It was such a comforting feeling. He had me completely fooled, I guess. Maybe I wanted to be fooled. I felt ashamed for not trusting him sooner. He told me his mother suffered from schizophrenia, that she was an inmate in the state insane asylum. I felt so sorry for him."

It is now about three o'clock in the morning. They've gone to the kitchen to raid the refrigerator. Mary and Sue Ellen are making ham and cheese sandwiches for everyone. They're all seated at the big kitchen table. Outside the rain has stopped. Water drips from the eaves.

David says, "That was pure bullshit. I guess you know that by now."

"No, I never heard anything different."

"Randy's mother left his daddy and went back home to her mother in Tennessee or Kentucky or some place like that. She wasn't insane. Hell, she was probably the sanest person in the family, which was why she left."

"Why would he lie to me about that?"

"To win your sympathy," Sue Ellen says. "Nobody can get into a girl's bloomers quicker than a great big boy nursing a little boy hurt."

Melissa takes a big bite of her sandwich and speaks out of the side of her mouth. "The wily bastard! Now I can chalk up one more reason to despise him." You'd think she's just now figuring out what a conniving and manipulative ass he is. Of course she had that figured out long ago, but now she is once again immersed in the moment, reliving her youth and experiencing the hurt and disillusionment and anger all over again. She says, "I really thought he was my one and only. If all the son of a bitch wanted was to get in my pants, goddammit, he was right there and didn't even know it. I was ready to jump his bones. Ready and willing."

She takes another big bite of her sandwich and chews sloppily. Her eyes are red and her nose is still slightly swollen from the car wreck, and she is masticating her ham and cheese like a dog attacking a bone, a smear of mayonnaise on her jaw. David thinks he has never seen her look less sexy, although there is a kind of tender appeal in the vulnerability she is displaying, which is something else he has never seen in her.

*

She can clearly recall every moment of that night. She remembers how dark it was. She remembers the sound of wind twanging a wire strung between light poles. It sounded like a reverberating guitar string. Like every once in a while one of the boys in the band inside the gym hit a

sour note and held it too long. With the windows in Randy's car open and
the double doors to the gym propped wide, they could hear the band. They
had been playing old songs: Bill Haley's "Rock Around the Clock," some
forgettable songs from the seventies, The Beatles, and just as they settled
into quiet after he told her the big lie about his mother, the one song she
thought was just about the most beautiful song ever— "Smoke Gets in
Your Eyes" sung in a not-bad imitation of The Platters. Outside the gym
the only light was from poles on the four corners of the lot. Randy
clutched the Styrofoam cup in both hands and held it in his lap. Even in
the semi-dark she could see that his hands were rough, swollen and red,
like the hands of an older man. From the way the light reflected in his eyes,
Melissa thought he was on the verge of crying. She reached to cup his
hands in hers. He set his cup in a cup holder and squeezed her hand. She
pulled his head down to her chest, and he nuzzled her breasts with his
cheeks, and they kissed. They kissed long and hard, and for the first time
ever she began to feel as if maybe, just maybe, her body was beginning to
respond to sensual touch the way she had dreamed it could. When his
hand reached for her chest, she imagined, moments ahead of his actual
touch, the feel of his gentle caress. She imagined the softness of silk, his
hand gently lifting the weight of her breast. But his actual touch when he
rammed his hand inside her sweater wasn't at all what she had just
imagined. It was rough and demanding, and she jerked away and shakily
said, "That's enough. Let's go back in."

That was their first date. It was a far cry from the tale she told
David and Mary back then, and a far cry from what she remembers now.
Memory, imagination and reality all distorted over time. David and Mary
remember Melissa regaling them with a story about how she fought off his
advances and then gave in to long and passionate kisses, and then fought
him off again when he became too aggressive. And they remember how
shocked they were when she announced that she and Randy were going
together, and they recall that during that time Melissa became strangely
reticent in their regular late night gab fests. She no longer wanted to talk
about Randy or her feelings for him or what they did on their dates.

By Christmas of that year, the six of them had become established couples, and when they all got together to hang out after school or double-and-triple date to the Friday night dances in the gym and the movies down at the Rialto, nothing much seemed to have changed in any of them other than the togetherness of the individual couples seemed more solid than before. David and Sue Ellen were comfortable with each other. Buddy remained as shy and polite as he had always been around others, but, according to Mary, was increasingly intense and desperate in his passion when the two of them were alone. Randy continued to be the arrogant but humorous guy he'd always been—one dirty joke or grossly inappropriate comment after another, some of which were admittedly funny but most of which they barely tolerated (David being more tolerant than the girls). But more and more over the course of that year Randy and Melissa went off on their on, and she seldom talked about what they did.

And now Melissa says, "I don't remember what I told you about that date, but here's what happened. For a little while it was really nice, and we started petting some, and then he got rough. I pushed him off. I said I wanted to go back in the dance. He begged me to stay, and he started pawing me. I couldn't get away from him. I tried to open the door to get out of his car and he grabbed me and pulled me away from the door. I thought he was going to rape me. I swear to God, it got really, really scary."

"And you never told us?" Mary asked, astonished.

"No, I couldn't. It was crazy. I was scared to say anything to anybody. He held on and wouldn't let go. I begged him to go back in the dance, and I tried to push him away, and then he said something that stopped me dead still. He called me a nigger. I don't remember the context, but I sure as hell remember that word. It came out of nowhere. I was astounded, and I guess he could see it in my eyes that he had shocked me into... not exactly submission, but something. I was stupefied. He had my undivided attention. He said, 'You're a little black girl trying to pass as white.' He said, 'What d'ya think David and Mary would say if they knew you were a nigger?'"

They're all quiet. Melissa takes a deep breath. "I said, 'Don't use that word again,' and I think I tried to slap him, but he held both of my wrists. I told him ya'll wouldn't care if I was black or white, and he said, 'Yeah, well you just might be in for a big surprise.' He said, 'You might think all your goody-goody white friends are all color blind and stuff, But they're still white Southerners and there's generations of racial hatred instilled deep in their hearts.'

"Can you believe it? He was going to screw me whether I wanted it or not, and somehow in his warped little brain he took that as proof that he wasn't racist."

"If you submitted to sex under that kind of threat, that's rape. He might as well have held a gun to your head," David says. "I wonder if you could still press charges. You'd have to find out if there's a statute of limitations."

"I don't want to charge him with rape or anything else. Not now. I'd like to scratch his goddamn eyes out. That's what I'd like to do. I'd like to hurt him. And I could now, now that my daddy's gone, there's no reason to keep his goddamn secret. I'd like to expose the bastard." She barely takes a breath between words. "The real horror was not just that he forced me to have sex with him, as if that wasn't bad enough. As if that wasn't painful and shameful."

"You never had anything to be ashamed of," Mary puts in.

"Yeah, I know. Now. But back then I was plenty ashamed. I was ashamed of myself for letting him touch me, no matter what the reason. But... but like I started to say, the real horror was that he made me his trophy girlfriend, a badge of honor just like his letter jacket. I had to pretend to be in love with him. And it wasn't just once or for just a little while, it was day after day after friggin' day. Ya'll know that. You were there. If I didn't go along he said he'd tell my secret and the people who were after my daddy would find out and force me to tell where he was."

"But you said you didn't know where he was," Mary says.

"I know, but I was confused and scared."

David and Mary and Sue Ellen all express their regret that they didn't know about it at the time and weren't able to do anything to help her.

Sue Ellen says, "None of us can know what we would have done in your shoes or what we might have done if you'd told us."

David says, "It's probably a good thing you didn't tell me. I might have killed the son of a bitch. Even now it's a good thing he's not here, 'cause I don't know what I might do."

The tension is beginning to abate. Humor sneaks in. "What would you like to do to the bastard?" Melissa asks.

"Oh, I dunno. Let me see. Hang him upside-down from the goal post on the football field, maybe."

"Naked," Melissa says.

"Oh yeah, definitely naked. With a target painted around his genitals."

"We could get dart guns and charge a nickel a shot. Give a big prize for hitting his bulls eye," Mary puts in.

"His balls eye," Sue Ellen says.

For a few minutes they further relieve the tension by fantasizing ever more horrible ways to hurt and humiliate good old Randy Moss. Finally, shortly before dawn, they wander off to bed—David and Sue Ellen in the guest room, which was once upon a time his bedroom, and the others in the girls' room.

*

The hurricane that brought torrential rains to the western tip of Cuba, the one that forecasters had feared would head on up to the Gulf Coast of the United States, has weakened to become, once again, a tropical storm and is not moving. It now looks like it will play itself out over Cuba. But the other storm has passed Puerto Rico, flooding sugar plantations and knocking out power for a few hundred homes west of San Juan. It blew north of the Dominican Republic and is building strength as it slowly inches northward to skirt the Bahamas on its way to the eastern shores of Florida. Sooner or later it's going to unleash its power somewhere over the southern United States. Everybody knows because Weatherman Donny says so. He said, "The tropical storm now slowly moving northward in the Bahamas is expected to make landfall as a category three hurricane somewhere between Key West and West Palm Beach around sunrise Saturday, although it could easily veer to the west and hit land anywhere along a path that follows the coastline from the Florida panhandle to Southeast Texas. All residents in the Gulf region are urged to stay tuned for possible evacuation notices."

It is now Wednesday evening. It's been a few hours since Weatherman Donny has announced any change in the forecast, even though he has announced frequent changes since Pop has been home from the hospital—four days now. The family is gathered in the living room, including Melissa and Sue Ellen, but not Buddy and his girls. Pop is feeling much better, despite being sick and tired of being on his back all day. He pushes himself up from the couch and shuffles over to his favorite recliner. Shelly jumps up and reaches to support him, but he swats her hands away. "Quit pawing at me, woman. You want to be helpful, go get me a beer."

She brings him a cold beer in the bottle. He takes a big swig and says, "Ah, now that's what I call good medicine."

He says it's good to have all the kids at home. "That goes for all of you," he says, "Y'all are all our kids." He seems to be including Sue Ellen as part of the family and even welcoming David back into the fold as if twenty years of antagonism are forgotten. "Hey, I know what we need to do. We need to have a hurricane party. Celebrate my recovery and ride out the storm."

"That's crazy," Shelly says. "You're not up to it, and besides, we might want to consider evacuating if the storm looks like it's going to hit here."

"Evacuate my ass," Pop snorts. "It's gonna take more than a measly little hurricane to run me off. We already rode out the biggest goddamn storms to ever hit the coast. There'll never be another storm like the last one, and even if there was, this damn house is a fortress. Nothing on God's green earth is gonna run Earl Ray Lawrence from his home."

"Famous last words," Shelly shoots back at him. "We were damn lucky the last time, but sooner or later luck always runs out."

David, Mary and Sue Ellen exchange winks. They know how stubborn the old man can be. They know he'll never listen to reason. Shelly will give in, she always does, and although they know riding out the storm in some drunken revelry might be crazy, they share Pop's optimistic belief that the Lawrence family is bullet proof. They simply can't believe that the house that has been unscathed through some of the worst hurricanes ever to hit the coast can possibly be hurt by this storm, which they figure will likely miss the whole area and make landfall somewhere in Texas anyway. That's what Weatherman Donny is now predicting as the most likely scenario, and as Mary points out, Weatherman Donny is seldom wrong.

Another thought nuzzles its way into David's mind, but he immediately slaps it away. It is the thought, which should be obvious to everyone, that there is no logical reason to think of the Lawrence house as a fortress. It's a wood frame house built on ground that is probably not too stable. It survived earlier storms by sheer good fortune.

Mary and David are seated on the couch, Melissa on the love seat by the sliding glass doors to the deck. Sue Ellen is on a throw pillow on the floor in front of David with her elbows resting on his thighs. Pop and Shelly are in their matching recliners, the ones that have been *their* chairs as long as anyone can remember. Nobody else is there. Mary's kids are home with their father, who has promised Mary he'll get them bathed and into bed early because it's a school night. Likewise, Sue Ellen's kids are with their father. It's a balmy September evening. The slight breeze outside gives no indication of the predicted storm. David says, "No sense in fighting it, mama. If he wants a party, we're going to have a party."

Sue Ellen says, "It sounds like fun to me. I remember the last hurricane party we went to. I wouldn't mind replaying that." She giggles.

Shelly seems perplexed. She shouldn't be. After watching David's monologue on DVD and listening to everyone's comments she should know exactly what Sue Ellen is referring to, but at the time she had clamped her hands over her ears and said, "Na, na, na, na, na. I don't want to hear it."

So for her elucidation Mary says, "She's talking about sex, mama. Remember the big storm our freshman year in college?"

"That piddly little thing," Pop interrupts. "It weren't nothing."

"Yeah. Well it tore the hell out of Randy Moss's beach house," Mary said. "That's where the hurricane party was, and guess what these two were doing while the house got blown away."

"That's probably none of your business," Shelly says. And then she asks, "Am I the only one that's afraid of this storm?"

"Yep," Pop says. "You're the only sissy in the house."

"Or the only person with a lick of sense."

"Good comeback, Mom," Davis says.

Feeling ganged up upon, Shelly gives in. "All right. You win. We'll have the damn party and just hope we don't get blown away."

Coordinating their plans with Weatherman Donny's prognostications, they decide the best time to throw the party would be Friday night or maybe during the day Saturday, depending on the weather.

Mary goes home and informs Buddy that they're going to have a hurricane party.

"Oh no we're not," he says. "We're not going to put Rhonda and Patricia in danger just because your father wants to have a goddamn party." Mary is stunned at his reaction, not only because he is standing up to her, something he has rarely done in all their years together, but because she knows in her heart that he is right. Riding out the storm is more than foolhardy, it's stupid and juvenile and dangerous. What kind of mother would subject her young daughters to such a danger? How could she have been so thoughtless?

"You're right," she admits. "We shouldn't put the girls at risk, but I can't abandon my parents either. You and the girls should go to your brother's place in Tupelo. But I have to stay here. If my whole family is going to ride out the storm, I think I have to be here."

Sulkily Buddy says, "Your last name is Boudreau, not Lawrence. You haven't been a Lawrence for a long time. *We* are your family, me and the girls, not your parents and your brother. Us, right here." He gathers Rhonda and Patricia into his arms like a hen gathering her chicks under her wing. They both shiver with fright.

After being subservient to Pop and in awe of the Lawrence legacy all his life, once Buddy stands up against them, resentments come pouring out. "What are you gonna be, a wife and mother or a little girl? God! Your hotshot movie star brother abandoned the family long ago, and your goddamn old man is crazy as a loon. He's had way too much influence on this family and the whole town for far too long. Don't let them bully you. Make a choice."

As impressive as his outburst is, it's ineffectual. Mary says, "I know you're right, honey, and I promise you that as soon as this is over I'll do whatever you want. Stay here, go somewhere else, start over, re-dedicate myself to you and the girls. But for now I've got to stay."

"Well I just pray they have a mother to come home to."

The one thing they both agree on at the moment is that they don't want Rhonda and Patricia to see them fighting. So they send them to bed with assurances that everything will be all right. Mary goes into the kitchen, grabs the gallon bucket of chocolate ice cream from the freezer and steps over to the dish cabinet and lifts the biggest bowl she can find from the shelf, piles it with ice cream and squirts chocolate syrup all over the top. Chocolate on chocolate. If she had sprinkles she'd put that on too.

Buddy is standing by the window digging fingernails into the meaty butt of his palms. He turns to the end table where he keeps his keys and change and pocket knife in a bowl, scoops them up and stuffs them in his pocket and walks out the door. "Don't wait up."

She carries her bowl of ice cream into the den and turns on the TV, flips through channels in search of an old movie. Her hands shake when she spoons the ice cream into her mouth. She hears the Jaguar start up and shortly after the squeal of tires.

He cranks the window down and feels the wind whip his hair, pounds his palm on the steering wheel to the tune in his head, some disco tune. He doesn't know the words. Soon he's at Little Don's nursing a beer at the counter. Keeps picking the beer bottle up and moving it spot to spot like it's his one remaining knight in a game of chess and he can't decide where to put it in order to threaten the black queen. He's creating a puddle of condensation rings on the countertop.

In a corner booth sit two men he vaguely recognizes. He thinks they work at the shipyard, probably just off shift. They work around the clock down there. Four teenage couples are in the booth next to them. Beulah's working behind the counter. She comes over to wipe up the water in front of Buddy. There goes his chess game. He eyes her ample cleavage. She keeps wiping the counter and he thinks she must know what he's looking at. Seems like she wants him to take a look. Her arms are chubby. A tattoo of a linked chain encircles her bicep, black ink on milk chocolate flesh. He thinks that if she weren't so darn near being a member of the family he might just put a move on. He's thinking she's looking better by the minute. This is not the first time he's thought about what's under those T-shirts and the tight jeans she always wears. If she was willing, would he? He knows he shouldn't but thinks he probably would.

"Want another?" she asks.

"Yeah, just one more. I oughta be getting on home pretty soon."

"Yeah, it's kinda late for a family man to be out all on his lonesome." She knows Buddy's reputation. She thinks it's kind of her duty as the girls' babysitter to remind him of his responsibilities. She asks, "Everything okay at home?"

"Oh yeah, just fine."

She pops open another bottle and sets it in front of him.

"Thanks, honey."

It's after midnight. Beulah's just waiting for the last customers to leave so she can lock up. The teenagers have already left. Nobody's there but the guys from the shipyard. One of them sticks spread fingers in his mouth and gives Beulah a whistle. Buddy watches her walk over, order pad in hand, looking plump and inviting from behind. The guys in the booth are flirting with her. They call her honey. They've got no right to call her honey, he thinks. *He's* got the right, but not them. One of them asks if she'd like to go out jukin' after she closes. "Thanks but no thanks," she says. "I'm pretty wore out, and I got classes in the morning."

The man on the side nearest to her looks like a scarecrow, got an old beat-up fedora cocked back on his head and jeans worn nearly white at the knees. He's wearing a corduroy sports coat with elbow patches. Buddy thinks that's the wrong look for a working man. Maybe he's a professor out slumming. He reaches for an inside pocket and pulls out a whiskey flask, pours a little in his coffee. "Care for a little snort, honey?" he asks.

"No thanks."

They ask what's for dessert.

"We got cobbler, peach or apple, and sweet potato pie."

"You got some ice cream to go on that cobbler?"

"Sure."

The skinny man puts a hand on her leg. She flinches away. He says, "Hey now, don't be so skittish, sweetie. I's just tryin' to be friendly like," and he puts his hand on her leg again.

Before she can scoot out of the way Buddy is there by her side. He doesn't say a word, but growls like a dog, a low and rumbling growl. He may not be the biggest man in town, but there's an icy glare to his eyes that's enough to give pause to the most foolhardy of men. The scarecrow slowly removes his hand, holds both hands up palms out to show he's backing off. But the other guy in the booth is not intimidated in the least by Buddy's maddog growl. Maybe he doesn't see the killer glare. Maybe he's just stupid. He reaches into his pocket and pulls out a switchblade and shows it to Buddy. He says, "Mister, you step back now and everything will be just hunky dory."

In a move so fast nobody sees what's happening, Buddy darts around Beulah and has an arm around the knife man and has his own knife in hand and at the startled man's throat. "Now here's what's going to happen," he says, "You're gonna leave that little pea sticker on the table, and we're gonna walk real slow out the door and ya'll are gonna get in your pickup and drive on the hell away and outta here."

"Yessir," they both say.

Buddy's hands are shaking and his voice trembles slightly, but the two men haven't noticed and he hopes they won't. Or that they don't foolishly mistake his adrenaline rush for fear. They don't. He walks them to the door and they take off. After they're gone Buddy says to Beulah, "I think it's about time you close up for the night."

"Oh yeah," she agrees. "I'm more than ready."

"Does this kind of thing happen often?"

"No, never. It's hardly ever anybody comes in here that I don't already know."

He offers to stick around until she closes. She thanks him for his help, and when he walks her to her car after she locks up, she stands on tip-toe and plants a kiss on his cheek, says, "You're my knight in shining armor tonight."

He follows her down Liberty to Freedom Lane and half a mile south to where she turns into her daddy's driveway. He toots his horn and waves as he passes by, then he heads on down to the coast and to the strip. He cruises the strip for a while and pulls up to the curb not far from the Rough Rider and shuts the motor off and lets the seat back to a reclining position. He's got his eye on a prostitute standing under the amber glow of a street lamp about thirty yards ahead. She has long legs and tight little silvery-looking shorts. Some kind of jacket, open in front with flouncy sleeves, looks like what flamingo dancers wear. A halter top underneath. It's unusually humid for this time of night. Buddy breaks out in a sweat. He unbuttons his shirt, lets it hang open, what little breeze there is licking his bare chest. He thinks, what if I got buck ass naked right here in the car, right here in public? Wouldn't that be wild? He slips a hand into his trousers. I could do it, he thinks. Do I have the nerve? Nah, maybe not. With my luck, a damn cop would catch me. I can see myself tryin' to explain it to Mary.

He watches the whore on the corner. Argues with himself over whether to pick her up or not. Bargains with himself. *I'll give it five minutes. If nobody else picks her up by then, I will. If they do, then I'll head on home.* And then: *One of these days, sooner than, later Mary's going find out. Somehow. She caught me the one time and I promised it'd never happen again. Man, would that ever come back and bite me on the butt.*

He pops open the snap on his pants (he's not wearing a belt) and unzips. Wiggles his pants down far enough that he's open to the night air. Nobody could tell unless they stuck their head in the window, and the whores are the only ones that do that. He looks at the dashboard clock. Three minutes have passed since he struck the five-minute bargain. He knows he doesn't really want the whore. It's not desire that's brought him to this. It never has been. It's compulsion. Something he doesn't seem to have any control over. He thinks of the possible side effects. So far, none. Nada. Not counting the one time Mary walked in on him. But she forgave him then, and he knows that if it comes down to it she will again— probably. The worst possible thing he can think of is catching some kind of STD, maybe even infecting Mary. But in spite of reason Buddy is convinced that nothing like that could ever happen to him, just like his crazy in-laws are convinced they can ride out a hurricane. His reasoning is that not the next time but the time after that could be the fatal one, so he'll just do it this one time and never again.

He can lie to himself, but he doesn't believe his lies. This time his better judgment wins out. He zips up, pulls his seat back into driving position and drives home. He congratulates himself for licking his compulsion, but he knows deep down that he hasn't really beat it, that he never will.

*

There are plenty of preparations to be made. Shelly gets on the phone and invites everyone she can think of who might want to come or who would feel slighted if they weren't invited. "I understand. Yes, yes, that's all right," she says to person after person who tells her they're escaping from the path of the storm. The day before the party Shelly makes a trip to the fish market and buys oysters and shrimp freshly pulled from the water. Everything else they get from their usual wholesalers: buckets of potato salad and coleslaw, frozen hamburger patties, hot dogs and buns, assorted chips, pickles, relish, mayonnaise and ketchup. Pop orders the beer, cases of three different brands: Schlitz, Jax and Budweiser, none of which David can stomach, so David and Sue Ellen drive store-to-store in search of drinkable beer, finally purchasing a six pack of Heineken at a store on the coast highway. It's not his favorite but it'll do.

*

More than ever, everyone within a hundred miles of the coast is glued to Weatherman Donny's "Storm Tracker" updates. Donny talks about tropical depressions and wind speed and surface analysis and satellite imagery, and his predictions keep changing and his viewers begin to think he doesn't know what he's talking about. They *hope* he doesn't know what he's talking about, and then again they hope he does, depending on his latest projection.

Many of Weatherman Donny's loyal viewers watch him from Little Don's, where they find comfort in the company of neighbors. It's standing room only. Everyone's talking about the storm. People are already starting to flee. Cars filled with evacuees and their hastily packed belongings clog the highways.

David and Buddy and Freight Train and Abdul sandbag around the store and nail plywood sheets to the windows; they spend all day Thursday and Friday going from house to house and store to store helping others secure against the coming surge of wind and water. Back at the Lawrence house they put plywood sheets on the sliding glass doors to the back deck. A single sheet covers all but a three-foot area where they can slip out onto the deck if they want to and duck back inside if and when the surge hits. They board up all the windows on the bay side, leaving the windows on the road side uncovered because they know which direction the wind will blow, and they want to be able to see the store across the street.

Jimmy Dale Patterson and his and Sue Ellen's boys have volunteered to help set up a Red Cross shelter thirty miles north in Saucier. They make trips back and forth hauling food and blankets and other goods in Jimmy Dale's pickup. Their daughter, Jeri, has gone to Laurel to stay with a cousin on her daddy's side of the family.

For those who are waiting for something to happen, minutes are like hours, and for those who are frantically preparing to secure their belongings and get out of town before the storm hits, hours are like minutes. For two days the storm swirls in a holding pattern off the coast of Florida feeding like a voracious animal on warm tropical air. Weatherman Donny says it will start to move north by northwest sometime Thursday afternoon and hit the coast between Miami and Fort Lauderdale at about midnight. That is the most likely scenario, Weatherman Donny says. Sustained winds at that time are expected to be around eighty to ninety miles per hour and gradually die down as the storm heads into Georgia. That's if it continues on a northerly path. If it takes the more westerly course it will cross the Florida peninsula and head into the Gulf of Mexico, where wind speeds can conceivably increase to as much as two-hundred miles per hour. The slower it moves to the northwest, the stronger it will become, a monster devouring energy pills in the form of tropical air.

At one o'clock Friday morning winds of up to one hundred miles per hour hit a small town on the Florida coast right on one of Weatherman Donny's projected paths. Store awnings are ripped to shreds and tin sheets fly down Main Street like serrated swords, fortunately not hitting a living soul since the downtown is deserted. Power lines down. Lights out throughout a ninety-mile swath of South Florida running east to west from Boca Rotan to Cape Coral. Palm trees stripped of their branches. Tons of beachfront sand lifted by wind and pounded back down by rain, but few human eyes to see it in the dark of night as there are no major cities in the hardest-hit areas. Florida residents will thank God for sparing them, unmindful of how capricious God must be. God rides a gale from the Caymans to Cuba, from Puerto Rico to Florida. He reaches down and lifts a boat from its mooring, destroying forever the livelihood of a poor fisherman's family; He rips up acres of sugar plantations and floods towns and villages and kills a few dark skinned men, but mercifully spares good Floridians who will live to praise His name while being interviewed for the evening news.

The storm loses strength as it crosses land, but builds up again when it heads northwest over the Gulf of Mexico.

Not many people in Freedom are watching television at daybreak when the local station interrupts the morning show with a breaking news story. "The Channel 7 news team is sad to say we've lost one of our own. Donald Sizemore, affectionately known around here as Weatherman Donny, passed away during the night. He was found by his wife of thirty-eight years, Sarah Sizemore, slumped over his desk, his head resting on a weather chart. The cause of death: apparently a heart attack. Weatherman Donny died doing what he loved, tracking a storm. The storm, which we at Channel 7 will forever after think of as Donny's storm, caused an estimated three million dollars in property damage to the state of Florida and is now headed right toward us with renewed strength. It's a shame that Weatherman Donny did not live to ride it out. Those of us here in the Channel 7 newsroom who knew and loved Donny will always picture him standing in front of an ocean pier, microphone in hand, barely able to stand upright in the wind and rain. Giving it his all for you the viewer.

"This storm is expected to make landfall within hours. If you have not already evacuated the area, stay inside and stay tuned to Channel 7. If we should go off the air tune your battery operated radios to the national emergency broadcast network."

*

"Well crapola, where the hell are all the people?" Pop demands to know when no one but family members and a few close friends show up for breakfast Friday morning. "I never known Freedom folks to be so fucking lily livered."

David quips, "I never knew 'em to be so fucking smart."

The residents of Freedom have ridden out one hurricane too many. Each of the last three storms has been stronger than predicted, so now many of the brave souls who used to routinely ride them out have taken flight.

The only people at the party are David, Sue Ellen, Mary, Pop, Shelly, Beulah, Abdul, Freight Train and Melissa. Nevertheless, they're in a party mood. With Channel 7 off the air and none of them knowing yet that Weatherman Donny has died, they tune in to a New Orleans station that is tracking the hurricane. Now listed as a category three, it is south of Mobile and headed northwest, expected to hit land near the Mississippi-Louisiana border. Florida was just a warm-up.

Outside the Lawrence house trees and grass bend in the wind and clouds race overhead. Thunder booms to the southeast. Waves pound against the retaining wall between the house and the bay, a wall that was erected after the last big flood but which, rather than preventing another flood, is sure to trap any water that does get in and keep it from flushing out into the gulf. Spray spouts high above the bulkhead.

Shelly dishes up pancakes, scrambled eggs, sausage and bacon with fluffy biscuits, and everybody eats—some at the kitchen table and some from lap-balanced plates in the living room, protected from the storm by the plywood sheets David and Abdul have nailed up. Overhead lights burn brightly. On the television hoards of twelve-year-olds in New York are now screaming at some boy band playing in Central Park, oblivious to what's going on twelve hundred miles south.

David stands by the door for a few minutes, balancing a plate in one hand and forking bites of pancake while watching the intermittent waves of spray over the seawall. He turns to face the room and says, "Sue Ellen and I have something to tell everybody." His words, with their solemn weight of pronouncement, capture everyone's attention. He says, "Sue Ellen's going to return home to L.A. with me. We're leaving Sunday. That's assuming the airports will still be operating and we survive Pop's little party."

"That's wonderful," Shelly says. "Is there a wedding in your plans?"

"Nah, they're just gonna shack up," Mary teases.

David and Sue Ellen explain that, no, they're not getting married. It's just going to be a trial run to see how things might work out (if, David thinks, he can figure out how to get Jasmine Jones out of his life). He knows everybody else is also wondering what he's going to do about his live-in, movie star girlfriend. Lord knows he and Sue Ellen have talked about it, but not in any great depth, and he knows his mother will worry about the morality of the whole thing and fear for his eternal soul—not to mention that he might hurt someone or be hurt. He knows that Jasmine already suspects something, but he really can't imagine how she might react. David's thoughts zoom through labyrinthine paths:

First the clothes again, Jasmine's clothes. He wonders why it is that every time he thinks about Jasmine he pictures her freakin' clothes. The black strapless, the six bikinis on hangers, a whole wardrobe of shorts and halters, the tight jeans and the loose jeans, the no telling how many shoes. Maybe because her stuff takes up nine-tenths of the hangers in their closet and most of the drawers in their dresser. He cleared out a drawer for her when she first started staying over nights, and then her stuff started spreading like algae in a lake. But her clothes aren't the half of it. Jasmine's all over the house. Her cosmetics in the bathroom, her jewelry. Her scent. A million e-mail messages in David's in-box signed Jaz. He imagines the first thing Sue Ellen will want to do when they get home will be to use his computer to check her own e-mail. So first thing she'll see will be a bunch of e-mails from jaz@aol.com. Any doubt who jaz@aol.com is? No way. She won't snoop, Sue Ellen's not like that; but seeing those e-mails will be a reminder of Jasmine's constancy in his life.

He knows there must be countless other reminders of Jasmine he can't even think of. Jasmine wouldn't have packed much for London. She'd have bought new stuff when she got there. Everything else will be at home. Maybe Sue Ellen could wear some of her stuff. She'd look good in that black dress Jasmine wore to the Academy Awards. But oh no, he thinks, that's way too much. Then there's—oh God, her diaphragm and contraceptive gel. Probably right there on top of the freakin' bedside table. Jaz wouldn't have even thought to put them in the drawer. She's so casual about that stuff. Besides, she'd never have thought about somebody else in their bedroom while she was gone. *It's not as if Sue Ellen doesn't already know we were sleeping together, but I don't want to slap her in the face with the evidence. Maybe Jasmine took that stuff with her. But why would she? That would mean she was thinking about getting laid in London. Well hell, I wouldn't put it past her. At least that would make the breakup easier.* And that thought spurs him to wonder just exactly how he is going to break it to her. In person? Clearly he can't do it over the phone. That just wouldn't be right. Maybe by e-mail? God, no. That would be a chicken's way out. No, it's got to be in person. He reassures himself that she'll take it just fine. Hell, she's probably thinking about how to break it off with me, he thinks. Or weighing the pros and cons between David and Spike Love.

He knows he'll never be able to work it out. When the time comes, he'll simply have to face Jasmine and play it by ear. He tells himself he'll have to be gentle with her.

*

First Abdul and Beulah and then Pop and David and Sue Ellen slip out on the deck to watch the majesty of the storm. There's electricity in the air, literally and figuratively. Crackling lightning in the distance. Pop brags that the new double pane windows are built to withstand a hurricane. Boards underfoot are slippery and Beulah skates on her rear end toward the railing when a gust of wind catches her unexpectedly. Both David and Abdul grab her and help her back to her feet. "Wow!" she exclaims. "That was something."

Everybody hugs the house. There's a half roof over the deck to protect them from rain and sun, but even up close to the house salty spray gets in their mouths and their eyes. Soon the battering of wind and rain becomes too strong for them to stay out on the deck, and they all go back inside. "I think we better board it the rest of the way," David says.

"Good idea," Pop says.

David asks Freight Train to give him a hand, and they gather hammer and nails and a half sheet of plywood from Pop's workshop. The workshop in the back of the garage opens onto a walkway along the side of the house, which gives them access to the deck and a way to get back in after they're done tacking up the plywood.

For about an hour none of them have very much to say to each other. They've exhausted the topic of David and Sue Ellen's romance, and they're just waiting for the next step in the storm. They can't see outside on the bayou side of the house now that the windows and doors on that side are boarded up, but on the side facing the road they watch the moving shadow of an oak tree, and every once in a while they see some object go hurling past, mostly things they can't identify in the few seconds it takes for them to sail by.

"When's it supposed to hit?" Mary asks.

"This is it," David answers. "Or at least this is the outer edge. I mean we're in it for the long haul."

Sue Ellen says, "It doesn't seem so strong."

"You weren't here for the last one," Pop says. He explains: "It's not like just one big blow and it's over. It could be hours. It's cumulative. It's like the big bad wolf trying to blow the house down, only in this case he doesn't give up after three measly huffs and puffs."

The distance from the eye of the storm, still out over the gulf, to its outer edge, which is already battering Freedom, and the ten- to twelve-foot-high waves of the storm surge, which is beginning to wash across Interstate 10, is about seventy miles. That means the whole witch's cauldron of mighty wind and rain covers an area 140 miles in diameter. To people who are easily frightened it's the wrath of God, but to those crazy, crazy people who are intoxicated by danger—and God knows there's more than a bit of that within the Lawrence household—it's like a big hit of mescaline or crack cocaine; it's like dancing to the beat of frenzied drums; it's an aphrodisiac. David and Sue Ellen keep eying the hallway thinking about the big bed in Mary's old room and remembering the last time they rode out a hurricane together.

Eighty miles north in Hattiesburg, all the fraternities and sororities at the University of Southern Mississippi are having parties. Daylight parties starting at an hour when they're usually still asleep.

They've brought in beer kegs and tapped them, and two of the frat houses have hired rock and roll bands for the occasion. Outside on campus a rag-tag contingent of the school's marching band is marching around campus playing disco tunes. At the Alpha Tau Omega house everyone's decked out in classic Roman togas (some traditions never die). The boys at the Kappa Alpha house across the street have rented a slew of disaster movies and are having a marathon movie fest. And the Phi Kappa Alphas plan to streak from fraternity row to the Hub and back at the peak of the storm—carrying a stolen ATΩ flag to pin it on the rival fraternity.

More beer kegs are in play on the beach at Pensacola, where sailors from the naval base are trying to keep a giant bonfire going in the rain.

In the basement of one of the old antebellum homes in Biloxi a dozen college students sit in a large circle on the floor and pass around bottles of whiskey and vodka while playing strip poker. One of the boys is already completely naked, so he's out of the game but still allowed to sit in the circle, and two of the girls are down to panties and bras, and one of them is about to lose her top and her composure, and when she flings off her bra she is going to start screaming, "We're gonna die! We're gonna die!" and everyone will think she's playing, but she won't be.

In the cafeteria at Coastal Medical Center where Pop had his bypass Doctor Duval is drinking a cup of decaf coffee and listening to weather reports on a radio station in Jackson. The hospital is running on emergency power, and Doctor Duval has cancelled a scheduled angioplasty, but will make his regular rounds to check on his patients and is on call with the emergency center.

Inside the closed and boarded-up Piggly Wiggly store in Freedom, Malcolm Ashton hunkers down in the employee's lounge with one other employee, Fred Dalton, his supervisor. They are armed with shotguns and are prepared to fend off looters. From their position inside they can hear the constant battering of wind and rain outside. Malcolm is cold. His hands are shaking. He keeps glancing Fred's way, trying to ascertain if his boss can tell he's scared. He wouldn't want to be thought a coward. Fred has not noticed Malcolm's nervousness but would not think badly of him if he did. And he would not believe it if someone told him that twenty-five years earlier Malcolm had been one of the young hoodlums who looted the town during a flood. After that, Malcolm had been caught holding up a 7-Eleven and spent five months in a juvenile detention center, and two years after that he had spent time in the penitentiary farm up north in Parchman for robbing a gas station and had gone through a twelve-step program for drug addiction. Finally clean and sober, he got a job as a stock boy at the Piggly Wiggly and married Bitsy Gardner and had three children, and has remained responsible and out of trouble ever since.

At the Lawrence house the doorbell rings. Shelly, who is stacking dishes in the kitchen, goes to answer it. It's Randy Moss. He's wearing a yellow slicker over his uniform. Static blares from the radio hooked to a strap on his shoulder. A waterfall cascades off the brim of his hat. His pants are dark with water halfway to his knees, as if he's been wading. "Are you folks all right?" he asks, huffing heavily.

"We're fine. Why don't you come on in?" Shelly says.

"Well, okay, but just for a little while. I'm on duty. I'm going house-to-house checking on folks."

"I heard everybody else cleared out long ago."

"Yes'um, that's about right. But 'cept there's probably some holdouts here and there."

"Well you ain't likely to find them now and couldn't do nothing for them anyway, so you might as well hang around. Come on in. Set a spell. I think we still got some eggs and sausage left, if you'd like. There's coffee in the pot."

Randy glances over Shelly's shoulder. He's standing in the foyer, which is next to the hallway and the stairs, and which is connected to the kitchen by an open archway. Through the arch he can see the coffee pot and piled remnants of breakfast. To his right is the large front room where all the others are gathered. They haven't yet acknowledged him. Randy stomps his boots to shake off the water.

"Don't worry about the water," Shelly says.

He shucks out of his rain slicker and hands it to her, and she drapes it on a hook in the vestibule. "I could use a shot of coffee," he says.

"Go on back to the kitchen and help yourself."

He goes through the archway instead of through the open front room. His boots squeak on the hardwood floor. He helps himself to coffee and then looks up as if slapped by the awkward silence. In the living area a few steps away from where he's standing with cup in hand, all talk has stopped. They're all staring at him. He says, "Oh, hi. Um, Shelly asked me to come in."

Not everyone returns his greeting. Pop and Freight Train are cordial but not overly friendly. David and Mary refuse to speak to him. Melissa turns her back on him and walks into the kitchen, brushing right past him, pours herself a big shot of straight whiskey and swigs it down, and then pours herself another and carries it down the hallway. She goes into a bedroom and kicks the door shut behind her.

A huge crack of thunder shakes the house. Outside the sky is almost as dark as night, but floodlights aimed at the front walk and out across the bay from the deserted deck highlight sheets of sideways rain that look like shimmering mercury. Another loud thunder boom rattles the house, and the lights go out. For a moment it is pitch black inside, until their eyes gradually adjust. Pop says, "David, go crank up the generator."

David heads out to the garage, where he starts up the generator. The lights come back on. Shelly wanders back to the bedroom, taps on the door and opens it. Melissa is sitting on the edge of the bed holding her drink in her hands. Her eyes are red. Shelly says, "Sweetie, how come you're in here drinking all alone? You're not going to let that Randy Moss ruin your day now, are you? You can't let your resentment ruin you."

"What do you mean?"

"I mean running away every time he comes around. I mean letting what's inside boil up like that water out there in the crab pot. Hiding from him don't hurt him one little bit, honey. You're the one it hurts. I know how you feel, and if you want to know the truth, I think you oughta confront him. Tell him why you're mad at him. Tell him right here in front of God and everybody. And then, as hard as it might seem, you got to forgive him. That's the only thing that'll bring you any peace. But whatever you do, you got to quit hiding from him. Look at what all you done missed 'cause a hiding from him. You missed Little Don's anniversary barbeque because you knew Randy was going to be there. You didn't even go to Barbara Brady's wedding for the same reason. You made up a stupid excuse that she seen right through, and now she's mad at you, and it's all because of him. You couldn't even stay in the room with us at the hospital when he came to visit. You went down to the cafeteria and sat there all by your lonesome. It's time you set it right with him. Get it all right out there in the open and deal with it."

For the longest time she doesn't react. She continues to stare at the drink in her hand. Then she looks up and there's a flicker of a smile, and she lifts her shoulders and looks Shelly fully in the eye and says, "You're right. Damn if you ain't. I'm going to do it. Right now."

"That a girl."

She tosses the rest of her drink down.

Outside the wind is growing stronger. Rain hits the deck like a hundred million spears of ice. The aluminum boat tied to the pier breaks loose and flies toward the house, crashing into the beams supporting the back deck. Inside they hear the crashing noise and feel the house buckle like an old man given out at the knees. But they can't see out because of the plywood. Pop laughs, "Don't know what the fuck just got busted, but at least we're still standing."

In the kitchen Melissa pours herself another drink, her third in fifteen minutes, and marches into the front room. "Hey everybody, listen up," she shouts over the howling wind. "We're going to play a game. It's called guess who's guilty. Y'all ever heard of that game?" The tone of her voice is manic, higher pitched than usual and unsteady. Shelly has followed her and stands close behind as if to prop her up.

Everyone stares at her in stunned silence, all but Pop who says, "Naw, I never heard of that game. How's it go?"

Melissa takes a stand in front of the fireplace, legs spread, chest outthrust. She says, "It's real simple. Everybody has to think of somebody they know who's guilty as hell about something. Anything. It don't matter what. Everybody's got a secret on somebody. So you tell the secret and then everybody's got to guess who's the guilty party."

She eyeballs person after person as if daring each not to chicken out. David breaks out in a beaming smile. He knows what's coming and he loves it. Randy senses what's coming, too. He says, "I don't know if y'all want to play this game."

"Shut up, asshole," Melissa hisses at him. "You don't get a say in this."

She pauses. Everybody waits. Randy looks like he's about to throw up. Melissa says, "I get to go first." She takes another swig of her drink and wipes her mouth with her sleeve. She says, "There was this guy, see, a white guy. It's important to know he was a white guy because he was a racist pig and…"

And she gets no further because a deafening roar like that of a speeding locomotive silences all speech. The air outside is a solid sheet of hurling water and debris as trees and shrubs and parts of piers on the bayou are lifted up and the retaining wall below the house breaks apart and chunks of concrete and dirt fly against the house. David shouts, "Get down!" He grabs Sue Ellen and dives to the floor with her as a sheet of wind and water slams against the back windows and glass shards from the hurricane-proof windows fly inward and pieces of trees and other debris come hurling into the house. Voices scream and bodies fly and the lights go out once again, and water gushes into the downstairs of the house. With a deafening sound of ripping and tearing, the whole house tilts like a giant gyroscope loosened from its moorings and tumbles down the embankment and into the bayou and spins like a stick caught in a whirlpool while David and Sue Ellen and Pop and Shelly and Melissa and Mary and Randy and Freight Train and Abdul and Beulah are tossed about like dice and deluged with water, water, water. The house is carried downstream to where, after just a few minutes, it slams to a stop in the cove a hundred yards south of where it once stood, jammed against a dam of fallen trees and the debris from their neighbors' homes.

Inside the house bodies are at the mercy of raging water for what seems like fifteen or twenty minutes of deafening chaos. Heads bob up like corks. They grab blindly for anything that might offer some stability and crab their way toward the stairway. Somehow most of them manage to find solid footing on the stairs leading up to the second floor, where they bobble while grasping the railing and holding each other. The wind outside has passed over and is heading farther inland. The brunt of the storm has passed. Their topsy-turvy world becomes quiet and still. Are they in the eye now or has it passed over? Nobody can even guess. Heads barely above water, they see that all around them the floodwater fills every space all the way to the first floor ceiling. The stairwell where they cling to each other is at an odd angle, almost parallel to what should be the floor's normal orientation. Light from outside filters in on oddly-angled beams, and throughout the house there is an eerie, dull greenish glow. David's eyes are still clinched shut from being underwater. He feels a throbbing pain in his left leg, and when he opens his eyes he sees that blood is oozing from a cut on his leg and another on his hand. His injuries seem minor. He sees silhouettes of bodies bobbing in the water around him like oil drums afloat. Everyone is scrambling toward the upstairs rooms. His foot grazes something soft. A body. He reaches down and feels around until he can grab an arm and lift. Fingers clutch his hand. Whoever it is is still alive. He pulls. Sue Ellen surfaces like a spouting dolphin, sputtering, gasping for breath. They can barely see. David and Sue Ellen support each other as they look for the others. They spot Shelly a few steps above them. She too is searching for heads above water. "Is everybody here?" David asks.

Mary, Randy and Beulah, Freight Train, they all speak up. They're clustered close together. "Pop's not here," Mary says, and Randy says, "Melissa. Where's Melissa?"

David immediately responds by diving underwater to search for Pop and Melissa. He knows he's got to find them fast if he's going to save them. Randy knows, too. Randy may have grown fat and slovenly and hateful, but he is still a law enforcement officer who, in addition to taking bribes and arresting bad guys (and sometimes not so bad guys) also saves lives in natural disasters, plus he is the man who once was the boy who used to race David underwater. He calls on whatever strength he still retains.

They swim through rubble, vision cloudy in the underwater world within the house. Nothing is recognizable. Nothing seems to be properly oriented with anything else. Diffracted light swims in odd channels illuminating unrecognizable furnishings. David is holding his breath. He turns to his right, pushes aside an overturned chair, sees nobody, turns to his left, sees Melissa in a doorway, her skirt and hair flowing clumps of seaweed. There is something holding her down. It looks like a broken door or window frame jammed into the doorway. He tries to push it away. His chest is beginning to hurt. He feels another body, cold and wet, slithering up against him. He turns to look and sees that it is Randy. He's reaching to tug Melissa free. They tug together, tug and tug and tug, trying to free her from her underwater entrapment. David can feel the pressure in his own lungs, and he knows Melissa has been underwater even longer. She's probably passed out already, lungs filled with water. She can't move, and they can't pull loose whatever it is that has her trapped. And David still hasn't seen his father. He knows he's got to help Randy free Melissa first. The first rule of triage: help the ones that can be helped, and then, if necessary, retrieve the bodies. He grabs hold of the splintered two-by-four that's jammed in the doorway and gives it a hard yank. It doesn't budge. He taps Randy on the shoulder and signals with a pumping motion for him to push the top part while he pulls the bottom sideways. He hopes Randy can read his signal. He jerks sideways. Nothing moves. He does it again. This time Randy has guessed what he's trying to do and puts his shoulder against the top of the door and pushes, and the whole thing gives way and floats upward to bump bump bump against the ceiling where there is about three inches of air above the water's surface. Randy and David quickly surface to swallow air and dive again and grab Melissa and free her, and David swims with her to the stairs.

Once he's halfway up the stairs and able to stick his head out of water. David says, "Take her from here." He's gulping air so desperately he can barely speak, but Randy gets the message. He drags Melissa upstairs and lays her out on the floor and begins blowing in her mouth and pushing on her chest. David gulps as much air as he can and dives underwater again.

In the upstairs hallway water gushes out of Melissa's mouth and she coughs violently and vomits up bits of egg and sausage. Randy smells the whiskey she drank. He wipes her mouth with the wet tail of his shirt.

In the murk below, David swims froglike through the house. Not only can he barely see, not only does nothing look familiar, but he feels disoriented to the point that he's not sure which direction is which. He tries to visualize: come downstairs, turn left through the archway into the kitchen or to the right into the living room area. If the house is turned around, he wonders, would that mean left is right and right is left? No, of course not, he decides. But what difference would it make anyway? Pop was in the living room when the surge hit, but he could have been washed into any other room or even out of the house. He could be halfway down to Bilbo Bayou. Or would it be *up* to Bilbo Bayou now? Again irrelevant, he tells himself, his stupid mind going bonkers, maybe from lack of oxygen. If David could see outside and if there were anything familiar out there with which to orient himself, which there may or may not be following a hurricane, he would know that the house was tipped partially to one side and is jammed with its south wall against the shore of Walker Cove half a mile south of where it stood before the storm hit. If he could somehow get out on the roof or onto the deck, he could jump to the ground. But no he couldn't. Because the ground would be ten feet underwater, just as the first floor of the house is. But if he could, what would he do then? Go for help? Where? The rest of Freedom is surely long since evacuated, so where would he look for help? It drives him crazy that he can't think clearly. He begins to panic. The simplest thought processes seem impossible. Nothing makes sense. He tells himself to calm down. Think. All of this time while he is trying to sort out his thoughts he is underwater, moving aimlessly, not so much swimming as propelling himself by pushing and pulling in and around chairs and tables and careening off walls. Boiled shrimp and hamburger patties swim with the fishes. He surfaces as best he can, gasping air in the few inches by the ceiling, and then dives again. He sees something huge and black in the muddy water. It's his mother's grand piano. It's turned sideways against a wall. The top of the piano has broken loose and is floating against the ceiling, but the mass of it is jammed underwater. He sees Pop's leg protruding from beneath the piano. He knows he can't lift it. Even if he were on dry land he couldn't get a firm footing to lift it. But if he could just break it loose from whatever was jamming it, wouldn't it simply float up? Does he have the strength to work it loose? Everyone knows that people are capable of inhuman feats of strength at such times. Who knows? Why not at least try? He grabs an edge of the piano and lifts, but of course it does not budge. Then he sees another body coming toward him. It's Randy. He's already helped save Melissa, and now he's diving in to help save Pop. He swims up alongside David and they nod heads in recognition that together they can do it. Friends or enemies, they nevertheless spent their youth together in these waters swimming long distances, holding their breath ungodly lengths of time and building the kind of strength and determination that just might help them conquer this challenge. Never mind that Randy has put on thirty pounds of pure fat and his once powerful muscles have gone to flab. They push together but they cannot move the piano. And then they see something that scares them both half to death. A giant fish has somehow gotten into the house, probably swimming right through the broken back door. It looks like a small whale or a dolphin. Oh God! Could it be a shark? It's coming right at them, and just when they are sure it is going to ram into them, they realize that it's not a fish at all. It is Freight Train Taylor, all three hundred pounds of him. With Freight Train's added heft they are able to push the piano off, and David lifts Pop and swims with him to the stairs. They carry him up to the second floor bedroom where Abdul and the women wait, and Shelly begins trying to resuscitate him.

Melissa, still groggy, lies on the bed, which is damp but still upright and jammed at an odd angle in a corner of the room. She shivers under heavy blankets. From the big cedar chest in the master bedroom Abdul and Beulah have dug blankets out for everyone. They're damp but better than nothing. David crawls to the bed and slings his arms across Melissa and rests his head next to hers on the big pillow, cheeks touching, and between deep gasping breaths asks, "Are you all right?"

"Y-ya-ya-Yeah, I'm f-f-f-f-fine. What about Pop?"

"I don't know."

Shelly has wrapped her arms around Pop from behind. She's trying to perform the Heimlich maneuver, jerking him around like a rag doll despite their huge difference in size. Dirty water mixed with undigested bits of shrimp leak from his mouth. She uses his own watersoaked shirt to clean up the vomit as she places him on his back and begins CPR.

Randy falls on the floor with his head propped against a wall and, like David, gasps to restore normal breathing. Freight Train, not quite so winded, hunkers down on his knees to watch as Shelly attempts to breathe life into Pop. Sue Ellen, Mary, Abdul and Beulah all stand by anxiously. For the longest time no one speaks. They listen and watch as Shelly tries to bring her husband, their friend and father, back to life. Shelly knows the procedure. She has taken classes at the YWCA and has practiced on dummies. Now she practices on her husband, patiently, tirelessly. Two breaths and then pump on his chest thirty times, repeat, repeat, repeat. All of this is happening in the murky light filtering in from outside. It's not even noon yet but it seems to everyone in the house that it must be getting on late into the evening.

When Shelly gets too tired to keep blowing and pushing, Abdul takes over. He's never done CPR before but he's learned from watching Shelly. He bends over the body intently, his braids falling in front of his face. Shelly pulls the braids from in front of his eyes and loops them together on top of his head. "How's that?" she asks.

"That's—huff, huff, fine—five six seven—thanks..."

After a few minutes Mary says, "He's gone. Let him go."

But Abdul ignores her. She says, "This is not a movie. This is real life. There are no miracles here."

But Abdul keeps breathing life into the old man, pushing and blowing and counting, and Shelly prays out loud. She has no illusions. She doesn't expect God to answer her prayers. She's not even sure that she believes in God. Her prayer is not really a prayer so much as it is an expression of her desperation vented for relief. Over and over she mumbles, "Let him live, let him live" in rhythm with Abdul's pumping motion.

Miraculously, the old man does regain consciousness. He coughs and gags and shivers. Abdul turns his head to let the water leak out, and then they sit him up and then lift him up and carry him to the bed, where they lay him down beside Melissa who has now sat up in bed. She is firmly swaddled in blankets and her violent shivering has slacked off. Melissa cuddles close to Pop to warm him with her own slowly-returning body heat. Now everyone is swaddled and warmth returns.

Twenty minutes go by with no working clock to tick them off. Half an hour, an hour. Pop has not moved, and he has not said a word, but he is breathing shallowly. "Is he unconscious?" Shelly asks.

"I think he's just asleep," Melissa whispers. She places her ear to his chest. "I feel him breathing. I can hear his heartbeat. It's weak, but it's there."

Everyone else seems to have survived intact. They've inventoried their various cuts and bruises, the worst being a gash on David's thigh, which Shelly has bandaged. The wind outside has died down. The sound of gently lapping waves. What little light there is comes from gaps in the side of the house where planks have been ripped off and from a broken window that is jammed up against what seems to be part of the bridge connecting Freedom with East Freedom, a bridge that, by any sensible reckoning anyone in the house can come up with, should be half a mile north of where they are. If that's what the mess outside really is. Angled across the window is a wooden beam six to eight inches thick and webbed with a tangle of steel cable and tree limbs. It completely blocks what looks like their only possible means of escape. If Pop and Melissa could see the web of cables from their position in bed, they would surely be reminded of the tangle of cables that held Pop's car when he drove it off the Casino.

Abdul peeks out the window as best he can. There's not enough room for anyone to squeeze out. "If we could get out, it's just a short drop to the ground," he says.

"But where would we go if we could get out?" Mary asks.

"Nowhere, I don't guess. Everything's under water anyway," Abdul says.

There is only the one bedroom upstairs in the Lawrence house, and that is where they are all gathered together. There is an attic accessible by way of a drop-down ladder. "Reckon there's an opening up there?" Randy asks.

"Not unless something punched a hole in the roof," David says. "I'll have a look."

He climbs to the attic and soon comes back to report that there is no way to get out from there. The only window they can reach is blocked, and the whole downstairs is flooded. It is clearly understood by all that there will be no means of escape until the water drains from the house. David and Randy, both powerful swimmers, could possibly swim underwater long enough to find an escape, but the women may not be able to make it out, and Pop cannot move at all. He's barely alive. His breathing is shallow, and when Shelly attempts to take his pulse, it is but a weak echo of a failing heart. If they do not get medical help soon he will surely die.

The hazy light through the window grows sharper as clouds dissipate. Mary says, "What do we do now?"

"Wait for the water to go down," David says.

"And while we wait?"

"Well I guess we talk to each other," Melissa says. "We are still capable of that, aren't we?"

Randy uprights an overturned chair and sits in it. Freight Train settles against a wall. Everyone else crowds onto the bed with Pop and

Melissa. Pop has the appearance of the half-dead, as if all of his systems—
his heart, his lungs, his nerves—are on stand-by. The strain has taken a
toll. His head rests against Shelly's chest. Shelly strokes his forehead,
repeatedly brushing with her finger a lock of hair that keeps falling over
his eyes. She can't tie the thin strands up the way she did with Abdul. It is
almost as if there are two Shellys: the one who absent-mindedly nurses her
broken husband and another one who talks to her son and daughters and
friends. This second Shelly says, "I want to hear the rest of what Melissa
started back before the ruckus hit."

"Are you kidding?" Mary exclaims. "Surely this is not the time."

"What better time?" Shelly says. "If she's up to it. We're stuck
together here. Heck, in some ways we've always been stuck together. In
more ways than you can shake a stick at, I guess, throughout all our
natural born days. We're family, we're kin. Those of us that ain't blood kin
are still like family just 'cause we all been friends and neighbors since
practically forever."

She looks David in the eye. "If you got anything to say to your
daddy while he's still alive, whether he can hear you now or not, this is the
time to get it said."

"I thought you wanted to play Melissa's gotcha game."

"That too." She glances back down tenderly at her husband and
then locks eyes again with her son. She says, "You've hated your father for
so long, I don't think you even remember why."

"I never hated him, mama. I've just been pissed off at him as long as
I can remember."

"Say it to him, goddammit." Shelly challenges.

It's clear to David that as far as his mother is concerned this is the
end of something, a way of living, perhaps. Surely it's the end of Pop, and
she wants the air cleared while there's still time.

David looks at his father, whose eyes are closed and whose breath
is so shallow he can't even see his scrawny chest rise and fall, and he says,
"I don't hate you, daddy. But I've been mad at you for such a long time. I
just wanted you to once in your life say something nice to me. Why did

you always think you had to be so freakin' tough? I guess you thought you had to make a man out of me. Your kind of man, I guess. But you expected so much. I could never measure up. You don't have to be Genghis Khan to be a man, but I don't reckon you ever understood that."

For so many years that he can hardly remember when it started, he has harbored the belief that the old man beat his mother and might have even molested Mary when she was young, but after talking to each of them about that over the past few days he has come to realize that those are scenes he has constructed in his head as a way of justifying his hate. He doesn't need to justify it. He just needs to express it and get on with it. And now that his justification is gone, it takes too much effort to hold onto the hate. But he doesn't regret it either. He turns to his mama again. "I don't know what you want me to say. If you want me to say I love him, well I don't know if I can."

Shelly says, "I don't know either. Maybe what you said is enough. I guess I was looking for closure, but I don't really know what that is, if there's even any such a thing."

Melissa jumps in and says, "Well I want some closure. I didn't get finished before."

"Oh crap," Randy mutters.

Mary says, "This better not turn out to be like... what was the game in the old Elizabeth Taylor movie?"

"Hump the hostess," David provides.

"Yeah," Melissa says, all the anger from before coming back into her voice, "only in this case we can call it hump the nigger."

"We don't use that word in this house," Shelly snaps.

"Oh yes we do," Melissa shoots back. "This time we do."

Abdul, Beulah and Freight Train look both shocked and perplexed. They've never heard Melissa utter that forbidden word, and they've never heard such venom in her voice. David thinks: They don't know Melissa's history. They think they're the only black people in the house, and they're probably thinking that the one white person they thought they could most trust has turned on them. Beulah sits quietly next to Abdul. They are holding hands. David wonders if they are a couple and if so why hadn't he realized it. It seems he hasn't heard Beulah say half a dozen words since he met her that first night at dinner. Apropos of the situation, he thinks of the old saying still waters run deep. But the waters they find themselves in are anything but still. He worries that thought into a possible opening for a new monologue.

Randy stands up. He stands upright but appears, due to the orientation of the house, to be slantwise like a tree on a hill, holding the back of the chair for balance. He says to Melissa, "I'm the one that's guilty. Let me tell it."

Mary says, "No. Both of you. We all know, or most of us know. And we don't need to go into all of that now."

"Maybe y'all don't need to hear it but I need to say it," Melissa insists.

Surprisingly to those who know what is coming, even Randy insists. The past has to be aired. Randy says, "She started to tell a tale about a white man who was a bigot. That was me. I was that bigot."

"And you couldn't wait to get yourself some hot nigger ass," Melissa says. She sees Beulah cringe.

Randy admits, "No I couldn't. And I'm just as sorry as I can be." Then he tells the story. He confesses that twenty-five years ago he blackmailed Melissa into having sex with him and forced her to pretend being in love with him. He offers weak excuses of his youth at the time and the corrosive influence of his father, whom he admits was "a first class son of a bitch."

He says, "Ya'll know this by now, I guess. It was my old man that told me Sugar Rogers was her father, and I used that knowledge to get in her pants, and Melissa let me do what I did because she was afraid for her father. I thought it was 'cause she was ashamed of her Negro blood. Stupid, stupid me. Didn't matter how much they shouted about black pride, I didn't think anybody could actually be proud of being black. My old man and them had put so much race hate in my head that, hell, I just raped her and thought she had it coming. That's right, I raped her. Ain't nothing else to call it. She was just a mulatto to me, or octoroon or, you know, whatever part black blood she was. Just some fine light skinned nigger pussy. And I thought the reason she let me do it was 'cause she didn't want anybody to know what she was."

It is clear to everyone that he is using such offensive racist phrases as a way of lashing out at himself. He's painting himself in the worse possible light, because he sincerely regrets what he did. Mary and David, who have known him better than anyone, realize that the guilt he has carried all these years has been punishment enough. Even Melissa seems to soften toward him, if only a little.

"It's time to forgive and forget," Shelly says, but nobody responds.

For a long time no one else says anything. It has now been many hours since the storm surge hit. Time for confessions and recriminations seems to have come and gone. Randy says he is going to check on the water level downstairs. With everything still topsy-turvy in the house, he has to prop against furniture and walls to make his way down the hall to the stairs. He inches his way down into the water and out of sight of the others. David has a momentary thought that maybe Randy is going to kill himself. He seemed that despondent while confessing to blackmailing Melissa. He could just walk out into the water and never come up again. He thinks for a moment about going after him but decides that he has to trust Randy to do what he said he was going to do, which is to check the water level and come back.

While Randy is out of hearing Shelly asks Melissa, "Do you think you can ever forgive him?"

"I don't know," she says.

With a bitter chuckle David says, "Maybe he'll arrest himself."

Randy comes back upstairs and announces that the water has gone down enough for them to leave. "It's just about chest high to me," he says. "Might still be a little deep for Mrs. Lawrence and Beulah, but I think we can make it. We can carry Mr. Lawrence."

"There's no need to move Earl Ray," Shelly says. "He's gone."

"Gone?" David asks.

"Gone to his maker," Shelly says. "He gave up the ghost a while back. He just quit breathing. There wasn't any reason to tell you. He went peacefully."

Randy says, "We have to dispose of the body somehow."

"How?" Shelly asks. "There's no town here. The funeral home will be flooded and abandoned, the cemetery underwater. There's no way to transport a body out of town."

But Randy insists that they have to remove Pop's body. Out of habit, he assumes authority. He takes charge in leading everyone out of the house. They make their way downstairs, where the water is now only waist high to the men, and on out to the deck where they take turns jumping off the five-foot drop to the muddy ground below. Abdul and Freight Train lift the smaller women down, and Abdul hands Pop's body to his father. The ground is a mud rug of woven grass and leaves and sticks. In the distance they see the flattened remains of houses. From where the Lawrence house once stood to the store across the street is a solid mat of strewn rubble, nothing taller than two or three feet above the ground. There is no sign of Randy's house across the bay. Freight Train lifts Pop in his arms and they all trudge the muddy ground a half mile to the site where the Lawrence house once stood, still the highest ground in Freedom.

Like soldiers surveying a battlefield after the fighting's done, as soldiers did back when wars were fought with handheld weapons, they survey all around from their slight height advantage. The Lawrence store still stands across the street. The awning has blown away and the front windows are shattered, but the building is mostly intact. They see figures slowly emerge from inside the store and head their way. There are four of them, a man, another man, and a couple holding on to each other. David thinks they look like movie zombies.

"Look, there's people," Shelly says.

They understand that the Lawrence store would be the place survivors would naturally gravitate to.

"That's Raymond Jenkins," Randy says.

Mary says, "And Mr. and Mrs. Short."

From far to the north two more people trudge their way. Randy identifies them as Malcolm Ashton and Fred Dalton. The battlefield may not be littered with corpses, but the survivors are shell shocked.

They have lain Pop on the ground. As the others gather round, Malcolm says, "Is he dead?"

"Yep," Randy answers.

"That's a shame. He coulda kilt me once when he had a right to, but he let me go."

Everyone looks to Randy for guidance. Under different circumstances Melissa's accusations would have shaken him so much he'd be unable to think rationally, but dealing with emergencies has been so ingrained in him that the opportunity to take charge is restorative. He fires specific and rational questions at the discombobulated survivors: "Is anyone injured? Have you seen anyone else? Does anyone have a walkie talkie or a working cell phone? (No, they don't.) Are there matches or cigarette lighters in the store? Lanterns of any type? Rope?"

"We can use the store as shelter," he says, "but first we have to bury Mr. Lawrence, and we have to find some way to signal a search party. Boats or helicopters will come soon. We need shovels. We need something to make a sign with. Brightly colored cans or boxes from the store oughta do if we can't find any paint. And something like a sheet on a pole to rig up as a big flag."

With scavenged shovels the men take turns digging a shallow grave, and they bury Pop. "I reckon it's the best we can do," Randy mutters.

"Thank you, Randy," Shelly says. "I would have left him where he was, but you knew best. This is where he belongs."

They put together letters made from cereal boxes and soup cans to spell out the word HELP on the ground, and they erect a flag of sorts. There's food enough in the store to sustain them until help arrives.

*

The storm surge was sixteen feet, winds two-hundred miles per hour, deaths attributed to the storm: seven. It hit land ten miles south of Freedom as seagulls fly. Huge chunks of commercial and residential properties were completely flattened, many of them properties that had been flooded, blown to smithereens and rebuilt before. Some more than once. Among the buildings that were destroyed was the funeral home founded by Riley Rogers. On a gurney in the funeral home, not yet prepared for burial, was the body of Weatherman Donny. It is assumed that his body was carried into a nearby bayou and then washed out to sea with the receding storm water.

More Water

Randy Moss took charge of rebuilding the town of Freedom, and four years later he ran for mayor and was easily elected. Murabbi Taylor won Randy's vacated post as sheriff. Many of the residents of Freedom decided to rebuild their lives somewhere else. The rebuilt town was barely more than half the size it had been before the hurricane. The two high schools were consolidated into one school and renamed Lawrence High, and the old Booker T became the town's combined elementary and middle school. No longer would there be football games between Booker T and Freedom.

Mary and Buddy moved to Mobile, where they both got jobs with Wal-Mart, Mary in their optical department and Buddy as a stock clerk. They bought an old house overlooking Mobile Bay, and Shelly moved in with them. Buddy quickly worked his way up to a management position. Beulah and Abdul remained friends but not a couple. Abdul went to college at Tulane on a football scholarship and made All-American his senior year, but when the NFL came courting he turned them down. He married a college classmate. Beulah discovered something she had suspected all along, which was that she was attracted to women, and she ended up partnering with an old schoolmate from Freedom, and they took over Little Don's when Little Don passed away at the age of ninety-three.

Melissa, who reclaimed the name Tashee, inherited Pop's interest in the Golden Eagle Casino.

*

It took David and Sue Ellen a couple of weeks to tie together loose ends and get ready to head to L.A. They caught the puddle jumper to Atlanta and from there they flew nonstop to Los Angeles and grabbed a cab to his Malibu house. He showed her around. They had a drink on the deck. Then, when she went to the bathroom, he rushed into the bedroom and jerked open the bedside stand to dispose of Jasmine's diaphragm before Sue Ellen had an occasion to see it. It wasn't there. Of course not. She would have taken it with her. He should have known.

After making love for what was their first time with no disruptions—neither from a hurricane nor a lecherous cop on the beach— and while lying in her arms for what was his first time with her or anyone else without a post-coital cigarette, he said, "You know, we have to go to London now. At least I do. I have to break it to Jasmine, and I'd like you to go with me."

"Jesus, no. You don't expect me to be with you when you break up, do you?"

"No, that's not what I mean." Suddenly he was dying for a cigarette, but he resisted the urge. He said, "I'll break it to her by myself. I just want you in London with me. For a vacation. You can go shopping or something while I talk to her. Then we can do all the touristy things. The Tower of London, maybe see Shakespeare at the Globe, take a tour to Stonehenge."

In London he met Jasmine on the set of *The Adventures of Tammy Jones*. She invited him to watch the rushes with her. God, he thought, was she ever sexy! She wears a huge blonde wig and a different elaborate gown in each scene, every dress one of those low-cut numbers that pushes the tits up so they look like double moons on the rise, and each gown quickly removed by a succession of cads and rakes and innkeepers and cooks and stable boys. If his mother thought the sex scenes in *Travlin' Light* and *Cold Justice* verged on the pornographic, she ought to see this one.

After the screening the director cornered David and talked to him about another project that he would be perfect for—another chance for him to work with Jasmine and "capitalize on that chemistry."

They caught a cab back to her hotel. In the cab they talked about the hurricane and his family, and she bitched about the film (the director was a flake and her co-star was a snotnose kid who was conceited and couldn't ever remember his lines). When they finally got a chance to be alone together, after dinner and while having drinks on the hotel balcony, he said, "Honey, I hate to tell you, but I've met someone."

She stared mouth agape and he amended that to, "not really *met* someone but reconnected. My old high school sweetheart. I'm sorry, honey, but we're in love."

She threw a hissy fit. "You bastard!" she screamed. "You sorry, sorry... how could you? You said there wasn't nothing between ya'll."

He got mad right back. He said, "At least I wasn't screwing a nineteen-year-old rock star. Spike Love, for god's sake. I bet you don't even know his real name."

"I do too. It's Randolph, uh, um... something or other. And he's twenty-five."

"It's Randolph Spaniel. He's a freakin' dog."

They shouted at each other until they were worn out, saying things they both knew weren't true and airing every little irritation they'd ever had with one another. The last thing she said before they went their separate ways was, "If I come back to get my stuff and I see her wearing my jewelry, I'll pull every hair out of her head."

"That went well," he told Sue Ellen back in their hotel room. "At least she didn't shoot me."

Three months later the producer of the Raymond Moon films approached him with a script for a new film in the series, insisting that they had to have Jasmine Jones as his girlfriend again. Professional enough to put their personal lives aside in order to work together, David and Jasmine agreed to do the film, and while shooting it they discovered that, as is so common with divorced couples, they could be much better friends than lovers.

Jasmine even befriended Sue Ellen, reluctantly at first, and the two women eventually discovered that they like each other.

David wrote and performed another monologue based on his return to Freedom. He called it *More Water*. He told all about his trip back home, including the hurricane and the death of his father. But he changed the story of Randy and Melissa to avoid embarrassing her.

The new monologue played to mixed reviews on Broadway and closed after six weeks. The DVD sold fairly well but was never as popular as *Water, Water*. He opened the new monologue with: "There's a saying down home, the closer to the water, the realer it gets. Everybody kind of knows what that means, but it's bigger than any definition. The lives of the people who live and work along the bayous and bays are like the lives of the shrimp and the crab and the flounder, profoundly affected by the ebb and flow of the coastal waters. And you just can't fake it when you're really in touch with that reality."

David said he had had to go back home in order to get real.

The problem with his new monologue was that he tried too hard to be philosophical, and that just wasn't his style or personality. In comparison to *Water Water*, the new monologue sounded pretentious. Besides, he had lost his edge. His life with Sue Ellen was too damn comfortable. You just can't create art from an easy chair.

8216553R0

Made in the USA
Charleston, SC
19 May 2011